REBEL OF ANTARES

by
Dray Prescot

Illustrated by
Jack Gaughan

DAW Books, Inc.
Donald A. Wollheim, Publisher

1633 Broadway, New York, N.Y. 10019

COVER ART BY KEN W. KELLY.

FIRST PRINTING, DECEMBER 1980

1 2 3 4 5 6 7 8 9

DAW TRADEMARK REGISTERED
U.S. PAT. OFF. MARCA
REGISTRADA. HECHO EN U.S.A.

PRINTED IN U.S.A.

SAN FRANCISCO, JULY 8TH 1993
TO: JOHN V. GUNTHER
FROM:
KYLE STEVENSON (STEVEN)
BREWSTER.

UNDER THE SUNS OF SCORPIO

Dray Prescot is a man scarred by a destiny that has hurled him four hundred light-years from Earth to the exotic world of Kregen orbiting the double star Antares. Assured of long life and vigorous health by the well-meaning Savanti nal Aphrasöe, now he is entrusted with the task of reuniting the island empire of Vallia and resisting the ambitions of the Empire of Hamal. From time to time he is called upon by the superhuman Star Lords to serve their mysterious purposes, and his relationship with them is entering upon a new phase.

To survive on Kregen Dray Prescot needed to be strong, resourceful, cunning and courageous. Yet there are more profound depths to his character than are called for by mere savage survival, and the tasks set to his hands and his experiences have changed him markedly. Educated in the harsh environment of Nelson's Navy, he is a man above middle height, with brown hair and eyes, the quiet movements of a hunting cat and a physique of exceptional power. Although he describes his face as "an ugly old beakhead," other sources state that his face is "noble and fierce." Expert with weapons and a master swordsman, he knows his own limitations. That he so often transcends them is a testament to his attitude toward life.

Prescot's loyalty to his friends is unbreakable. In the island realm of Hyrklana, off the east coast of the southern continent of Havilfar, he may now return home to Vallia. Many of the incidents of his varied career on Kregen are now falling into place in the grand design, and the reasons for his involvement are becoming clearer. At once, as is the happy way on Kregen, he is hurled headlong into new adventures under the Suns of Scorpio.

"The beast leaped clean through the open door."

Table of Contents

List of Illustrations

Chapter One

Sorcerers in the Souk

I have often been in two places at once; the superhuman powers of the Star Lords can arrange that little trick without trouble. Less frequently have there been two different versions of myself in the same place at the same time.

Walking along in the bustle of the city of Huringa, I was under the impression that to solve half of the problems confronting me I had only to bid farewell to my comrades Tyfar and Jaezila, secure an airboat and fly home to Vallia. The other half of the problems limped along spryly at my side, chattering away, and without a doubt presented the much more intractable half.

Unmok the Nets and I had become partners in the wild-animal business, dealing fairly with each other, and he expected us to set off on a new voyage to collect a fresh selection of savage beasts for the Arena. If ever there had been an occasion for two of me to be in the same place at the same time—then it was now.

As we passed under a balcony from which a cascade of multicolored flowers scented the air, I said, "Don't look back, Unmok. There is an unpleasant-looking fellow dogging our footsteps and I think he means us a mischief."

That, then, was an extra little problem for the evening.

Presently Unmok contrived a glance back as we neared the arched entrance to the Souk of Trifles. The twin Suns of Scorpio were almost gone and the sky blazed in cloud-banded jade and ruby.

"A nasty, devilish-looking customer, Jak."

"Just walk along quietly. We'll dodge into the Souk of Trifles. It might be interesting to play this fellow. Find out why he follows us like a burr in a blanket."

"Aye, it will be fun to bedevil him—"

"I said nothing about fun."

Unmok had no need to laugh. He might be a little six-limbed Och not above four feet six inches tall, and with a stump in place of his middle left limb; he was accustomed to handling the ferocious beasts employed in the Arena here.

"I know you, Jak the Shot," he said, sidestepping a man rolling an amphora along, single-mindedly concentrating on his rhythm. "You will play him and suck him dry, aye, and have fun in the doing of it."

"And if he is an assassin?"

"You have your sword, as I have mine."

Torches threw ragged light into the shadows cast by the declining suns. People bustled everywhere, intent at this time on finishing up their labors and enjoying themselves, and on offering a multitude of services to entertain and to relieve their customers of their cash. The Arena had, this day, remained empty and silent. People were dry-throat thirsty for sensation. At the entrance of the Souk, situated between three-story buildings of gray brick, the nearest stall furnished, as it were, a foretaste of what lay beyond. This stall, partially covered by a striped awning, piled with ankle-bells whose qualities were touted in unbell-like bellowings by a woman whose bodice strained with lung power, offered us concealment as we struck off down the Souk. At once we were engulfed in a jostling tide of humanity.

"Perhaps," said Unmok as we edged our way through the throngs, "there are others with him."

"The thought is in my mind."

The noise of hundreds of people shouting and laughing, chaffering and bartering, bounced from the crystal roof. With the last of the daylight, the mineral-oil lamps were lit. They depended on brass chains, high above, and as the agile monkeylike girls and boys clambered among the girders and chains with nerveless skill, the light within the Souk brightened. The vista of those long lines of light, the hanging chains, brought a vivid image of the Swinging City of Aphrasöe to my mind.

"Well, I can't see anyone else with the rast."

"They'll hang back and await his signal—if there are any more assassins with him." I could feel the soreness of the wounds I had taken still on me. I would not welcome another fight. All day Unmok and I had spent resting at our camp well outside the city walls, and we needed that rest. Froshak the Shine and the slaves waited for us, and Unmok had insisted he would go with me into Huringa. As for our gold, that was buried just outside the camp. If these assassins dogging our footsteps wanted that, they would be unlucky.

"So," I said, continuing the thought, "what does this fellow want of us?"

Unmok dodged a blundering Gon carrying a tray filled with sweetmeats. His little Och face screwed up. "Rather, who would want us killed?"

"Noran, for one. Vad Noran, for falsely taking the credit for fighting the schrepims in his private arena yesterday. His honor was very touchy on the matter."

"Perhaps. I was convinced when he paid us, for the animals and for the fight, that was the end of it. But you never can tell with these nobles."

"Aye."

This Vad Noran, a puffed-up bladder, but a bladder with much power, had bought many of the animals Unmok and I had brought into Huringa. When the schrepims, fearsome scaled warriors, had broken free and sought to slay anyone in their path and we had been forced to put them down, Vad Noran had, willy-nilly, been credited with the victory. It had been called a jikai, a warrior triumph. Perhaps he wanted to shut our mouths, in case we talked and revealed the hollowness of his claims.

An excited bunch of people wearing blue favors crowded in a rowdy uproar, laughing, already very merry, a whole mixture of races united in their partisanship for the Sapphire Graint. The blues rode at the highest point of the victory totems just now, their prianum filled with trophies of triumph. This mob was celebrating and didn't mind who knew.

"The Sapphire Graint! Kaidur!" they yodeled, reeling along, shouting, waving bottles, pushing people out of the way. It was all good-natured fun, and nothing untoward. I looked back.

The man who followed us so tenaciously persisted, waiting by a booth, crossing to the other side of the Souk, forcing his way through folk who, after one look, gave him plenty of room. He was an apim, a member of Homo sapiens, wearing nondescript brown clothes, a brass-studded jerkin and pleated kilt and with a Hyrklanian hat pulled low. I caught only the jut of a dark beard. He wore sword belts strapped diagonally over his shoulders.

"He sticks with us." Unmok's middle left stump gave that small characteristic twitch, a reflex he could not control, a pointer to his state of mind. That limb, the middle, set between the upper and the lower, is used as either a leg or an arm by Ochs, who are sprightly, agile folk. Unmok's middle left had been chewed off by a wild animal—before he earned the sobriquet of Unmok the Nets.

"He knows his trade."

"And I know mine. He is ripe for netting, that one."

Along each side of the Souk extended arcades, each a heaped treasure-house of Trifles. Extending the illumination of the high suspended lamps, myriad torches and cheap mineral lamps cast ruddy light upon the scene. Multicolored clothes, the glint of jewelry, the massy banks of hanging carpets, the furtive glitter of teeth and eyes, the smile that concealed, the merry jingle of coins, the uproar of bartering, all the normal everyday chaos of a busy bazaar flowed about us. The smells were quite comfortable, spicy, tangy, quite unlike some of the more odiferous of the Souks of Huringa.

"Out at the other end, Unmok, then double back and—"

"And find out what his tripes look like."

A sharp-toothed angerim, all hair and ears, spat at us for jostling his stall, where an untidy mixture of pots and pans and cutlery rang and chimed together. Angerims as a race of people are singularly messy in their life-style.

"Easy, dom," said Unmok quickly. "No harm done."

"Fuddled Ochs, clumsy apims," said the angerim. And then: "Buy a pot—here is a fine brass pot chased in Cervantern style, cheap for you, doms, a quality piece for your fire."

We walked on past hanging drapes of cheap cloth of brash color and pattern festooning the next stall. The angerim spat after us, wiping swatches of hair across his ears. The man who patiently dogged our footsteps padded on, keeping to the shadows.

The uproar within the Souk of Trifles continued and increased. A multitude of people from many of the fabulous races of Kregen presented an unforgettable spectacle, vivid with life and energy, laughing, bartering, quarreling, shouting, but alive, alive! At the far end the Souk opened out onto the Street of Running Werstings. Other bazaars riddled this area with noise and color and confusion. We passed under an overhanging balcony protruding from the level over the arcades, which are often called Monhan terraces. A woman leaned over and emptied a pot. To her evident disappointment, the pot's contents missed us. The splash cleared a circle.

A mob of people running wildly and screaming in fear scattered back from the exit to the Souk. They were all a mixture of races and colored favors and they pushed on blindly, their faces contorted, their eyes staring, their mouths open, screaming. The throngs picked up the panic. They began to recoil, and turn, and join in the flight. An enormous Rapa whose beaked face stuck up, surrounded by bristling feathers, blundered past and knocked Unmok flying. The little Och skidded back into a confusion of basket-protected amphorae. He flailed about, trying to get his balance, as the crowds streamed past. I had to skip smartly to get out of the line of stampede, and hitched myself up under a beam from the arcade.

"Hold on, Unmok! Stop thrashing about like a stranded fish."

"That Rapa—I'll—"

Unmok got his feet under him and staggered up and was immediately knocked over again by a fleeing Rhaclaw, whose immense domed head tried pathetically to twist on the pitiful plate of gristle that passed for its neck to stare back. The Rhaclaw wore armor and swords, and he ran with the rest, ran in blind panic.

The words the crowd was shouting spurted up mingled with the shrieking.

"Sorcerers! Wizards! Run! Flee! *Sorcerers*!"

Well, I generally steered clear of sorcerers myself, unless they were friendly.

The scattering of basket-protected amphorae dislodged by Unmok at last made a kind of breastwork. He staggered out, wild, flailing his arms about. When folk with three or four arms do that it makes you blink. He looked down the Souk and then up at me as I dropped down to join him.

"The rast is still there, Jak. Crouched in a doorway on this side—"

"I saw him. And his fellows are with him now."

"Aye."

"Do you fancy assassins or sorcerers?"

"You give a man a hard choice. If there is nothing else for it—"

"Unless you can batter a way through the walls."

He took the suggestion seriously, in that dour way some Ochs have, but he knew the thickness of the walls needed to uphold the overarching crystal. "Unless we find a door, we'll never knock a hole through in time."

"I judge the same."

The rout streaming past thinned and a last few crazed individuals fled past, sobbing, casting agonized glances back. We looked along the Souk under the lights and the crystal roof toward the end that gave egress onto the Street of Running Werstings.

Two beings stood there in the puddled light, facing each other. It was a Confrontation.

One of the figures stood tall and robust and encased in a solidly glittering robe. A splendid figure, a dominating figure, one who commanded and knew nothing of disobedience, one who wore splendid vestments of silk and gems and gold thread, this one was a Sorcerer of the Cult of Almuensis. For the briefest of moments I fancied he was San Yagno, who had disappeared down the Moder, but he was not. His face, lined with the seasons of knowledge and power, bore a fierce, predatory look as he intoned the spells from the great book in his beringed fingers. The book was covered in lizard skin, gold-bound, gold-locked and fastened to his belt by golden chains. From this book, this hyr-lif, came the sorcerer's very real powers.

The Sorcerer of the Cult of Almuensis sparkled with the radiance of power within the lights of the bazaar.

The other figure presented the most marked contrast.

This was an Adept of the Doxology of San Destinakon. His gown swathed his figure in a drab but bewildering array of brown and black lozenges. The hood peaked to his right, for a woflovol perched on his left shoulder, the little batlike animal's membraneous wings now extended and fluttering in echo of the rage suffusing his master. The woflovol was chained to the Adept's waist by a slender bronze linkage. In the sorcerer's right hand, a hand devoid of ornamentation, a wooden-hafted bronze flail, a scourge, was uplifted, for the followers of San Destinakon are not above the outrage of physical chastisement. Now the bronze flail hung limp, but it quivered with the passions of the Adept.

Two figures in marked contrast, yes. But they held and controlled power, undeniably. Between them, shimmering and sparkling, grew a dish-shaped circle of light. Constantly changing in color and texture, shooting forth rays of brilliance, the center of the conflict between the two sorcerers shifted back and forth and spat fire, crackling with the dissipation of energy.

Unmok gulped.

"An Almuensin and a Destinakon! This is no place for an honest man, Jak. Let us—"

"Loosen your sword and let us hit the damned assassins first—"

"Yes! As Ochenshum is my witness, let us die by an assassin's hand as by the malignancy of a wizard!"

Just like Unmok the Nets. I knew him to be brave and loyal, but brave only when he had to be and loyal only to those he valued. If he could have paid some of his good red gold to a fine gang of cutthroats to insure his safety out of here, he would have done so, faster without another thought. Well, and wasn't that the sensible course?

"Sink me!" I said. "We won't get ourselves killed. Come on. Let us hit them fast and break through and then—"

"*Run*!"

"Aye!"

Then a noise broke about our heads like the last trump. The colossal smash of sound bore in on us and made our heads jump on our shoulders. I thought the sound more like a battery of thirty-pounder Parrotts all firing together right beside us than a battery of twelve-pounder Napoleons. The air in the Souk was thick and the noise bellowed along, amplified and channeled and directed personally, so it seemed, at every individual's eardrums. But, on Kregen, they had not yet developed gunpowder or guns. This was no battery of cannon firing, this was sorcery venting in deafening discharges the overflowing plasma of thaumaturgy. I glanced up.

The crystal roof split.

In spinning sheets of crystal, in razor-edged plates of shimmering fireglass, the roof collapsed. It rippled as though shaken. The metal supports buckled. Over an area a full hundred paces long and the full width of the Souk, the roof fell in.

Unmok let out a screech and dived for the upended barrow that had contained the amphorae. I wasted no time in joining him. Together, heads down, we crouched in the hellish din.

Sharp slivers of crystal slashed into the paving. Chips flew like shrapnel. The uproar smashed at us so that we gasped for air. The barrow and the amphorae clattered with the scattering crystal chips. Amphorae exploded. Wine gushed forth, staining the basketwork and the straw and running gleaming red across the paving. The whole place quivered as though in the grip of an earthquake.

The avalanche of crystal thundered down for what seemed an eternity of Kregan nights and days. At last in a final clashing of shining slivers the noise ceased. Unmok lifted his head.

"If that is what the end of the world is going to be like, I do not believe I will wait around to see it."

"Sensible," I said, brushing dust from my clothes.

We crawled out from under the barrow and shook our heads, bloated with sound.

The order in which we took stock of the situation might have reflected a mutual dependence in a coming battle; it could just as easily have revealed our nervous preoccupations. Unmok peered through the swirls of dust toward the two wizards. I looked back into the Souk for the assassins.

Assassins are hardy souls, the stikitches' trade being of a demanding nature, and two leather- and bronze-clad men still sheltered in an arcade opening, peering out at us. Their beards showed black against the pallor of their skin. The rest of the gang had fled; at least, they were nowhere in sight. Leaving my observation of the assassins and that problem, I turned to look where Unmok stared, rigid with a terror he made valiant attempts to conceal.

The two sorcerers had by no means finished their altercation. The disc of light spun between them, coruscating and throwing off streams of radiant matter as though a Catherine Wheel spun to a crazy destruction. The shards of light struck the walls of the Souk with thunderclap noises. Chunks of masonry were blasted away. Dust sifted among the wreaths of smoke.

"Let us—" said Unmok, and he swallowed and wet his lips before he could continue. "Let us get away!"

I nodded. The wizards' quarrel was no concern of ours and we were like to be harmed by its side effects. The assassins presented a simpler and more approachable problem, for all that I had looked their way first. I have no truck with sorcerers unless I count them as friends or must use them despite all.

We began to move back down the Souk.

The crackle of splintered crystal under our feet sounded like mahogany leaves. The assassins eased out from their arcade.

"Two," said Unmok. "I think we will be able."

The assassins bared their swords, the weapons glinting in the light of the sorcerer's quarrel.

The Souk presented a melancholy spectacle, empty of people apart from us four, with the paving strewn with smashed Trifles, stalls overturned, bales of cloth unrolled and abandoned in serpentine meanderings, smashed glass and pottery, feathers and ivory and knickknacks scattered everywhere. The noise and light at our backs persisted. We moved on.

"*Are* they assassins?" asked Unmok, as the two men ahead of us hesitated. They began to withdraw, steadily, their weapons lifted, going slowly, but they drew back before us as we advanced.

Without looking back, and just to cheer up Unmok's little Och heart, I said, "They need not be retreating because of us."

Unmok burst out with a comment that almost made me smile. He whirled to look back.

"The sorcerers still fight, Jak—you devil! You had me going then . . ."

"True."

"Tell me why I shouldn't throw you into one of my wild-beast cages."

"Riddles were never one of my easiest marks."

The assassins—if they were stikitches—halted again and then once more drew off. They moved with purpose.

"It could be they seek to lure us on—"

"On to our doom!" Unmok cast another look back. "Well, there is no getting out that way."

Keeping a very sharp lookout in all the nooks and crannies of the Souk, bathed in that supernatural fire, we pressed on.

The occult radiance drove our shadows ahead of us, long and dark and leaping, seeming to draw us on as the fires forced flames and smoke into the Souk. The mineral-oil lamps cast gobbets of flame as they fell in the continuing crashing destruction of the roof. We were running now, leaping obstacles and diving past overturned stalls as the crystal burst and the lamps showered down and the fires raged.

We must have looked like two phantom figures bursting through veils of smoke from some time of forbidden lore, some realm of ancient magic. The assassins hovered, their steel glinting. Then they swung away, looking back for only heartbeats; Unmok ripped out his sword and waved it—and the assassins fled.

"That," said Unmok with immense satisfaction, "has seen them off."

"By Harg!" I said, leaping forward. "I want to know more about this—who sent them—what the hell they're up to!"

"Jak—"

The backs of the assassins leaped and dived among the Trifles scattered over the Souk. The roof fell in successive crashings. The fire crackled. Smoke streamered in long layers, stinging the eyes and making us cough. I roared after the fleeing assassins.

The whole area had been cleared of people, and any thoughts that the first roof-falls had finished the business were now seen to be ill-founded. What the sorcerers had begun the fire and the domino effect along the roof would finish.

One of the men running ahead of us skidded on a mess of squishes upended from a basket. His arms flailed. He staggered into a rack of cheap zorca trappings, and before he could recover I put my fist around his neck. He squeaked like a rabbit.

"Let me go!" he shrieked. "The sorcerers—"

I let my dagger make an acquaintance with the space between his third and fourth ribs. "Do not fret over the wizards, dom. They quarrel between themselves. You should rather fear for your fate—" the dagger twitched "—here and now."

He gasped, twisting, trying to kick, trying to bite. I moved the dagger.

"Tell me who sent you, and I will let you live."

"I cannot—"

"Very well. You have your stikitche honor. You may adhere to your code and die, here and now. I do not care. I will find your comrades. One will tell me."

"You devil!"

"So I am told."

"I cannot tell you!"

"You mean that for a short moment you will not."

"Listen, dom—take that dagger away. It is sharp!"

"A blunt dagger is like a grave without a corpse."

He knew that old Kregish saying, which may be taken in two ways, both of them apposite. He went limp in my fist.

"If—"

"Just speak up."

"I am no stikitche."

Unmok arrived then and made a disgusted sound.

"We guessed as much. As assassins you would make passable dung-sweepers."

"So," I said, "Vad Noran sent you. And you've failed him."

I felt the quiver of him in my grip. "I did not tell you that! I did not! As Havil is my witness, I did not speak!"

I gave him a resounding kick up the backside and let him go. He had merely confirmed what we suspected. I bellowed after him as he scampered off.

"If you dare to face Noran, tell him we will keep our silence. We will keep that and the gold. Tell him."

He did not answer, did not look back. He just ran.

Unmok rubbed his middle right across his face; his upper right still gripped his sword. "Now that I've seen him close to, I do recognize him. He's one of Noran's men, all right. They call him Hue the Grasshopper. But the others with him . . ."

"Of a tougher frame of mind, I would think. But if they are not assassins, I, for one, am profoundly grateful."

There was no need for me to elaborate. Once stikitches take out a contract, they will, within the framework of their so-called honor codes, fulfill it, or arrange the recompense on annulment. If I was to do what I had to do in Huringa, I did not want a horde of hairy, unwashed assassins breathing down my neck all the time.

What I had to do now was to find some way of taking my leave of Unmok the Nets so that I could bid farewell to Tyfar and Jaezila. If one problem had been resolved, the rest remained.

All the same . . . "I wonder—" I said as we dusted ourselves off and started off toward the far end of the Souk. "I wonder what the quarrel was between the two sorcerers."

Unmok gave a little cluck of sound, a dutifully respectful and at the same time dismissive appraisal of all wizardly doings.

"Who can say? They are unto themselves—thank all the gods."

People began to move about at the far end, creeping out of hiding places, standing up to look with bewildered horror upon the catastrophe. The fires burned fiercely at our backs. We went on and found an arcade with an opening onto a narrow side alley. One or two people evidenced a desire to talk to us; we had no wish to engage them in conversation. By Krun, no!

The fires burst through between the empty walls and threw orange and crimson weals against the evening sky. We dodged along the alley and turned right and then left between shuttered buildings and came out onto the Street of Condiments where people stood about, staring up, talking among themselves, watching the fires. The conflagration would be brought under control by fat Queen Fahia's officials, for like most monarchs of important cities, Fahia kept up services to deal with emergencies of this kind.

Ashes blew on the evening breeze. We went through the throngs, their eternal chatter about the Arena for the moment forgotten, and thought about a wet.

"My throat is as dry as a Herrelldrin Hell," said Unmok.

"There's a swinging flagon."

We went into the low-arched opening and sat at a wooden table, and the Fristle fifi brought us a jug and two flagons. Unmok poured and we drank. By Vox! I was thirsty. My Och companion scattered a few copper coins on the table, a handful of obs, and we refilled the flagons.

"Talking of money," said Unmok, which was a perfectly logical process of thought for him, "I am in poor case to see Avec. He will think my talk of gold a cod to catch him." He started again to bang at his clothes and to pull and tweak them about to make them fit better.

"We have the gold now, Unmok, and no man will quibble when his hand jingles the bag of yellows. Just tell him straight out."

"I will. You are right."

Unmok the Nets was a wily enough fellow when it came to money matters, and his banking connections with Avec Parlin, I fancied, would not altogether favor the banker. Unmok's burning desire now was to buy a cage voller, an airboat fitted for the carriage of wild beasts. With such an airboat in his possession, with his connections, he ought to make money like wildfire.

The Fristle fifi in her yellow apron—for she was not a slave—came over with a wooden tray filled with odds and ends of munchables, and we popped a few into our mouths and chewed as we talked. The wine, a middling Stuvan, lowered in the jug.

"Avec will know the best bargains," said Unmok, with confidence. "We need a large vessel, but she must be economical to run. A few deldys more on the initial costs to insure that will pay dividends."

I fretted within myself, for I had more or less promised Unmok I would ship out with him on his next voyage, and yet I could not in all conscience do so. I knew that, although my own country of Vallia was in good and capable hands, I wanted to return there and finish up the business of uniting the land and turning out the villains who had so destroyed and brought low the Empire of Vallia. I sipped wine to conceal the turmoil of my thoughts, and Unmok burbled cheerfully on, already in command of his famous cage voller and soaring through the skies with a full cargo of fearsome, snarling, savage beasts.

Then he stopped talking, and his jowly Och face changed, a frown of concentration drawing down his brows.

"Hue the Grasshopper—Vad Noran's man you lifted up to inspect—may not have been a stikitche, being at best a stable hand. But the man who followed us, dogging our footsteps—he was an altogether more ugly customer."

So I guessed Unmok had seen this altogether more ugly customer pass outside the tavern, still seeking us, no doubt.

I felt relief.

The persistence of this tracker afforded me a chance to postpone telling Unmok that I would not be shipping out with him, that our partnership was ended unless he chose to go with me. I stood up.

"Jak?"

"You go and see Avec Parlin. Make sure he lays his hands on the very best cage voller we can afford. All the gold is yours. I may not be able to ship out with you—"

"Jak!"

"—But I will see you again. You know you have my word on that. Now, which way did this ugly customer go? I will sort him out—"

"*Jak*!"

"—So there is no good arguing, there's a good fellow."

Unmok swelled out those jowly Och chops and tilted his head back to look at me. He did not stand up, and in that I felt the smaller of the two of us.

"He went along toward the Avenue of Sleeths. No, there is no profit in arguing with you. You have secrets, that I do know. I will see Avec and arrange the cage voller. After that—you must decide. As for me, we are partners, and remain so."

Little, are Ochs, puffy and with six limbs, and not apims like me at all. But in that moment Unmok the Nets displayed a dignity surpassing many and many a blowhard apim lout I have known. And that thought should surprise no one in two worlds.

"Although—" and here Unmok shivered his whole body, as though gripped by a vampire spider of Chem. "Although if you go away I will take it hard. We have been partners for only a small length of time, as these things are measured, and yet in that time we have been through much together. It is of value to me to think of that, and those times . . ."

"It is of value to me, also. I think you know that." The lamplight glittered on the bronze studs of Unmok's jerkin beneath the opened fold of his tunic. "Secrets—yes, we all have secrets. It is difficult for me to explain. I believe you would find it well-nigh impossible to credit. But explain I will. I will."

His regard of me did not waver.

"May the hands of all the gods rest lightly on you, Jak the Shot, and may Ochenshum have you in his keeping."

I nodded and without the usual rememberees on parting, I went out and along the street toward the Avenue of Sleeths.

After all, as I tried to tell myself with some hollow vehemence, how could a partnership with a little Och wild-beast catcher and a half-promise to him possibly weigh in the balance against the preoccupations of an emperor and the fate of an empire?

Chapter Two

A Rapier Twinkles at Dinner

The quarrel between the two sorcerers and the resultant disastrous fire forced animation on the people of the city. Parties of the queen's guards galloped along the streets. The flames continued to light the night sky. People talked of the catastrophe, agog, joying that their premises had not been consumed. I walked along at a good pace, heading went out and along the street toward the Avenue of Sleeths.

Huringa, the capital city of Hyrklana, is not one of the largest capitals of Kregen, but it is impressive in its own way, dominated by the imposing pile of the queen's palace, the Hakal, with the ominous bulk of the Arena, called the Jikhorkdun, alongside. From the Arena the four main boulevards, lighted by gas, stretch toward the cardinal points of the compass. I saw no sign of the man who had been following us and whom I now followed in order, as I had told Unmok, to settle this business. I did not know, myself, if this were true . . .

Anyway, if I did not find him I was going in the right direction for the promised meeting with Tyfar and Jaezila.

The idea that I ought to take a part in the fire-fighting occurred to me. I dismissed it immediately. The authorities charged by fat Queen Fahia with fire-fighting duties would be adequately capable. She'd have them thrown to her pet neemus if they were not.

Moving along among the folk out strolling in this early evening preparation period for the night's entertainments, I kept a wary lookout. The fourth moon of Kregen, She of the Veils, sent down smoky pinkish rays, wavering and erratic in the smoke pall, paling beside the lurid glow of the fire. Keeping out of the way of sorcerers had always seemed a sound practice, and this latest imbroglio merely confirmed that. The disc of radiance balanced between the two opposed powers of the wizards and casting off the chunks of incendiary material was in itself a potent force.

That occult disc of light is called The Quern of Gramarye. When it grinds opposed magics the very fabric of time and space is distorted and fractured.

The Avenue of Sleeths ran straight between private houses fronted by gardens for over five hundred paces. Here lived some of those inhabitants of Huringa who were bracketed in the middling wealthy class, with slaves and carriages and fine clothes, whose tables were well-laden. Down at the far end, a crossing place where the Street of Sleeths joined the east boulevard was always crowded with idlers and ruffians patronizing the taverns and inns there. So it was from gentility into abandonment I walked. And still no sign of the fellow who had dogged our footsteps.

Many torches and lanterns lit up the crossing place which formed a kind of square or kyro, and the taverns stood cheek by jowl. Most strollers approached this place, the Kyro of the Happy Calsany, along the boulevard. When the amphitheater turned out after the games, the place became choked. Amid all the uproar I fancied there would be little chance of spotting my man, so I set off directly for the travern, the Faerling's Feathers, where I was to meet Jaezila and Tyfar.

The great cross of the boulevards, with the Jikhorkdun and the high fortress of the Hakal at the center, imposed a certain order on Huringa's street planning, but the mixtilinear walls made of the alleys and streets in the outer portions of the quarters a mass of interconnected labyrinths. A general assault on this city would be held up there unless airborne troops could land in rear of the defenses.

Wondering why that particular thought had crossed my mind just then, I walked up to The Faerling's Feathers. We of Vallia had no wish to go to war with Hyrklana; quite the reverse. Tyfar and Jaezila were talking together, engrossed in each other's company. I looked at them with great pleasure. And I was come to say good-bye!

They sat at a small table under a climbing vine smothered in blue flowers; above their heads a balcony depended silken shawls and tasseled scarves. The light from She of the Veils glowed warmly from the stucco wall. The table was set for three; the empty chair waited for me.

I shook my head as though to clear away cobwebs. I knew that saying good-bye to these two would be a wrench, and now that I watched them as they talked so closely, I realized afresh just how much I did not want to part from them. Blade comrades are rare, and I have been blessed and more than blessed with true blade comrades on the wonderful and terrible world of Kregen. For a true blade comrade one would lay down one's own life without a second thought, and for these two, for Jaezila and Tyfar, I would—with only the first thought for my Delia to halt me—go through the fire. Delia, Delia of the Blue Mountains, Delia of Delphond, always stood foremost in my thoughts, and against our love I measured all my actions.

The task of saying good-bye would not be easy for another reason. Prince Tyfar, with his shining honor and ideas of upright dealing with all men and women, and Jaezila, with her willful ways and quick bright grasp on living, would certainly attempt to detain me. They had work to do here in Huringa for their own country of Hamal. Hamal was at war with my own country of Vallia, and that was all a stupid nonsense; these two were comrades and we had lived and walked close to the edge of death together.

Jaezila tossed her head back so that her brown hair rippled all gleaming in the moonlight. She laughed full-throated. And, so laughing, saw me.

"Jak!"

"Well, Jak," said Tyfar, scraping his chair back and standing up to greet me, "and have you freed yourself of your entanglement outside the city? Do you come to stay with us?"

"Lahal, you two," I said, walking up and grasping Tyfar's hand, leaning down to kiss Jaezila. "No. I'm not clear yet." I sat down and the wine was poured as I pulled the chair forward. "But I joy to see you—"

I had told them only the most superficial account of my true life and circumstances out of necessity. They knew I was happily married, although I had—prudently—given Delia a different name. I had said—and I would not want Delia to learn this too swiftly—that her name was Thylda. That was a good name in Hamal. You see what petty shifts one is driven to when friendship is sullied by these monumentally idiotic politics of war! So they knew that my entanglement outside the city was not with a woman.

I asked after the fliers they had come here to buy, and heard that the work proceeded slowly, for the people of Hyrklana deeply resented having to build airboats for Hamal. Only fear of that great empire on the mainland opposite, and its mad Empress Thyllis, kept the Hyrklanians polite to Hamalese in their midst.

"Although," said Tyfar, looking flushed and annoyed, "a factory was burned to the ground today—ten fliers were lost. They go in for fires in Huringa, I see."

I told them that the fire in the Souk of Trifles had been started by two sorcerers quarreling.

"Their damned Quern of Gramarye, I suppose?"

"Yes."

Now that I had joined them, the slaves could bring the food. One thing was sure, despite the enormous difficulties, when Vallia had triumphed over Hamal—as we would!—we'd stop all this slavery. The transformation of a slave-owning society into a free society was causing difficulties in Vallia, and the problems would be worse in Hamal. But in Opaz's good time, the task would be done.

Jaezila wore a deep crimson evening robe, just such a gown as Delia had once worn here in Huringa, and with a narrow golden belt from which swung not a silly ornate curved dagger but a solid workmanlike rapier and main gauche. She looked stunning. And yet still she teased Tyfar, and tweaked him and, as I looked at them and saw, she was more attached to him that she probably realized. As for Tyfar, his dark blue evening robe concealed a harness of mesh link, I did not doubt; his rapier and main gauche swung from his belts outside the robe. Under the folds of cloth I also did not doubt he had his axe about him. He was not willingly parted from that axe, was Prince Tyfar of Hamal.

Toward the end of the meal he kept darting puzzled looks over my left shoulder. A wary expression crossed his face and then he returned to the squish pie. But again he looked up. Open and frank, bold and fearless—these words describe Tyfar as he carried himself with us, for we were comrades. With his father, Prince Nedfar, and the high notables, Tyfar tended to the withdrawn, the aloof. A bookish man, he had taken up the axe as a kind of defiance of those forces seeking to mold him into the run-of-the-mill Hamalese prince. A good man in a library and a good man to have at your back in a fight, Prince Tyfar.

He said, "I think—"

Then he stood up, very quickly, overturning his glass of wine. His rapier snicked out and thrust past my ear as he flung himself forward. I was off my chair and rolling on the ground, without thought. I heard the scream of surprised pain and then I was up, rapier in hand, to see that damned assassin fellow who had been following Unmok and me writhing with Tyfar's rapier through his guts.

Jaezila's own sword flicked about, checking the sudden surge of interest from other diners at adjoining tables.

The wretch skewered so neatly fell down. Tyfar withdrew.

"Friend of yours, Jak?"

"My thanks, Tyfar—not exactly. He's been following us—me—around Huringa tonight. I'm glad I know where he is now."

"He's on his way to the Ice Floes of Sicce, that's where."

"May his ib rest in peace—although I do not think that likely."

"Pay the reckoning, Ty, and let's go." Jaezila spoke evenly.

"Agreed."

I started to shuffle coins out and the prince checked me, as he always did in these matters. He was a real prince.

The landlord waddled up, protesting, but a dead man who might or might not be an assassin was no new thing in this Kyro of the Happy Calsany. A few gold coins jingling, a smile and a word or two, and the matter was settled. We were known to be strangers, and rotten damned Hamalese at that, but gold was gold.

We walked away, and Jaezila picked up a ripe shonage to eat as we went along.

So I told them about my dealings with Vad Noran.

"Unmok the Nets and I sold Noran a parcel of wild beasts. We were up at his villa when the slaves broke out." I didn't tell him why the slaves had escaped. "Some schrepims were released from their cage and the reptilian warriors went berserk."

"Schrepims," said Tyfar. He pursed his lips. "Nasty."

"Quite. Unmok and I managed to beat them off with the aid of a lion-man, and this great Vad Noran appeared and was given the credit for the fight. We did not care. Unmok just wanted his money and to get out, and the numim escaped, for he had been a slave there. So now, I think, Noran wants to shut our mouths in case we spread the true story. He has been dubbed a great jikai because of his supposed fight—"

Jaezila laughed, striding along, munching shonage, the juices running down her chin. "It is strange, for we have heard of the jikai Vad Noran performed. And it was like that!"

"We heard more about this Noran, also," said Tyfar, and he spoke seriously.

"He builds vollers and no doubt sells the airboats to you?"

"Yes. It was not his factory that was burned to the ground. But—"

"But he seemed most pleased that the vollers had been destroyed." Jaezila wiped juice. "No. Not seemed. He was damned pleased—and it is easy to see why."

These two blade comrades of mine believed that I worked in secret for the Empress Thyllis—a lie I had been forced to for the sake of friendship and a whole skin—and that I was Hamalese as they were. At least, as Tyfar was. Jaezila might not be Hamalese but she labored for that evil empire just the same. So I could say, with a grimace, "Because they hate us."

"They do hate us. And again, it is easy to see why."

Once more we were on thin ice. I guessed that Tyfar's father, Prince Nedfar, did not share the grandiose ideas of conquest harbored by Thyllis. Hamal had extended out to north and south, laying waste lands and islands, sending her iron legions to destroy all the might sent against them. Well, we in Vallia were checking that onward march. But south of Hamal, in the Dawn Lands, the Iron Legions of Hamal surged on in blood and death. The invasion to the west of Hamal into the Wild Lands had been halted some time ago. To the east, across the sea to the island of Hyrklana . . . Well, would not Hamal seek to conquer Hyrklana in the fullness of time? Unless mad Empress Thyllis was stopped? There must be many men in Hamal who wished to check the empress and could not. And I had said—or implied—that I worked secretly for Thyllis. Tyfar's father opposed Thyllis—again in secret. Yes, thin ice, damned thin ice . . .

"The empress is like a dark center of contagion," said Jaezila. I looked at her sharply. Tyfar's face remained wooden. I guessed they had talked long and deeply on this. Now, how was I supposed to react?

"I once said that revolution might not be the way. I once said—"

"Yes, Jak the Sturr?"

"I do not like wars and killing and all the horrors they

bring in train. If they could be halted . . ." I paused. "If they could, the world would smile again."

"But Thyllis is strong. My father extends feelers, but he must move cautiously." Tyfar looked at me and his brows drew down. "We are blade comrades, Jak. Yet you work for the empress, personally—"

"We are blade comrades. You are aware that my opinion of your father is that he is a great man. I would like—" Again I paused. "Prince Nedfar is a man among men." Was the idea so ridiculous, so impossible? Would it be beyond the bounds of reason to imagine the Empress Thyllis deposed and Prince Nedfar installed as king and emperor? The war would end then, instantly. Vallia and Hamal could shake the right hand of friendship and turn to the more pressing problems of the reivers from over the curve of the world, the dark cloud of horror that threatened all these bright lands of Paz on this side of Kregen.

I harbored the suspicion that Tyfar's sense of honor would prevent him from raising his hand against his empress.

Feeling cautious, I said, "It is said in many of the old writings that a man's allegiance to his country must outweigh any friendship for an individual." Tyfar remained unresponsive. "Other wise men say that friendship overrides all other considerations. Does loyalty without friendship constitute reason enough?"

"Loyalty—" Tyfar would have gone on, but Jaezila burst out passionately: "I hate this stupid war. Thyllis should have had her backside slapped when she was younger, been made to realize a few things."

"Now, Zila . . ." Tyfar was not so much outraged as amused. I perked up. For a high and mighty prince of Hamal that was a good sign. And Tyfar was no high and mighty prince in that petty and world-weary way; he was alive and eager and filled with the conviction that, as the gods had seen fit to make him a prince, he was obliged to honor that position of trust.

We had talked up the east boulevard heading west, toward the somber bulk of the Arena. The outer courts of the Jikhorkdun would at this hour still be crammed with throngs seeking a continuation of the thrills of blood and death, catching a glimpse of their favorite kaidur, seeing an animal trainer, doing business with a slaver, organizing the eternal wagers, perhaps taking up swords and venturing into small practice rings to pit strength and skill against professionals.

Now shouts lifted at our backs and we turned about, wary and alert to possible danger. It was just a miserable coffle of arena fodder, being prodded along toward their destinies.

"Klactoils," said Tyfar. His face expressed a distaste I knew to be for the institution of the Arena and which people who did not know him and reacted as the common run of folk react would have taken for disgust at these chalk-white Klactoils. A strange kind of diff, the Klactoil, parchment white, only around three feet tall, with a thick ridged array of spines down the backbone and a walloping great tail that could take your ankles off. There is a fishy look to a Klactoil's face quite different from most of the faces of Paz. They keep themselves to themselves in out-of-the-way places, ruins like the Lily City Klana were infested with them. It was said—and at the time I was not aware any more than anyone else of the truth of the saying—that they were either a decadent remnant of a marooned band of marauding Shanks from over the curve of the world or else and more darkly a product of miscegenation of Shanks and some doomed race now long extinct.

Whatever the truth of that, these Klactoils were whipped and prodded along the boulevard headed for the Arena. The guards did not spare their whips. Most of the time I noticed that the lashes fell relatively harmlessly across that barrier ridge of spines along the diffs' backbones.

"Let the bosks at them!" a fat man declaimed, licking his lips. "That'll be rare sport!" He watched, safely away from them.

"No," disagreed his companion, nudging him. "Let the chavonths chew them up."

"If you ask me—" said a thin woman with a down-drawn mouth, one or other of the men being unfortunate enough to claim her for wife. "If you ask me, they should be tied two and two, and then tied two and two, until there is only one left."

"Yes?"

"*Then* let your bosks or your chavonths at him."

Jaezila made a disgusted sound, and we walked on. No,

the institution of the Jikhorkdun in Huringa, the capital of Hyrklana, was not a pretty affair at all.

Of course, it was not beyond the bounds of possibility that one of those Klactoils might succeed in the Arena, might win his victories, advancing from coy to apprentice, to kaidur, and then, if the gods smiled on him and he trusted in Beng Thrax, he might become a hyr-kaidur. Then his fortune would be made. Of the fifty or so I did not think more than one percent would do that; which meant not one would succeed in the Jikhorkdun. The opposition would be just too fierce, from savage animals and giant beasts to extraordinary proficient and cunning kaidurs who'd have their tripes out as they stood on the silver sand gawping at the crowds and the color and the noise and the whole impressive and diabolical display.

The life of a hyr-kaidur could be alluring. I knew that. Once you had made your mark, achieved your victories, stayed alive, you were a man set apart. The life could suck you in and overwhelm you with sensory impressions, with the fierce surge of combat, with the ferocious partisanship and courage that sought victory for your color. The Mystique of the Arena might possibly transcend areas amenable to reasonable analysis; it existed. I had been a hyr-kaidur in Huringa at a time that, with the stink of the place in my nostrils, did not seem at all long ago . . . Yes, the Jikhorkdun possessed its aura, and between harshly defined limits the Arena did have a genuine feeling, a sense of passion in victory, an involvement with means which, in themselves, created a mystery above reason, even if the ends were despicable to me. I wanted nothing more of the Jikhorkdun, where I had been known as Drak the Sword.

Jaezila threw down the remnants of the shonage. "All the same," she said in her bright, no-nonsense voice, "the Jikhorkdun in Ruathytu is far more bloody than the one here in Huringa."

Tyfar hunched a shoulder. "True."

Ruathytu, the capital city of the Empire of Hamal, was well-known to me. I had visited the arena there, unwillingly.

"We were interrupted at table," I said. "Let us find a fresh bottle."

"And we can talk more about this Vad Noran. You know him well?"

"No, Jaezila. Only to sell wild beasts to." I laughed, shaking off the dark mood. "Oh, and to provide him with a vicarious jikai." We jested, between ourselves, in an easy companionable way, and made light of ponderous matters. But the ponderous matters pressed in hard.

We found a small tavern that was not too congested and a bottle of red Corandian, very low in alcoholic content, and split it between us. "And did you see this mysterious swordsman, this Gochert with one eye and the other all covered with crusted diamonds and emeralds?" Jaezila lifted her glass and before she drank, added, "I am intrigued how a one-eyed man can be so sure with a blade."

"As to his prowess as a bladesman, that I cannot say," I said. "But, yes, I did see him. He moved with a deliberateness, rather like a stalking leem, very quiet and smooth. He wore good blades. He dressed austerely. And he was thin, by Krun! At the time I remember I thought he looked like a starving ferret."

Jaezila laughed. Tyfar nodded. "Such men are quick with a blade."

"I'll tell you one thing. He gave Vad Noran the Jikai* for the fight with the schrepims. But I don't think he could believe Noran had really done what was claimed. He looked at me with his one eye, very fishy."

"A Klactoil eye!"

"Precisely."

"But he was apim, like us?"

"Assuredly. What do you know of him? For I confess, he intrigues me."

"I know little and that little bodes ill for Hamal." Tyfar lifted the bottle, which was empty, and signaled the serving girl, who was a Gonell slave with silver hair wound around her body three times. The fresh bottle opened, Tyfar said, "My people here keep their eyes and ears open. They tell me this Gochert is a part of a conspiracy against Hamal."

This sounded promising. Maybe Gochert had been too harshly judged. Anyone willing to strike a blow against Hamal would, in Vallia's present circumstances, be regarded as an ally. And then Jaezila put the question that was crucial for any decision.

* Jikai: A word of complex meaning. Used in different forms means: "Kill!" "Attack to the death!" "A warrior." "A noble feat of arms." "Bravo!" and many related concepts to do with honor and pride and warrior status.
—A.B.A.

and others of that ilk. He knew I had done business with Noran and so he warned me in friendship. I agree the conspirators are foolish. I do not think that news is general knowledge."

"For your sake, I hope not—"

"My sake, Jak! Have I not just explained—?"

"Noran strikes me as a weak man who vents his pettiness in vicious attacks against those weaker than himself. If Avec dies, the papers may burn."

"Not Avec Parlin. He is too shrewd for that." But I could see the notion did not please Unmok. He twitched his middle left stump and threw his plate at the slaves with his middle right, at the same time picking his teeth with his upper right. His upper left brushed worriedly over his forehead where the lines stood deeply incised.

"Slit his throat," said Froshak the Shine.

This Froshak had been about to be put to the question, up at Vad Noran's villa, when the schrepims escaped. I'd thrown him my knife and helped him escape, and in the subsequent action he had been exculpated of the crime of freeing the schrepims. I viewed him with favor, for we had fought shoulder-to-shoulder, and I think—I hope—that he bore me a certain fellow-feeling.

Where your normal camp boss might have stood up and said something like, "Well, time to be up and doing," Froshak the Shine just stood up and got on with it. The cages stood about, empty. Our mercenary guards had been discharged and the few tame slaves, who had been with Unmok some time, had little to do. The institution of slavery is abhorrent to me, but in this instance of Unmok and his tame slaves, a relationship had developed that, while still unpleasant, is perhaps less of a blot on humanity than slavery as a whole. Certainly, this kind of valued family-retainer kind of slavery is often trumpeted in extenuation of the whole vile business. As far as my friends and I in Vallia were concerned, it wouldn't wash. Slavery was going to be eradicated.

And there spoke the great idealist with stars in his eyes and blood on his hands and mud on his boots, by Vox!

A pottery dish of palines afforded Unmok the chance to remain seated, looking at me. He popped a paline into his mouth and chewed. I followed his example, savoring the taste. Chewing, he said, "I spent some time thinking over what passed when we first went to see Noran and sold him the thomplods. I think he believes you are employed in some secret capacity by Queen Fahia."

"I gave him that impression. It helped the bargaining."

"It did that all right. But Jak, if he is plotting against the queen then he will regard you even more as an enemy to be put down."

"You could have the right of it, Unmok! It could be that is why he sent those assassins, and not to silence our mouths about his vain claim to the jikai!"

Solemnly, Unmok chewed and nodded.

"Then until this matter is settled, you and I must part company. He has no quarrel with you."

"If you think, you hairy apim, that I will—"

"I know. I had promised to introduce you to my friends this afternoon. But now, I think . . ."

Saying good-bye to Tyfar and Jaezila had been pushed from my head by what they had said. Huringa seethed with plots and moils, and now Unmok was telling me of another. If fat Queen Fahia could be brought down I could play a part in that, then this was where I belonged. Vallia was in good hands, as I kept on telling myself, fretting that I was not there. Tyfar was expecting news this day, and from what he said the news might give us the chance to join in a plot that was, so Tyfar said, the most promising. The future filled with visions. There was much to be done here. But—

"If word is spread about that you and I have quarreled, and I have left the partnership, Noran should not trouble you further."

Unmok stared at me in comical dismay.

"You—you—if only we had that damned cage voller!"

"You have all your equipment, the cages and the draught animals and the beast handlers. Froshak is a good man. You can start a fresh trip right away. Or," I said, jocularly scathing at his funny ways, "you could take up the latest scheme you have to change your profession."

"Jak! You wound me!"

"I intended to."

"Well, you won't break the partnership like that."

"You are always talking about giving up the wild-beast business and going in for a new line. Or an old one. They are never the same two sennights running. Now is your chance."

He clamped down on a handful of palines, the rich juice spurting, and he glared at me in his funny Och way.

I sighed.

"Look, Unmok . . . It makes sense."

Suddenly he brightened. He swallowed. He jiggled with excited realization. "I have it! We spread the story of this quarrel and our parting. I take the cages back to the coast and there you join me and we sail off together! Capital! Capital!"

The immediate thought that shot into my head was vile. I couldn't do that to Unmok, could I? But, a little Och and a partnership, against the fate of empire? Could I?

I stood up. Emperors have to make decisions all the time, right or wrong, it is part of the job. Given the importance in material terms of the two conflicting courses open to me, I knew I was choosing the right one. In almost any other terms I chose wrong.

"A good idea, Unmok. I'll draw Noran off. He ought not to molest you and you can get the caravan down to the river and hire craft to take us to the coast. I'll meet you on the waterfront. And you mind you take care. Froshak—"

"It is in my mind to hire guards now. The caravan will be empty, the worth nothing, but a few hired swords will afford a comfort to a five-limbed Och."

"Yes. I won't pick you up at Ingadot where you contract for the ship but at the mouth of the river. They always take on water last thing. It will be safer. And Unmok, watch out for the Forest of the Departed."

"I will. But it is caravans coming the other way that interest the bandits."

"And because of that, if you hire swords, keep them out of sight. They will make the bandits think you conceal wealth in what appears to be an empty caravan. Yes?"

"You are a good partner, Jak."

"Unless," I said, continuing the thought, "being a little five-limbed Och, you hire so many guards they would frighten a queen's regiment of crossbowmen away."

He threw the paline dish at me, whereat I felt the enormity of my underhanded treatment of him, for, of course, I had no intention whatsoever of meeting him where the ships took on water.

Unmok remained very cheerful as we said the remberees. We thought it prudent to begin the deception at once; thus, when we went down into the city we went separately. Froshak the Shine was apprised of the plan, and he said, in his usual way, nothing. I left the camp which had been moved away by the officials from the transit area. Once a caravan discharged its cargo it must make way for a new. We were a thousand paces or so up the road, sheltered in a nice little nook between fragrant clarsian bushes and the next nearest camp a good five hundred paces off. A stream ran paralleling the road here. I looked back as I crossed the rustic wooden bridge, looking at the row of cages, the tethered draught animals, seeing the huge, patient old quoffas with their wise enormous faces, seeing the thin stream of smoke from the campfire, and Froshak busily polishing up a krahnik harness brass. Well, I was saying good-bye to all that, and damned unhappy about the way of saying it.

I nudged the urvivel between my knees and he clip-clopped on across the bridge. Unmok and I had decided not to buy expensive zorcas as mounts, and I'd left him the freymuls. So astride an urvivel I rode along the road toward Huringa. We'd felt that the preysany was, just a little, not up to the impression we'd wished to create as businessmen. Kregen teems with splendid animals of all kinds, and all kinds are used, by Vox, for riding, flying, hunting and sport. For work the choice is just as vast.

My head was filled with jangling thoughts as I rode along, grandiose schemes to topple Queen Fahia and encourage the island realm of Hyrklana to resist the Empire of Hamal. Hamal's iron laws held sway over many lands, but by that token, resistance must exist. We in Vallia resisted, stubbornly and savagely. If Hyrklana could be coaxed into defying Hamal, one course of supply of the vital airboats would be cut off. If, then, Hyrklana would sell her vollers to Vallia . . .! That was an old dream. I knew my people in Vallia had tried to do business with Hyrklana, but the threat of Hamal had brutally snuffed out all hopes of that.

The rounded hill which obscured sight of Huringa from the transit camp unrolled its dusty road and gradually the city came into view. The fires were out. Queen Fahia had been extremely wroth at the two sorcerers, Unmok had learned, and had they been persons of ordinary quality who had become such wanton incendiaries, they would have been roasted alive. As it was, they had been asked to leave the city. The glittering, imposing figure of the Sorcerer of the Cult of Almuensis, high-powered and haughty in his book-magics, had been indisputably humbled, so the story going the rounds said. The Adept of the Doxology of

San Destinakon, by contrast, had been scornful, uncaring of the destruction, threatening retribution against the Almuensian, and of being told that the queen's court wizards would have to intervene if he did not obey. Fahia had gone in for sorcerers of late.

The urvivel was a good strong beast, brownish with yellow splotches and pricked ears, and he was called Snowdrop—why, I do not know. His saddle was cheap and a trifle uncomfortable and my gear in saddlebags and knapsacks dangled alarmingly between his legs. As for weapons for what might befall me, I had the rapier and main gauche, still unfamiliar weapons in Hyrklana, and a Havilfarese thaxter, a good stout cut and thruster that had seen useful service. Froshak had returned my sailor knife. The small wardrobe Unmok had provided had, in the nature of things, expanded, but I took only a few clothes. I had the feeling that I would be involved in more than a little hop, skip and jumping and wanted to be encumbered as little as possible. On Earth there used to be a saying: "Clothes maketh the man." On Kregen you would be fully entitled to imagine that the equivalent saying might be: "Weapons maketh the man." But Kregens are more subtle than that. They are aware that clothes can make a man look what he is not but weapons speak a truer tale when it comes to the test.

These jangling thoughts of mine veered away from clothes and weapons and sorcerers. The concerns over my country of Vallia never lay very far below the surface. If only . . . ! If only all this grouping of islands and continents called Paz could join together in friendship, then the menace of the Shanks from over the rim of the world could be met and fronted as a union. But the Empire of Hamal sought personal aggrandizement, and many other lands were at each other's throats. Hamal had to be dealt with first. And very first of all, Vallia had to be made safe.

My son Drak, my eldest, stern and serious, could run the empire; I knew that, his mother knew that, he knew that. But he stubbornly insisted he would not take over while Delia and I lived. Well, I'd as pig-headedly made up my mind that I would renounce the throne and crown and hand it all over to Drak when Vallia was once again in a fit state. That was settled, at least in my mind. My middle son, Zeg, was now king in Zandikar, miles and miles away in the Eye of the World. And my youngest son, that right tearaway Jaidur, was Opaz knew where, gallivanting around at the behest of his mother and the Sisters of the Rose. That secret organization of women ran far more damned things than many a mere male would credit.

The Sisters of the Rose had educated the three twin sisters of those three strapping sons of mine. Zeg's twin, Velia, had died away there in the Eye of the World, and her husband too, Gafard, the King's Striker, Sea Zhantil. The black agony tortured me still, whenever my thoughts turned toward them.

As for Dayra, Jaidur's twin, I fancied the problems she presented would solve themselves in time. She was called Ros the Claw, as she wore a razored steel claw on her left hand. At Lancival they had taught her how to employ those talons to shocking purpose.

So that left my eldest daughter, Lela, to worry me, for I had not seen her for long and long. Zair knew where she was now. All I knew was that she was away adventuring for the Sisters of the Rose. Her twin, Drak, had failed to recognize me when we'd met again, and I did not think Lela would know me, as I was confident, to my remorse, I would not recognize her now that she was grown up.

What it is to be a father separated from his children and hurled four hundred light-years across the gulfs between the stars!

People moved along the road toward the city, and I gave them all a wide berth. I was in no mood for idle chatter. Among the farm carts and peddlers and business folk and those pressing forward eagerly for the Games, marched formed bodies of troops returning to barracks after the night's patroling. No caravans of wild beasts were in sight. The suns of Antares shone, the air smelled sweet, music and laughter sounded all about me and I wore a blackly hating look and down-drawn brows, and, by the disgusting diseased liver and lights of Makki Grodno, I was in a right turmoil.

Unmok the Nets, stump left middle and all, could fend for himself, couldn't he? Of course he could. He had Froshak. He'd done it before we'd met and formed our partnership. And Vallia could fend for herself, couldn't she? Even with the outrages daily committed by reiving mercenaries and slavers? With great-hearted men like Seg and Inch, and Turko and Korero, and all the others, surely my Vallia could be trusted to them?

I hauled on Snowdrop's reins.

By Zair! Was I or was I not the Emperor of Vallia?

Well, then, if I was, couldn't I trust my blade comrades there? I knew I could. Each one knew what was at stake. Each one would give his life for me and for each other. I sat humped on Snowdrop's back and twitched the rapier in and out of the scabbard, and scowled. A passing Relt squeaked and stumbled on, his beaked face averted, the features quivering. I must have looked a sight!

"Sink me!" I burst out. And: "By the Black Chunkrah!" And: "By Zim Zair!" How could a little crippled Och beast-handler stand between me and my manifest destiny as an emperor?

How?

As I hauled on the reins and swung Snowdrop back the way we had come, I knew how—too damned easily how.

I'd given Unmok my pledge. Even an empire couldn't stand before that, could it? Well, of course it could. My pledge given to a foeman, or under duress, is broken as swiftly as a faulty blade in battle . . . Even my pledge to a friend, if greater forces supervene, would be broken. Regretfully. But then, I do not pretend to be your gallant gentleman. The only real regret I suffered as I started off back to the camp and Unmok was that I was delaying seeing Delia. But even then, you see, she'd probably be off about some derring-do for the Sisters of the Rose . . .

As I rode back to the camp quite expecting to see Unmok riding toward me on his way to Huringa to settle accounts and to hire mercenaries, I decided what I would do. It was a simple statement of alternatives, something I had been unable to do before. Unmok could make up his own mind. He could choose to carry on in the beast-handling business. Or he could choose to go to Vallia. I would not have to explain everything, merely indicate that my secret was of sufficient size to encompass his well-being for the future. Unmok and Froshak, both. Yes.

Feeling the weight of indecision sloughing away made me brisk up wonderfully. Shilly-shallying about was a sin to which I owned, and detested, recognizing the symptoms. Now that I'd made up my mind, the world took on brighter colors and the air smelled even sweeter and the laughter and music from the bands of people going toward the city fell on my ears most melodiously.

Even my urvivel, Snowdrop, welcomed this early return and he trotted along cheerfully.

The wooden bridge over the stream clattered a welcome as Snowdrop trotted across. But it was not quite the welcome I expected. One of Unmok's tame slaves lay on his face on the farther bank, with a tall brown-fletched arrow protruding from the middle of his back.

Even as I looked up from the slave's dead body toward the camp past the edge of the bushes, a cacophony of sadistic yells shivered into the air.

Chapter Four

Of the Simple Pleasures of Bandits

They'd locked Unmok into one half of an iron-barred cage with a savage beast in the other half and they were having great fun lifting the iron grille separating man and beast and letting it go, and lifting again, and letting go. Great fun.

As the chain rattled up, the wild animal—he was a hexagon-patterned chavonth—leaped slavering for Unmok, and down would come the grille with a crash. The great cat hit the iron bars in a bundle of spitting snarling fur, and a taloned paw raked through trying to reach Unmok. When the chavonth drew off, baffled, the chain would rattle again. His fur in the pattern of gray, blue and black hexagons gleamed in the lights of the suns. His six legs spurted sand as he sprang.

The grille dividing the cage lifted to chest height and as the chavonth leaped the iron clanged down, infuriating the beast even more and arousing it to frustrated frenzy. He was just a killer denied his kill. The men clustered around the cage and roaring their amusement as Unmok jumped in time to the grille were worse than mere killers in the scales of inhumanity. Froshak was tied insensible to another cage. Insensible or dead, I couldn't tell from where I watched from the cover of the bushes. The large area where fur was missing from his face revealing the membrane beneath did not glisten pink. It shone a vivid red. That was why Froshak was called Froshak the Shine.

There were eight or nine men taunting Unmok. I felt myself chill, there in the bushes. Not good enough. In a situation like this, an estimate of numbers was just not good enough. I counted more carefully. Nine. Right. I had no bow so could not fletch a few of them before I charged. Just how long I had before they hauled up the chain for good I didn't know. Judging from previous experience with unpleasant gentry of similiar inclinations, they'd carry on the joke—their idea of a jest—for as long as they could. Probably until Unmok passed out.

Froshak presented a problem, but if he remained insensible he ought to be all right.

These men were the usual mix of diff and apim. They were dressed in gaudy finery, with much cheap jewelry and an awesome assortment of weaponry in the Kregan fashion. Their leader wore a bright blue and yellow tunic over a brigandine, and he was exceedingly hairy. He was an angerim and his enormous ears had been cropped. They were mere flat ridges alongside his skull. So I knew who he was from what Unmok had told me.

This Maglo the Ears preyed on honest traders. He took the wild beasts from their caravans and sold them in Huringa as his own. No one had caught him. He had a finite way with him. Also, I did not doubt that as he could sell at a hundred percent profit, he could afford to distribute bribes on a scale lavish beyond the means of traders like Unmok. I frowned. Our cages were empty. So that could only mean that Maglo, coming along toward Huringa with a stolen caravan, had stumbled across Unmok and was dealing in this unholy fashion with a man with whom he'd tangled before. That explained the presence of the chavonth. The grille lifted, higher this time, and Unmok stumbled back to the far side of his cage, and the grille came down only just in time to halt the chavonth in mid leap. The screech of baffled fury spat like the scintillant bolts from the sorcerers' Quern of Gramarye.

"Finish him off!" yelled some of the men.

"Play him longer!" shrilled others.

Maglo the Ears strutted. He wore three swords on his left side, and they jutted up all at different angles. He was a big man, a spitting barbaric angerim, and he gloated in his power.

Working my way around between the clustering clarsian bushes, I momentarily lost sight of the cage. I could still hear the shouts of the men and the spitting fury of the chavonth. When I was positioned directly abaft the cage and cautiously peered out, Maglo was just walking across to the men on the chain. I guessed he meant to pull the chain for the last lethal time himself.

My first leap took me to the cage. The second landed me on the iron bars along the top and I plunged down and sprawled out flat. The door at the front was fastened by an iron staple. The staple came out in a long screech of metal on metal. I hurled the staple full at Maglo. Without pausing to see if it hit him or not, I drew my thraxter and reached down through the bars and hit the chavonth an almighty thwack up the rump.

The beast shrieked and spat and then, in a single sinuous bound, leaped clean through the open door.

The men screamed, and ran, and fell over, and goggled terror. A Rapa's head went one way as a taloned paw swiped, and his body toppled the other. A big Brokelsh stumbled and fanged jaws crunched. Dust smoked into the bright air. The noise racketed among the bushes. Unmok yelled. Froshak dangled in his bonds, and began to stir, lifting his cat's head.

"Stay still, Froshak, as you value your life!"

The Fristle had handled big cats for a long time. He did not move a muscle. Of us all, now, Unmok was in the safest spot.

Being a prudent man despite all seeming to the contrary, I stayed where I was. The chavonth went about his task of destruction with the unleashed fury of a cyclone. Men ran or died. The chavonth was in no mood to settle down with a nice juicy chunk of meat between his paws. Treacherous are chavonths, and this one vented his spleen in awesome fashion.

He vanished up the road after the last of the fleeing men. I hopped off the cage and slashed Froshak's bonds free. Then the chain was lifted and Unmok walked out. He was dazed.

"That Maglo!" We walked across and looked down on the bandit chief—or what was left of him. The chavonth had taken a bite in passing.

"You've one less damned animal bandit to worry about now."

"Aye, Jak. And, but for you . . ."

"Say nothing—"

Froshak joined in. I said, curtly, "Is there a caravan?"

"Maglo taunted me." Unmok cradled his middle left stump. He'd had a shock. "Down the road a space, out of earshot. He sent my tame slaves there, all except poor Nog who tried to run."

"I saw him. Let us take weapons and pay a call on Maglo's caravan. It will have been thieved by him."

"And we," quoth Froshak, abruptly pleased, "will take it for ourselves."

"Well, now," said Unmok as we stared about. "It won't be as easy as that. But—" He brightened. "May Ochenshum be my witness! We deserve it."

So, making sure none of the bandits still infested the place, and keeping a sharp lookout for the chavonth, we set off.

After the initial shock, these two got over the incident quickly. In one way, that merely reflected the hard knocks of their lives. When Unmok asked me why I'd come back, when we'd concocted a plan, I merely promised to tell him when we'd sorted out the matter in hand. At that point we had to skirt the remains of a Fristle, and so we pressed on with our swords clear of the scabbards.

The late Maglo the Ears had parked his stolen caravan beside the road and the uproar from the animals brought a quick frown to Unmok's face. "They are starving! That bastard Maglo—he kills the caravan owners and steals their wares, and then he does not feed them! Froshak—we'll have to see about this."

"Aye," quoth Froshak. "If there is food here."

If there was not, that would present a poser. The slaves huddled at the side of the road. They'd found shoots in the hedge and were chewing them and spitting green. Froshak roused them and they went off to attend to the animals. There was no sign of any of the bandits or the escaped chavonth.

"He is no longer hungry. He will probably not return."

"If he does, his hunger will be appeased and we can catch him as we would any stray."

Unmok yelled at a slave, a stranger, hurrying past with a bucket and a broom. The slave trotted up, half-bent, cowed, a once burly Brokelsh but now a man much fallen away. He mumbled his jaws and clenched and unclenched his fist on the bucket handle.

"Yes, masters. Ungarvitch the Whip. He was our master. The drikingers killed him. There was much blood."

"So you are a masterless man now, until your late master's creditors sell you."

The slave merely blinked his granulated eyelids and nodded.

I said, "Get Avec to find a good lawyer. You will have a claim on the animals, at the least."

"I will, Jak, I will. And we do, we do. I think I will leave Froshak in charge to get things sorted out. I am for Huringa and Avec and the law. There is gold in this."

I did not smile, but I felt like smiling. Good old Unmok!

"And you, Jak. What is it all about, hey?"

Very carefully, I said, "If there were a certainty that you would be received with great honor in a certain country, where you could take up whatever profession you desired according to your abilities, and Froshak with you, and where your position would bring copious quantities of gold, would you give up the animal-catching business—as you have promised time and again?"

He stared up at me with his quizzical Och face only half-puzzled. If I chose to speak in riddles, he seemed to be saying, that was my business. As for him, he had important affairs to conduct. "Well, Jak, if you will not tell me, I must see Avec and—"

"I am trying to tell you, you five-limbed infuriating Och!"

"For a great hairy apim, you bluster tolerably well."

I had not really regarded Unmok as a blade comrade. But I warmed to him, I warmed to him. A thought occurred to me.

"I suppose you can fly a voller?"

"Naturally."

Well, it wasn't really naturally, but in Vallia it was uncommon among the generality of folk to find airboat pilots. Herein Havilfar piloting was much more common. And I fancied in this I could, as Seg Segutorio would say, take two korfs with a single shaft.

"I am hardly likely to buy a voller I could not test fly myself. Now, if you have enjoyed your jest—"

"I do not jest, Unmok. I give you my word on this. Before I decide what is best to do, we must thrash out the whole business of the partnership—"

"You wish to terminate our agreement?"

"No, by Harg, no!"

"Well?"

"Leave it until the arrangements with Avec are made. But think on my words. It is you who must make up your mind, you and Froshak. Think of what is offered—assuming—assuming—"

"Assuming what?"

"Assuming I live to tell you."

There was no answer Unmok could make to that beyond the conventional one that I should confide my fate into the hands of Ochenshum and Havil the Green—and any other gods who would look kindly upon me.

A hullabaloo broke out with much shouting and cracking of whips, and presently Froshak came up to say the chavonth had been taken and placed back in his cage. We all breathed easier.

Froshak looked tensed up with excitement, and he spoke at a rate that, for him, was loquacious. "Come and have a look at this. It is remarkable. Come and see."

Unmok regarded the big Fristle with his eyebrows drawn down. "Come and look at what? You're being very mysterious."

"Come and look!"

"Do I, Froshak, or do I not, employ you and treat you well and pay you out of all proportion? I do, indeed I do. So no more of this mysterious nonsense. Tell me!"

But Froshak's fierce cat's face wrinkled up, his whiskers quivered, his bald membrane glistened, and he just nodded his head and started off, beckoning to us to follow along the line of cages. Unmok looked helplessly at me, and I set off after Froshak, so Unmok trailed on, loudly lamenting the evil days and the way loyal retainers had fallen away in the duty they owed their kind employers.

Halting before a large cage, Froshak pointed. He had all the air of a proud proprietor showing off his choicest wares.

We looked into the cage.

Well.

Unmok swallowed. He swelled. Tears stood in his eyes.

"Poor Ungarvitch the Whip!" That was his thought. "To have secured such a prize, and then to be killed! How he must have regretted not being able to go into Huringa as he died!"

Froshak beamed, as though the proud proprietor had pleased his clientele. "She is a magnificent churmod, such a churmod as I have never seen before, and I have handled three in my time in the trade."

I looked at Froshak in genuine amusement. This savage and malevolent wild beast had roused him and loosened his tongue. Unmok continued to stare into the cage. He shook his head slowly, and I could see he could hardly credit his good fortune.

"Look at the way she puts her eight legs down, and the size of her, and the talons! She could rip a boloth to shreds! And those jaws—she will fetch a fortune." He glanced up at me. "A word of caution, Jak. Churmods are unpleasant beasts, surly and sadistic and vicious. Never trust one. Never take your eyes off one unless strong bars protect you."

"Aye," amplified Froshak. "Churmods are beasts from the depths of Cottmer's Caverns. Nasty."

"And valuable," I said.

"Queen Fahia. She, alone, must be offered this churmod. To do aught else would be foolish." Unmok waved his stump about, letting the excitement out. This ferocious and malignant wild beast would make a man's fortune. The lawyers Avec Parlin found on our behalf would fight hard for this prize.

The churmod turned her head and stared at us. She did not rise, but her eight sets of claws extended, curved and shining, and she stretched with arrogant laziness. Her hide was all a silky slatey-blue, uniform, without patterning, and she looked like a silent silvery-blue ghost there in the center of the cage.

Her eyes were mere slits of lambent crimson in the blunt head. She looked magnificent and, at the same time, profoundly repellent. She was larger than a well-grown leem; but much as I detest leems I found another altogether more pungent feeling of distaste for this churmod rising in me and, displeased on that account, as though it demeaned my own sense of fair play, I turned away abruptly.

"Yes, Jak," said Froshak in this new loquacious way, "they do work on a fellow. Just watch yourself with her, all the time."

Fascinating though this splendid and vicious wild animal might be, we all felt that repugnance, and soon we moved away and Unmok and Froshak fell into a one-sided conversation about the running of the caravan and camp while Unmok was away in Huringa. He suggested we ride in together, and fake our quarrel there before witnesses. This was agreeable to me. If we could draw off Vad Noran's antipathy from Unmok onto me, that suited me. Unmok, to give him credit, did not see it like that. He saw the practical side of being able to manage our affairs in peace.

We walked down the road toward our camp and this time the swords were safely snugged in their sheaths. As we went I turned for a last look at the menacing slate-blue form with those smoldering crimson eyes.

Chapter Five

Valona

"A churmod," said Jaezila. "Your partner will make a packet with him."

"She's a her. And I hope Unmok does. He deserves to."

"Just steer well clear of them, that's all I will say," said Tyfar, and his mouth closed up tightly.

"Agreed. Have you had the news you expected yet?"

"I await the spy—" Here Tyfar looked around quickly. We were not overheard. The twin Suns of Scorpio, Zim and Genodras, flooded down their streaming mingled lights and filled the air with glory. We stood at one of the little open-air bars, a mere hole in a wall with a counter, where refreshing drinks could be had for the price of a copper ob or two. No one else was within earshot, and the crone serving the drinks had gone into the back at the wailing cry of a baby. Tyfar went on: "Just what it is about I am not sure. But fat old Homan ham Ambath won't let me meet the fellow anywhere near the embassy."

"That makes sense," said Jaezila, and she sipped her sazz.

"It is just as well he did not arrange to meet near the Kyro of the Happy Calsany. I do not think we would be welcomed there."

"We are not welcome anywhere in Huringa in Hyrklana," said Jaezila. She drank off her sazz with a defiant gesture.

"And this stupid protocol demands that our comrades Kaldu and Barkindrar the Bullet and Nath the Shaft must wait apart from us merely because they are your retainers." I half turned to lean back against the bar and so looked across the suns-drenched square toward another bar in the adjacent building where our three comrades stood, drinking easily, and keeping a watchful eye out. These finicky matters of rank seem to mean—by Krun, do mean—a great deal to most Havilfarese.

As I watched, a slinky sylvie, exhibiting all the flaunted sexuality of the sylvies, undulated up to the bar and engaged the three men in conversation. They did not stop looking out and keeping an eye on us, but they were engrossed with the sylvie, which was natural, given that they were men and she was a sylvie. She wore a dazzling garment of a rich dark blue, slit to the upper thigh, and her gems—imitation, of course—glistened in the light of the suns. She was probably a respectable girl who worked locally, out for a breath of air and a break from routine.

Jaezila drew her brows down. "Many girls say that the sylvies make them feel less than feminine."

"I do not think your Kaldu will—" began Tyfar.

"No. Nor your Nath or Barkindrar. But who could blame them?"

They were laughing together over at the other bar. A file of slaves carrying amphorae wended past, and a totrix clip-clopped six-legged along, his rider slumped in the saddle with his broad-brimmed straw hat pulled over his nose. The day seemed perfectly ordinary.

Tyfar squinted sideways up at the suns. By the position of the red and green suns Kregans can tell the time with wonderful accuracy. "In a few murs he will be here, if he keeps his appointment punctually."

Even as Tyfar spoke, a bent figure in a brown tunic and straw hat walked slowly toward the bar at which we stood. He carried a staff with which he assisted his movements. He looked completely inoffensive. So, naturally, we all became alert.

The sylvie laughed and danced a few steps away, and then walked in that undulating way they have around the corner. The bent figure halted at the bar. "Is the sazz here good?"

"As good as the parclear," said Tyfar.

That, then, was the secret exchange.

"Follow me, horters, hortera.* It is not far."

We finished the drinks and walked slowly after the man

* Horter: Hamalese and Hyrklanian for gentleman, equating with the Vallian koter. Feminine is hortera and kotera. —A.B.A.

in the brown tunic. I own I let my hand brush across the hilt of my sword.

There was no doubt that Hamal kept up a secret network of spies in Hyrklana. That was mere common sense. If there were plots against Queen Fahia the Hamalese would demand to know what the plots were and how best they might profit from them. Tyfar, now, might decide to help bring down Fahia, or he might decide it was better for his country for the fat queen to remain in power. Despite my feelings of intense affection for Tyfar and Jaezila, despite that they were blade comrades with whom I had gone through the fire, in these intrigues I would put Vallia first, always providing no harm befell Jaezila or Tyfar.

The opposite side of the small square was occupied by an arcade of shops nearly all selling religious trinkets and votive offerings. The fourth side was dominated by the bulk of a temple to Malab the Kazzin. Part of the side wall had fallen in and workmen had been killed in a second fall during repairs. Blocks of stone and bricks in ungainly heaps filled the side street. No work went forward until the queen's inspectors had surveyed the fabric. Malab is a relatively respectable religious figure. He is often called Malab the Wounded, or Malab the Fount, his believers seeking mercy and wisdom, luck and health in the blood that pours from his wounded head. He is not, of course, Malab the Kazzur, for that means bloody, and Kazzin means bloody, although the two meanings are very different. Our guide led us past the tangles of broken scaffolding and piles of brick. Dust tanged on the tongue. We went in through a low-arched doorway. The interior struck gloomily after the brilliance of the suns.

"Loosen your swords," said Tyfar in a low voice.

He went first, as was his right as a prince, Jaezila followed, and I tagged along at the rear. At that, I kept screwing my head around to inspect the way we had come for hidden assassins.

We climbed wooden stairs that creaked. The dust lay thickly. I could see only one set of footprints in the dust ahead of us, going up. Broken windows allowed light to sift in.

We came out onto a landing and a corridor with doors leading no doubt to the cells of devotees, or the quarters of the acolytes. The whole place lay silent and deserted apart from us intruders and whoever waited for us.

At the far end of the corridor the guide pushed open a door covered in red baize and studded with brass buttons. The door creaked in protest. Light washed out in a fan.

The guide passed through the opening, followed by Tyfar and Jaezila. Both gripped their sword hilts although they had not yet drawn. I paused. A sound wafted ghostlike up from the corridor. I looked back. A glimpse of a fierce Brokelsh face, of intent staring eyes, told me Barkindrar the Bullet led on our comrades to afford us protection. And, I own it, I felt the comfort of that. I went past the red-baize door. I left it open.

A vaulted space lay before us, long and high. The slates had fallen from the roof some twenty paces ahead so that the blaze of suns light fell like a curtain across the chamber. The myriad dancing dust motes within the wall of light, the brightness of that radiance itself, contained in a narrow slot, prevented any clear impression of what lay beyond. The proportions of the room suggested the slates had fallen near the middle and there was at least as much space again beyond. The door slammed at my back.

Whirling around was, as usual in these circumstances, entirely useless. This side of the door was solid iron.

The guide half-turned and beckoned us on.

At once I knew. Jaezila and Tyfar, also, at once saw what that indifference to the closing of the door must mean. The guide, in his turn, realized he had betrayed himself. With a cry he leaped headlong, vanished like a plunging swimmer into the curtain of light. Tyfar ripped out his blade and ran after him with Jaezila at his heels. I followed and my brand was in my fist.

The light dazzled only momentarily, for I had half-closed my eyes against the glare. The space beyond duplicated the first and boxes and bales lay scattered about, with a two-wheeled handcart upended at one side. Tyfar stood peering about, looking this way and that, his sword snouting. Jaezila was nowhere to be seen. A hole in the floor between Tyfar and me puffed a little dust turning and floating and sinking.

"Jaezila!" I yelled.

Tyfar looked at the hole. I saw his face. The shock, the despair and then the anger flooded into that face of his. His rapier shook.

"I heard nothing, Jak! Nothing! She must have—"

"Yes."

I ran to the hole, carefully, for the floorboards might be

rotten, and looked down. Only darkness down there. Not a speck of light. Our blade comrade Jaezila had fallen down through a devilish trapdoor in the floor.

Tyfar edged closer. He gathered himself. He was going to throw himself down, without hesitation, gathering himself as a professional diver gathers himself before launching off a high cliff into a narrow slot of rock-infested water.

Before Tyfar took that plunge a figure rose from the cover of an upturned bale at his back. A blade glimmered. The figure screeched wildly and hurtled forward, the sword aimed directly for Tyfar's back.

The trap had been sprung.

I cannot say if I shouted first or jumped first. Everything happened at once.

"Your back, Tyfar!" I leaped.

I leaped. "Your back, Tyfar!"

Whatever the order, Tyfar heard me and rolled away and I landed awkwardly on the edge of the trap and got my rapier up in time to parry that cowardly thrust.

The man was a superb swordsman, that was apparent in the first passage, and he pressed in again hard, silently, swirling his brown cloak with his left hand to dazzle me. I fended him off, feeling for a secure foothold at the trap edge.

"Jak!" Tyfar raged forward.

"Jaezila," I shouted, "go on, go on!"

Tyfar hesitated no longer. Instead of leaping in to fight with me, as he had automatically begun to do, being a blade comrade, he jumped bodily down through the trap. I did not envy him the decision he had had to make, but he had made the right one. When there are three blade comrades and you have to choose which one to stand alongside in a fight to the death, all the gods must needs smile for you to choose right.

A second figure joined in against me, and this was the guide, bent over no longer, but young and lithe and, his staff cast away, boring in with a skillful flourish of a rapier fighter.

Circling, I cleared that dangerous trapdoor. I foined and then a thrust intended to skewer the guts of the first fighter scored all along his arm as he riffled the cloak. He let out a yell and staggered back in that moment I stepped in and, most unbladesmanlike, hit the guide alongside the jaw with my left fist. He fell down.

"So that is how you damned Hamalese fight!" said a light voice at my side.

I didn't hang around. I leaped away, ducking, and a blow from some solid gleaming object whistled past, missing me by the thickness of a copper ob.

"Gouge the rast's eyes out, Valona!" yelped the man with the gashed arm. He started to come in again, the cloak now wrapped clumsily around wrist and arm to stanch the blood.

The girl who, after her first blow had missed, had sprung back to clear a space between us, lifted her rapier in her right fist. Her left arm was held down behind her back. For a moment we stood, fronting one another.

"I can take care of this Hamalese cramph, Erndor. Get after that corrupt prince! Stick him! He is the man we want."

"Quidang!"* said this Erndor. He ran and jumped down through the hole

I said, "I admire your self-confidence, Valona. You Hyrklese hate Hamalese very deeply—or some of you." I wanted to annoy her. I studied her as she stared in open anger and contempt upon me. She wore a loose blue tunic and her legs were bare. Her legs were very long and lovely. Her brown hair was fastened by a fillet. Her face was regular and beautiful, with widely spaced brown eyes, and the redness of her lips in the radiance from the roof glistened with full passion. Some peculiarity in her face, some characteristic, struck me with a chord of memory. I did not know her, but I felt I ought to know her, although we had never met before now.

"The Hyrklese hate the Hamalese, some of them, as you say, rast. But I am not of Hyrklana."

And she sprang.

As she leaped so she foined with the rapier and then—and then!

Her left arm whipped up. Her left hand reached for my face.

Razored steel flashed before my eyes. Her left hand was sheathed in talons, steel tiger-claws that could shred and rip and blind. And I knew she was exceedingly cunning in the use of this metal claw.

* Quidang!: The formal acknowledgment of an order and the promise it will be faithfully carried out. Equivalent to "Aye, aye, sir!" "To hear is to obey!" —A.B.A.

Without hesitation I leaped away, jangling the rapiers, and moving off and away from her. I did not wish to kill her. I could not, seeing she was of Vallia, and a sister of the Sisters of the Rose.

"I am not of Hamal," I said. I know I spoke breathily, caught up in the wonder of a girl of the SoR being here, here in the capital of Hyrklana.

"A cowardly lie to save yourself. You are Hamalese and therefore you will die."

"You are wrong on both counts."

I moved away, circling, the rapier up. I was ready for her next spring, rapier and claw working together sweetly, to lunge and to rip.

"Your armies have laid waste to my land and you, at least, will pay the price, here and now. Die, Hamalese!"

The rapier moved with precision, the feint lunge coming in exactly so, and the claw striking across with a glitter of steel. I made no attempt to parry but leaped away.

Again, we fronted each other.

"You are a man. Why do you not stand and fight? Do you fear my claw so much?"

"I am a Vallian—"

"You lie, rast! You lie!"

"I know you are of the Sisters of the Rose—"

"That is easy enough to discern. It is common knowledge, who I must be. Even you cramphs in Hamal have heard of the SoR—to your sorrow!"

This was becoming farcical. Here was this splendid girl trying to send me down to the Ice Floes of Sicce, and her deadly companions were off chasing Tyfar and Jaezila, and who knew how many more of them there were waiting below? I had to settle this, and settle it fast.

"Look, Valona the Claw—"

"That is not my name." But she hesitated.

"Valona, then. Listen, girl. Forget your preconceptions. Yes, the two who came here with me are Hamalese. But I play them, as I must. There is much at stake—you are here, far from Vallia. You must understand that . . . Perhaps you know of Naghan Vanki?"

"I know the name." Now her rapier lowered.

Naghan Vanki was the chief spymaster of Vallia. I wasn't going to say that, just in case she did not know. If she did not know I did not want her to have that information, and should she know, then Vanki was probably her employer. I knew he had spies in every country of importance to us. And if she was one of Vanki's people, she would understand what I was talking about.

She swung the razored claw about. "My father has a friend called Naghan Vanki. Not that my father knows much about what I do. But I do not think I believe you. I think you are a damned Hamalese spy who knows more than he should. It is the Ice Floes of Sicce for you, Jak the Hamalese rast!"

She was going to spring in the next instant.

I said, "There is no time to waste any longer on you, young lady. I know that you have been through Lancival . . ." Lancival was the place where the Sisters of the Rose were trained up to use the claw, those that did so, for not all the girls of the SoR wore the claw. No one would tell me where the place was, would not even tell the Emperor of Vallia. But the name itself, alone, might cause this Valona, who was not Valona the Claw, to stop and think.

The hammering on the door that was subdued red baize with brass studding on one side and solid iron on the other increased. The door shook. It had been designed to keep out thieves from this store chamber, but Barkindrar and Nath and Kaldu would break it down in only heartbeats.

"I have met young ladies who have been trained up at Lancival before. I am honored they count me as a friend. Now do you—"

She had stopped dead when I used the name of Lancival. Now she broke in, roughly, flourishing her claw. "What do you know of Lancival? How could you know. . . ?"

"Because I am what I told you I am! It is in my mind I know your father, for you bring someone to my mind. But there is no time for that now. I give you my most solemn oath, as the Invisible Twins made manifest in the light of Opaz are my judge! I am Vallian and dedicated to the Empress Delia."

"The Empress Delia! You dare use *her* name—"

"Stand aside from the men who are breaking the door in. For all your claw—and you have no whip? I see not. For all your razor-talons they will eat you up and spit out the pips. Now I am going down to try to stop honest Vallians from murdering those two poor damned Hamalese down there." I couldn't say that I was in agony for the fate of my blade comrades, my friends, Tyfar and Jaezila.

"I cannot believe you! You must give me more proof!"

"No time, no time."

I had worked us around during this conversation so that the open trapdoor lay at my back. I lifted the rapier in salute. She anticipated an attack and came on guard instantly. Then she saw what I purported—too late. She tried to get at me before I retired from the scene. Her exertions during the pseudo-fight had broken the latches of her tunic and as it gaped I caught the sheen of black leather beneath. A real she-cat, tiger-girl, this Valona!

I could not refrain from calling, "You fight well, by Vox. Take your friend the guide and go, for those men breaking the door down will deal harshly with you. Remberee!"

Then I leaped into the open trapdoor and fell headlong into blackness.

Chapter Six

Froshak the Shine

The thump of landing was not overly painful. The place was little more than a closet, dark and dank. I kicked out and a wooden panel nearly broke my toe. The square of light over my head remained clear: I half expected Valona to jump down after me. I kicked again at the next wall, more cautiously. A distant crash from above was followed by voices raised intemperately.

"Where are they?"

"There goes someone—after them!"

"Get on, get on! The prince is in danger!"

I leaned more gently against the third wall and fell all sprawling out into a lighted corridor. I did not want Kaldu and Nath the Shaft and Barkindrar the Bullet with me now. I did not want those three blade comrades, Hamalese, assisting me to slay Vallians.

The panel revolved and shut. I looked up and down and saw a dead man slumped against the wall. He sat with his head on his chest and his arms lax at his sides. He wore inconspicuous clothes. I did not know him. I hoped he was not a Vallian and guessed he was probably the Hamalese spy Tyfar had come here to see. Valona and her merry men had gotten wind of the meeting, had slain the spy and sent their man as a guide to bring us to the trap. Well, the trap had not yet failed. I ran full speed in the direction pointed by the dead man.

I wondered how Erndor, whom Valona had sent off after Tyfar, would fare against that puissant prince of Hamal. The guide must have been shaken into sense by Valona and the pair of them run off to a prepared bolthole as our three comrades burst in. Now, Erndor is a Valkan name, and I am the Lord of Valka. But, equally, as the Strom of Valka I cannot know the face of every Valkan, as everyone of that superlative island cannot know the face of his strom. The likenesses on coins are not reliable guides to recognition. If Erndor and Tyfar clashed, rapier against axe, it would make a pretty fight, a fight that would chill me to the core. I had to prevent that confrontation if I could.

The corridor ended at a door and I simply bashed it open and roared through. Torches in bracketed sconces lit up an area that curved in a subtle way like a crown rink, so that I guessed I was over the side porch of the great hall of Malab's Temple. Dust choked everywhere. I saw no more bodies, for which I was profoundly grateful.

A distant noise, like a clink of metal against stone, floating from the opposite side made me hare over the shallow dome, kicking dust. By the time I reached the opposite door, passing the ranked cubbyholes stuffed with skulls and skeletons, there was sign of no one. The torches were all burned low, some guttering. No doubt they afforded light to the watchkeepers of the dead. The believers in the power of Malab's Blood wished to remain in his temple when they were dead and not to be buried in the ranked mausoleums of the Forest of the Departed. As for Malab, your ordinary uncouth fellow like myself will quaff a good measure of Malab's Blood, and comment on the quality of the wine. Such is one belief to an unbeliever. As for Malab's Blood itself, as a wine I drink it when there is nothing finer to be had.

Stairs led down beyond the door. They would open up to the little porch that gave ingress to the major porch on this undamaged side of the temple. I rattled down the stairs quickly, but I went silently and my rapier snickered out before me as I went.

No one waited for me at the foot of the stairs.

Another damned door and this time I was out in the street.

The side alley was shadowed in the lights of the suns. I ducked back and went the other way, skirting around behind the pierced traceries, searching the ground floor of the temple. I could see no one, yet there had been that clink of steel on stone.

Back and forth I went, and nothing. Again I climbed, this time creeping out along the crazy half-exposed stairway where the other side wall had fallen away. Nothing. Back again in the vast and shadowed Great Hall of the temple, with all the fine furnishings removed, the idol missing from the alcove above the altar, the floor dusty and slick, I stared about.

Three men advanced toward me in the shadowed light.

I said—very damned quickly!—"It's me. Jak."

Barkindrar's sling stopped its whirling, and Nath's bow lowered.

"You were nearly feathered there, Jak," said Nath.

"After my shot had squashed his brains in," said Barkindrar.

"This is no time for a professional argument." I spoke more sharply than I intended. But I felt the pressures. "Where are Tyfar and Jaezila?"

They did not know.

So, once again, we went through Malab's Temple. Nothing.

At last I said, "Very well. They are not here. They will have escaped. They must have!"

"Of course," said Kaldu in his heavy assertive way. He was Jaezila's personal retainer, a big-boned, powerful man, who wore his brown beard trimmed to a point. He was capable of such anger when aroused in defense of his mistress that he could tear a savage beast in half with his bare hands, or so it was said. "All the same," said Kaldu, looking about. "It is passing strange."

"Deuced strange."

"They could have gone back to the tavern," said Nath. "But it is hardly likely—"

"They would not run off and leave us," said Barkindrar.

That, we all agreed, was most unlikely.

So, once again, we searched.

This time, in that same damned crown rink of a place above the porch, where the moldering bones glinted in the light of guttering torches, we heard a choked cry. Instantly

Kaldu was tearing at the nearest heaps of bones, flinging them about in careless savagery. He hauled a pile of skulls away and Tyfar's face showed, the eyes fairly sticking out, the cheeks scarlet, and the gag partly wrenched away from his mouth. He was making the most ferocious sounds beneath the gag.

I stared at him. As they hauled him out I saw he was unharmed, if covered in skeleton dust. I felt such a heart-melting sense of relief I took a deep breath. So that made me say, "Just a moment, before you remove the gag. The prince may do himself an injury if he is allowed to vent his feelings too soon."

Barkindrar and Nath, being Tyfar's men, could hardly let their amusement appear too obvious. Kaldu, feeling with us all the same sense of relief, allowed a smile to cross his savage face.

Then I said, "Now, now Tyfar, my prince, rest easy. We will take the gag off as soon as we may, although the knot is difficult."

I thought Tyfar would explode. His eyes fairly bulged.

When we got the gag off he took in a whooping breath, and stood up and flexed his arms, and then—and then he laughed.

"By Krun, Jak! You try a fellow sorely!" He looked about. "Where is Jaezila?"

Kaldu let out a screech and began to hurl the skeletons about in a paroxysm of rage. We joined in, searching among all the old bones, not uncaring that we violated sacred remains, since we were forced by the urgent necessities of the occasion. Jaezila was found, at the far end, piled under bones, bound and gagged.

We pulled her out. She looked dazed.

After a time we got it all sorted out, or as sorted out as it seemed possible to sort out so improbable a tale.

"All I know," said Jaezila, "is that I fell down a damned great hole and woke up under these skeletons."

"And I was leaped on by a man with a rapier and we were having a great set to, when three others appeared to assist him." Tyfar held his axe. The blade was steel bright. "One of them threw a brick at me." He sounded offended. "I was just about to enjoy showing them how an axeman tackles swordsmen when they ruined it all by throwing the brick. I woke up here, managed to chew or twist some of my gag away and yelled. I heard some fools blundering past three times. Three times. Before they heard me. I think I must still be suffering from concussion. Otherwise I would be extremely wroth with them."

Nath and Barkindrar found it necessary to study the angle of the roof above their heads with great attention.

Not for the first time I reflected that Prince Tyfar had grown in stature over the time of our adventures together. He had always been a man of honor, filled with noble ideas of virtue and right dealing, but now he was more contained, more sure, and where your run-of-the-mill prince would have lambasted into his men for failing to find him sooner, Tyfar could see the jest and relish it for itself. I looked on him with great kindness, and he looked at Jaezila with emotions far beyond kindness. She looked puzzled.

"I fell down the trap—and if it was a trap, why did they not kill us?"

We couldn't fathom out the answer to that.

Refusing to become maudlin over my sentiments for these two, I brisked them up. "We are not dead, thank Krun. Why we were not slain must remain for the moment a mystery. Now we had best go."

"Let us go to The Silver Fluttrell and get cleaned up," said Jaezila. "I feel positively grimy."

We were all smothered in dust and festooned in cobwebs. So off we went to The Silver Fluttrell, the quiet inn where they were waiting rather than avail themselves of the mansion they might have used as emissaries of Hamal. Their ambassador hadn't liked that.

When we were washed and they had changed into clean clothes, although I'd had to make do with giving mine a good brush, we sat in their airy upstairs sitting room, drinking superb Kregan tea, and eating a substantial meal—call it lunch, if you will—and talked the thing through.

"The devil of it is," said Tyfar, "we do not know what the spy was bringing." The man I had seen dead against the wall beyond the trap had been the Hamalese spy.

"And we do not know who killed him. Who it was who tried to trap us." I spoke normally, but the answers to those questions, known to me, must not be revealed to my comrades. Be sure I felt the degradation of this shabby double-dealing. But unless Tyfar and Jaezila ran into danger so great there was nothing else for me to do, I must put the well-being of Vallia first. I felt the coldness. By Zair! But they'd so nearly been killed. Why they hadn't been I had no idea. Certainly Valona had given Erndor sharp enough instructions, exact and explicit. Then why had those men simply chucked a brick at him and tied him up?

Presently I excused myself and said I must be going. If I was to play the spy in Huringa I wanted to settle the business with Unmok and Froshak. As for Vad Noran, I did not think he could have had a hand in the trap sprung in Malab's Temple. And if he had, he'd have killed the lot of us, and giggled in the doing of it.

"When you have finished this business with Unmok," said Jaezila, "then you will join us? Here, I mean."

"Thank you. Yes. And a thought occurs to me. This Vad Noran. I heard that he is involved in a plot against the queen."

They reacted to this very coolly.

"Of course," I went on, "it could be that plots like this are two a penny. There are many who do not like the queen."

"And many who will fight for her, in expectation of reward." Tyfar saw I had been a trifle put out. "But we ought to investigate every story. Suppose my poor dead spy was going to tell us of Noran's plot?"

"Entirely possible. But I hardly think it would be Noran's plot. There are stronger men using him."

"Gochert?" said Jaezila.

"Possibly. He struck me as a man capable of a great deal."

"Well, then," said Tyfar. He looked pleased, and lifted a handful of palines, holding them cupped on his palm so that the yellow berries rolled. "I have a plan of my own, that might serve. Also, it is time we had a plan of our own instead of others."

"Go on, Ty."

"I am here in Huringa to buy vollers. Everyone knows that. Vad Noran expects a visit from me at some time. I think I will pay him that visit and sound him out—"

"Oh—Ty!"

"Steady, steady," I said. I looked at Jaezila and saw she shared my concern. "If you are incautious you might find yourself minus a head, or loosed into the Arena—or thrown to Fahia's pet neemus."

It was very necessary for me to be circumspect. I did not wish to reveal the extent of my knowledge of Huringa, acquired during my previous residence here when I was

Drak the Sword, a hyr-kaidur. But if my impetuous comrade was going to thrust his head into a noose, I was bound to loosen the rope, by Krun, yes.

"He would not move against me, surely?"

"Not openly. But he employs assassins, we know that."

"Then that settles it." Tyfar's air of pleasure increased. "If I convince him of our integrity, he will call off the stikitches he has set on you. So that is that."

"I see why he would do that." Jaezila put her head on one side. "But if what we suspect of him is true, he will prove a broken reed in times of trouble."

"I'll—" began Tyfar.

I stood up. "Promise me you will not sound out Noran until we have spoken again."

Jaezila nodded vigorously. "I agree."

Tyfar stared from Jaezila to me and back again. He flipped a paline into the air—and caught it in his other hand. Not for a prince of Hamal the indelicate business of paline popping in these serious circumstances. When he spoke he sounded somber.

"I take your meaning exactly. We are comrades, and we have been through much together. I think we value one another, and I do not intend to belabor the point. But I am a prince and if I see my duty plain I must do that. My duty tells me now that if I am able to get Noran to call his bloodhounds off you, Jak, then that is what I must do. And, betwixt you and me and Beng Dalty, I think he will listen to me."

"Oh, *Ty*!" exclaimed Jaezila.

"You—" I said. I took a breath.

"There is no more to be said." Tyfar placed a paline into his mouth and chewed. He chewed with great determination.

"All right. Then when you go to see him, I will accompany you—"

"And me!"

"And there is no more to be said on that subject."

Prince Tyfar of Hamal laughed.

When I took my leave of them I sought out their three retainers, who, scrubbed and polished, were stuffing themselves in their quarters at the side of the principal room. I was short and to the point.

"Very well, Jak. It does make sense." And: "Aye, Jak, we will." And; "Good, Jak. We will keep an exceedingly sharp observation."

So, satisfied that Kaldu and Nath and Barkindrar would not allow Tyfar to go wandering off by himself, I went out. If they knew where he was likely to go and he tried to give them the slip, they'd know where to find him. Or so I hoped.

The urvivel took me along to Tazll Kyro where the mercenaries temporarily without employment waited to see what turned up. Not for them the rigorous formality of employment bureaus; they would sit at the tables circling the square or stand at the bars, and they'd drink and ogle the girls and talk and quarrel and there'd be one or two fights per diem. People wishing to hire paktuns would look over these hard-swearing, ruffling, swashbuckling fellows, and take their pick, and haggle over the price. I looked but could see no sign of Unmok, and presently a one-eyed shaven-pated Gon with a kax fashioned from bronze, and two enormous swords, told me that, yes, a little five-limbed Och had been there and hired stupid Bargle the Drop and anxious Nath the Quick and cunning Kardol the Red who was a Khibil and would slit his grandmother's throat for a silver sinver.

I forbore to inquire why Unmok, if he had picked up so unlikely a bunch, had failed to hire this one-eyed Gon. I thanked him civilly and mounted up and clip-clopped back out of Huringa toward our camp. I would have preferred to have caught Unmok before he'd hired his mercenaries, but they could be paid off and no harm done—if Unmok agreed with my scheme.

Now you will have gathered by this time that I regarded Unmok as a very shrewd businessman. When I got back to the camp and saw what these mercenaries Unmok had hired were up to, I began to come to the conclusion that perhaps the one-eyed Gon had been right. They were certainly a pack of idiots.

An enormous spitting splintered the air.

Beside the cage containing the churmod the mercenaries were laughing and catcalling and poking their swords and spears through the bars. They were stirring the slatey-blue animal into a vicious temper. Her crimson eyes were mere slits of smoldering hate.

Jeering and taunting, the mercenaries tickled up the churmod and she slashed spitefully with her front two paws. The talons glinted. She knocked a spear away, the Brokelsh laughed and jabbed it back. When he withdrew, the tip showed a spot of red. The churmod hissed and slashed and the spear shivered in two.

A fire burned nearby with a cauldron bubbling away. One or two slaves stood, agape, transfixed by the behavior of these swaggering bully-boys. I cocked my leg over Snowdrop's back and jumped off.

Froshak the Shine appeared around the cage. He saw what the mercenaries were up to and he ran forward, shouting and waving his arms.

"Idiots!" he yelled. "Haven't you any more sense?"

He pushed the big reddish Khibil, who pushed him back.

"Keep away from her!" shouted Froshak, incensed.

He shoved up before the man, his arms outstretched—both to show he had no weapons and to shepherd them away. They sneered at him, calling that he was a spoil-sport.

"Stand back!" shouted Froshak.

I saw it.

"Froshak, jump clear!" I bellowed with all the force of my lungs. "*Froshak!*"

The churmod's claws raked between the bars and fastened on Froshak's neck. Her other paw slashed around. She held the Fristle's body against the bars, and her two second front paws menaced us. It was clear that Froshak was dead. He hung with her claws through his neck, and the blood dripped from what had been his face. Then, holding him against the bars, the churmod thrust her muzzle as far as she could and began to chew on him.

The mercenaries stumbled back. They were screaming now.

Attracted by all the din, Unmok appeared. He saw. He did not fall down, but he shook.

"Froshak!" But he could only whisper.

The horrendous grunts and savage snarlings of the churmod sicked us. Froshak was being chewed up.

"We can't leave him—"

"Rather him than me!" said the reddish Khibil. He was not so red now.

I walked forward. I said in a voice that made them jump, "You are all discharged, now, instantly, without pay. Get out of my sight. Get out now. Or I will surely slay you all."

Then I took no more notice of them.

The fire crackled. I picked up the unburned end of a

hefty branch and swung it about so that the other end flared brightly. Holding the brand before me, I advanced on the cage. The second pair of forepaws slashed the air between the bars. It was death to reach out for the dead Fristle.

Savagely, as filled with bestial anger as the churmod herself, I thrust the brand at her. I dug it in and jerked it back, and it flared and spat sparks into those lambent crimson slits she had for eyes. She snarled and hissed and slashed the air before me. I thrust the blazing brand and swung it and scattered sparks. I reached out with my left hand and a set of talons raked and I snatched my hand back. Again I thrust the burning branch. This time I drove it with intent to hit the churmod in the face and force her back, force her to relinquish her prey.

She flinched.

She snarled a bubble of hatred at me, and she released Froshak. The dead Fristle fell in a heap. The churmod backed off. She looked at me. Those twin slits of crimson spurted hellish reflections as though the flames of the torch were caught and hurled back at me.

I stared malevolently back.

I thrust the fire through the bars, trying to burn her, making her back off. Then, trembling, I controlled myself. It is often this way with churmods, and was why the mercenaries had taunted her when they would leave a chavonth or a strigicaw alone. She slunk back, belly low, a smoldering silver-blue ghost of malignant power.

Froshak was carried away, tenderly, and laid on the ground. He looked dreadful. Unmok stood beside the body of the cat-man he had employed, and who had remained so silent under Unmok's proprietorial mewlings. I stood by Unmok. There was nothing of any use or sense we could say to each other.

I looked at the little five-limbed Och.

Tears coursed down Unmok's face, and he dropped to his knees, sobbing.

Chapter Seven

Of Letters and Remberees

Froshak the Shine was buried with all respect and reverence in the Forest of the Departed. Unmok lavished his hoarded gold to buy and furnish a tomb that, as he said, was not good enough for his friend. The gold should have been spent on Froshak when he was alive; now that it was too late for that, Unmok would embellish the Fristle's tomb in sumptuous fashion and give his ib surcease in the long journey to his Fristle paradise.

Leaving Unmok for the next few days was quite out of the question. He had shrunk. He looked a small pale ghost of the shrewd, businesslike Unmok I had known.

We went to see Avec Parlin together and Unmok took no joy from the money he received for the safe return of Ungarvitch the Whip's caravan. The animals were sold off in the usual way and, not surprisingly, the churmod was reserved for Queen Fahia. Unmok's tame slaves were housed in a cheap lodging, for he would not avail himself of the services of the bagnio. During all this time the suns shone, Zim and Genodras, casting down their mingled ruby and jade, and the seven moons of Kregen rose and set, the stars glittered and the breezes blew and men and women went about their daily lives, and it might all have gone hang for Unmok the Nets.

Nothing would rouse him. Even when Avec Parlin announced that he had heard of a good-quality secondhand cage voller that was not required by Hamal for her Air Service, Unmok merely nodded absently. "That is nice," he said, in his choked whisper.

"And when will you need her?" Parlin, the lawyer, an apim, treated Unmok with great civility. Had he not done so, I verily think, he would have had the rough side of my tongue, if not worse.

"When? Oh, I do not—I do not know—"

I said, "As soon as the sale is made, Avec, we will need

the cage voller. Can you see that she is properly surveyed and then provisioned? You know the gold is available."

He nodded. Then he screwed up his eyes. "Unmok has told me of Vad Noran. You walk perilously, Horter Jak."

"I thank you for your concern. Tell me, does the plot against the queen prosper? Or is it all a phantom, a Drig's Lantern?"

We walked along the north boulevard and the streets were hot under the suns and few people were abroad. The beast roar from the Arena told where the citizens of Huringa were spending the day.

"The plot is real. I will have nothing of it. But as for Vad Noran—he is a man led by the nose."

"And who does the leading? Gochert?"

"Gochert? No." Parlin looked surprised. "My informant says that Gochert warned Noran most seriously. The one-eyed man refused to have anything to do with such a hare-brained scheme."

That did not square with the impression I had received, but I let it pass. Gochert struck me as an antagonist worth ten Norans.

"Who, then?"

Parlin hitched up his shoulders and lifted his hands, palms up. "You are abrupt, Horter Jak. Such knowledge could bring a man to the Arena."

With the civility that was not altogether feigned, I said, "I crave your pardon, Horter Parlin, but the matter is of moment, as you understand."

"Assuredly. The fact is, I do not know. I have heard rumors that a great noble presses to take over the throne from Queen Fahia—"

"Someone with a legitimate claim? That would narrow the field."

"When the queen came to the throne she was severe with her family. Many died. Her husband is a nonentity."

I drew in my breath. "There is her twin sister, Princess Lilah."

In the long ago I had saved Princess Lilah of Hyrklana from the Manhounds. She had disappeared and no one I had spoken to had heard of her fate. Could she still be alive, and plotting against her sister? I devoutly hoped so, by Vox!

Again Parlin spread his hands. "It could not be. Princess Lilah disappeared seasons ago. Whoever plots against the queen and employs Noran as his tool is a man in the limelight who wishes to cloak his designs. That seems sure."

At another time and place in the long ago I had, because I was at first bored and then because I saw it was my duty, made myself King of Djanduin. Djanduin lay in the far southwest of the continent of Havilfar. The fearsome four-armed Djangs were among the most superb fighting men of all Kregen. They were fanatically loyal to me, as loyal as the ferocious Clansmen of the Great Plains of Segesthes. I did not toy with the notion that I, Dray Prescot, Krozair of Zy, Lord of Strombor, might make myself King of Hyrklana. I had done with titles. Now I would seek to exert my influence in uniting all of Paz against the Leem-Loving Shanks who raided our coasts, from the shadows and through emperors and kings and queens who saw the true path that the peoples of Paz must follow. Megalomania? If you wish. I did not care about that. All I knew was that if the Star Lords, who could fling me about Kregen on a whim or dispatch me back to Earth out of spite, left me alone to get on with the work which fate or destiny had set to my hands, I would carry on that good work with all the skill and dedication in me.

By Zair! The task was colossal and I a mere mortal man. But I could see no other reason for all the things that had happened to me. Well, as you will hear, I could see only a tithe, and a dark tithe at that, of what destiny had in store for me.

If uniting this great grouping of islands and continents in friendship was a fool's dream, then I was the fool, the onker, I have so many times been dubbed. I did not want a uniform grayness, a drabness. Havilfar was Havilfar, as Segesthes was Segesthes. Loh would remain a mysterious continent. The islands of Pandahem and Vallia would retain their identities. But we would cease from fighting among ourselves. We would turn all our energies toward ridding ourselves of the slavers and the aragorn, slavemasters and scum, and toward freeing ourselves of the grip of the Shanks. If that is idealistic nonsense, so be it.

At the time of which I speak, it was the guiding principle of everything I did and attempted on Kregen. Everything save one thing. And that was the happiness and well-being of Delia, Empress of Vallia. The welfare of Delia, Delia of Delphond, Delia of the Blue Mountains, and of our family and friends, for this I would see the rest go hang.

Such is the crumbling of high-minded principle when personal desires supervene!

As for all this not-really-but-almost nonsense of holding responsibilities in faraway lands by being the king or lord of them, as you will readily perceive, I was usually in constant communication by flier-borne letters and messengers with my folk in Djanduin, in Zenicce, among the Clans of the Great Plains. I knew what went on there, and the men and women charged with running those places to the standards we agreed knew my thoughts and carried out my wishes, as I confirmed my pleasure in their own ambitions and labors. On Kregen, with fliers to whisk you from one end of Paz to another, handling a widely flung empire was not anywhere near the enormously difficult undertaking the Romans had faced, or the Mongols, or Charlemagne. Napoleon would have relished instant news from Spain when he was in Poland—or, given *that* situation, perhaps not. The point is that although the image does not please me, I was like a spider at the center of a web, and I could feel the vibrations from all sides. Of course, when I went off adventuring, as I loved to do, the situation was more difficult. But now, with Unmok shattered by the death of Froshak, with my decision to send him to Vallia, and with a fine cage-voller to provide transport, I took full advantage of those assets.

A whole day was consumed in writing letters. I sent one of Unmok's slaves with a letter around to The Silver Fluttrell pleading that unexpectedly I had been detained. I would join Tyfar and Jaezila as soon as my duties were honorably discharged. I made no bones about it with Unmok. He continued in his dazed state, and I seriously considered flying with him back to Vallia myself. But that would be ducking what I had to do here in Hyrklana. Lackadaisically he agreed to go. He could hardly take in what I was saying, but I told him to go and see Enevon Ob-Eye. Enevon, as my Chief Stylor, would take care of everything. I fancied Unmok would get on better with him.

"And Unmok, fly directly there and do not land at all. Here is a satchel. Give it to Enevon. And guard it well."

"All right, Jak. But—"

The satchel bulged with a day's letters. Missives to my folk scattered across the breadth of Paz—but no letter addressed to Paline Valley, for that place lay in Hamal.

"Enevon is a good friend. The Lord Farris, too." I

handed Unmok a separate, smaller letter folded and securely sealed. "If you cannot find anyone there—then take this letter to the empress or one of her handmaids. Otherwise—burn it!"

"Yes, Jak."

He shook his head. This was beyond him. But he would fly to Vallia in the new voller and there, as I devoutly hoped, he would begin a new life. As for me, I had plots and ploys to work here in Huringa.

As I looked ahead, the future appalled me. There was so much to do. The tasks to which I had set myself were enormous. And yet: "Sink me!" I burst out to myself. "It's got to be done! We have to scupper mad Empress Thyllis and smash Hamal so that we can turn to the more important tasks ahead." I could feel my fingernails gripping into my palms. I forced myself to relax those constricting fists. Hamal under the imperious sway of Thyllis was again growing stronger, and with sorcerous help could smash up Vallia. If Queen Fahia of Huringa was one of the keys to help unlock the torrent of opposition to Hamal, then Queen Fahia would have to turn, like it or not.

Much though I detest fighting and warfare, I admit that the thought of a powerful army from Hyrklana landing on the coast of Hamal and marching inland to Ruathytu filled me with what I see to be an unholy glee.

"You are—feeling all right, Jak?"

"Yes, Unmok. It is you who—" Trust the little Och to see I was burdened with other problems. I still had not told him what he so grandiloquently called "my secret" and he'd find out quite enough when he arrived in Vondium, capital of Vallia.

The cage-voller had been a splendid flyer; she was still sound but worn. The cages gaped emptily. Unmok's slaves would spell him on the flight. "You'll have to manumit your slaves in Vallia. But that will be no hardship."

"Agreed. And you are not coming?" Unmok cradled his middle left stump with his middle right, and wiped his upper left over his forehead. His upper right was extended toward me. "I don't know why I'm going off and leaving you, anyway. What am I doing?" He would have gone on.

There was no time for him to indulge in deep personal philosophy and inquiry. I bundled him aboard, saw that the slaves were all there, stood back, waving.

"Remberee, Unmok the Nets!"

"Remberee, Jak the Shot!"

The cage-voller lifted off, fleeted into the streaming mingled lights of the Suns of Scorpio.

Chapter Eight

We Plot Against the Queen

We threw ourselves into the business of plotting against Queen Fahia with tremendous zest.

We did go to see Vad Noran, and Tyfar convinced the nobleman that I was not a queen's man, that I worked for Prince Tyfar of Hamal, and that we ardently wished to assist Vad Noran in any way we could. He preened and primped and, because it was the easiest course, accepted our proposals. Money lay near the heart, of course, but the promise of swords tipped the balance.

No wonder Noran had been flustered when I'd suggested I worked for Queen Fahia! No wonder he'd tried to have me assassinated! Now he was revealed in his true colors, his attitude changed. We were all conspirators together.

I had given Tyfar and Jaezila the impression I worked for their mad Empress Thyllis; at the time the ploy had seemed clever enough and had served, as I judged, to ease my position. Later, when I gauged more accurately Tyfar's own tortured doubts of his empress and the course his country was set on, my own supposed cleverness was revealed as being too damned clever by half. I did not think that Tyfar or Jaezila would swallow any story I might try to sell them, that I had renounced allegiance to Thyllis, in the same way that Vad Noran had swallowed the story I spun him.

Another side of Noran's character was revealed on the day when Jaezila and I went up to see him at his villa, Tyfar being obliged to inspect the latest progress on the airboats being built at another yard. Dorval, one of Noran's cronies and a man who did not recognize me, called me into the armory where he made a fuss over showing me some brand-new rapiers just arrived from

Zenicce. I admired them. I whisked them about, feeling the balance. When, at last, we left the armory, I saw Jaezila marching along the covered gallery toward us. She was pulling her tunic up; its latches were broken. Her color was high, very high.

Going forward, careful not to appear overexcited, I said, "Yes, Jaezila?"

"That man!" Then, seeing Dorval going past toward the door from which Vad Noran was just emerging, Jaezila said, quickly and in a low voice, "Nothing. It is nothing, Jak. For the sake of Tyfar. Leave it."

Vad Noran sported the beginnings of a fruity black eye.

Jaezila saw my hand twitch uncontrollably toward my rapier.

"Jak! Nothing happened! For all our sakes—please!"

Noran passed the matter off—something about a door being ajar—and since Tyfar's reactions would be well understood by Jaezila and me if he got into this, I, perforce, acquiesced, and let it lie.

To have made an issue of the incident would have impugned Jaezila's honor. She had requested me to do nothing. There was Tyfar to consider. So, even though it may seem strange conduct for Dray Prescot, nothing was what I did. All the same, Jaezila was relieved to be out of Noran's villa for that day.

"Do take the scowl off your face, Jak! Noran will—"

"Very well."

My old beak-head of a face can assume so ferocious an expression, so I am told, that it will stop a dinosaur in its tracks. So I am told. My comrade, Deb-Lu-Quienyin, who was now one of the two resident Wizards of Loh in Vallia, had given me the secret of altering my facial appearance. I say given and secret. By Vox! It was a most painful experience at first, like having a swarm of bees stinging me. But I had practiced and could now hold a new face for a goodly length of time, so that I could pass unrecognized. So now I assumed a face of docility that was still me, still Dray Prescot, in a mood of sweetness and light. Ha!

"Anyway," said Jaezila, "there is good news. Noran has arranged a meeting for the day after tomorrow. It does really seem as though we are getting somewhere."

Tyfar fired up at the news.

"At last!" Then his expression grew grim. "A new spymaster has been appointed. He flew in from Hamal. It seems that our operations here have been penetrated by those Vallian devils. They were probably responsible for the attack on us in Malab's Temple."

"Then," I said, desperately wanting to keep my Vallians and my Hamalese comrades away from one another's neck, "we had best keep our plotting to ourselves."

"By Krun! Yes!"

The situation in which I found myself was not an impossible one, although near enough to being impossible; it was most certainly a false position. This whole thing could explode around my ears, as the Quern of Gramarye had exploded the Souk of Trifles. I could be left surrounded by blood and dead bodies—and those corpses would be my comrades and my countrymen.

"This new spymaster has other disturbing news."

"Yes?" said Jaezila. She spoke casually. "What does he call himself?"

"Oh, Nath the Eye."

The name Nath on Kregen is like John on Earth. A pseudonym, without doubt. Jaezila nodded and Tyfar went on.

"There is something called Spikatur Hunting Sword."

I held myself still. I listened.

"Nath the Eye knows little. Some Hamalese nobles have been murdered, foully done to death. A man was caught. Under the Question he confessed to this Spikatur Hunting Sword. But he knew little, being a mere villainous hired stikitche, murdering innocent people for pay."

"I dislike assassins," said Jaezila.

"So do I." Tyfar looked angry and ashamed. "Yet, also, I dislike torturing people. Who can say that the answers are true, or shrieked in fear and agony, the poor wight saying anything he is led to say by his interrogators?"

I knew Tyfar well enough by now to know that his dislike of torture was not occasioned merely because the truth might not be extracted. He hated torture for the foul thing it was.

The reason for Prince Tyfar's mission to Hyrklana was to buy vollers and this was no fake assignment, for Hamal desperately needed fliers. Well, so did we all, by Krun. His involvement with the plot to topple the queen was a bonus on that. So, the next day, we went along to the voller yards where a ship had, at last, been completed. She was a fine large craft, with two decks and a high forecastle and poop, equipped with fighting tops and galleries. She could carry two hundred or so aerial soldiers, voswods, as well as her crew. Tyfar beamed on her proudly as the handing-over ceremonies were concluded. She fluttered a myriad flags from her staffs; those flag mocked me with the purple and gold of the Empress Thyllis. Had they been the new Union flag of Vallia, the yellow cross and saltire on the red field, I would have jumped for joy.

"A splendid craft," said Jaezila. She looked up expectantly.

The crew from Hamal who were to fly her back stood in a neat blue line. The shipyard workers, including many slaves, looked more sullen than Tyfar liked. But they could do nothing. Bands played. The breeze blew. All around the yard stood guards. Alongside the landing ramp the solid mass of a formed regiment of men from Hamal obtruded—brutally—the power of that empire here. They were here on the express invitation of Queen Fahia, so it was given out. As always, the swods of the iron legions of Hamal looked splendid, compact, formed and dressed, professionals to a man. They'd have short shrift with any disturbance. And, too, Fahia probably did not realize, these were some of the swords promised by Tyfar to Noran and his principals . . .

The crew stood in their neat line, but the voller began to lift.

People cried out. They pointed up, yelling. A man fell from the ship, his arms and legs spread-eagled. She rose slowly into the air. I saw Tyfar look aghast, and then furious, and then determined. At his side Jaezila gazed up with a ferocious expression I found difficult to decipher.

"She is being stolen!" Tyfar shouted. "Under our very noses!"

The band stopped playing. More bodies fell from the ship. We could hear the strife of combat aboard her, ringing out along her decks. I stared aloft, controlling myself, quivering with joy. I knew! Those gallant secret spies from Vallia had a hand in this! Perhaps Valona herself was up there, taking this splendid airboat for Vallia!

The ship hovered some fifty feet overhead. "If they don't get away soon," I said, aloud, wrought up, "they never will!"

Patrol vollers were shooting across. Soon the decks of the new ship would fill with fighting men and the handful of secret agents from Vallia would be slain.

"You sound—" said Jaezila.

"They're done for," said the owner of the yard, fat and

ubiquitous Kov Naghan na Hanak. He was puffed up and proud with himself. "If a job has to be done, willy-nilly, then do it right, is what I say, by Harg, yes!"

"What, notor, did you do?" I spoke normally.

"Why, stuffed her with guards, hidden. I had an idea something would happen. Look—there they come atumbling down!"

I turned away, feeling sick. Those bodies falling to earth were Vallians—people who had thought to take away a precious airboat from hated Hamal. Now they were flung callously to the ground. The ship began to descend. I hoped, I prayed, that there had been few Vallians aboard. And, a treacherous and demeaning thought, I hoped Valona had not been among them.

Then Prince Tyfar once again proved himself. He looked somber. "It was a foolhardy attempt. A handful of people however brave and cunning, how could they hope to succeed? But I own I am sorry they died. They were a very gallant company."

Jaezila turned away.

Stealing airboats from Hyrklana had become a much more difficult and dangerous pastime than ever it had been, as I had discovered. Now, when—not if, when—I took a flier I would, besides paying the owner for her, concoct a plan that with much forethought and cunning could not fail. Whoever had made this doomed attempt had failed not from want of courage but from lack of planning. My Vallians! Reckless, gallant, and yet shrewd and practical men and women, accustomed to the ways of trade and commerce, they still had not fully realized that when you fight yourself for your country instead of hiring mercenaries, there are many painful and difficult lessons to be learned.

The men of the Hamalian Air Service boarded the ship; the guards positioned by Kov Naghan na Hanak marched out. You couldn't really fault him in that, although a few quiet words in his ear explaining the situation more fully might have helped in skyjacking his newly built flier. That could be a part of this wonderful plan it was necessary to concoct. And, too, the guards of all the voller yards of Huringa would redouble their vigilance now.

The rest of the ceremony went off without a hitch and the ship, flying her new colors, flew off to join the Hamalian Air Service. No doubt she would soon be in action casting down sundry nasties on Hamal's foes—on our allies! I swallowed. The day was coming. It had to be coming. The dignitaries accompanying Prince Tyfar had by now grown more accustomed to his ways, and so were no longer surprised that he withdrew from them, that he put up at The Silver Fluttrell instead of the embassy. We rode back in a silence that lacked some of the old companionableness, and this, without doubt, was caused by the tragic incident we had just witnessed. Tyfar took no real pleasure from dead men, whether or not they were Vallian or any other of his supposed enemies.

The moment we reached the tavern Jaezila excused herself and retired to her room. Tyfar glanced at the wall clepsydra.

"I have just a bur and a half to snatch a meal. Then I must see Orlan Mahmud. He understood that we could not impose on his hospitality for too long. He has a magnificent palace; but we find this tavern comfortable."

"As the queen's chief minister he must keep up appearances."

"You should meet him, Jak. You would like him."

I nodded. This Orlan Mahmud nal Yrmcelt was hardly likely to recognize me. He had seen me seasons ago for a brief space when the Star Lords had sent me to Hyrklana. I had held up a massive slate slab so that the conspirators against the queen, of whom Orlan had been one, could escape. My scarlet breechclout had dropped around my ankles, and I'd been taken up in nets and sent to the Arena. I did not think Orlan would recognize me. Even if he did, he would not want to acknowledge an escapade of his youth before he'd succeeded his father Ord as the queen's Chief Pallan.

A stir at the door of our room heralded the appearance of the landlord and a messenger from Vad Noran. The meeting had been unexpectedly brought forward. We were asked to go up to Noran's villa right away. Tyfar made a face.

"I must see Orlan Mahmud. You go on, Jak, and I will join you as soon as I am able. Jaezila must rest."

"Very well. I just hope it is good news."

"Things are moving, Jak. Things are going to go our way!"

"I'm sure you're right."

On the way up to Noran's villa I passed a gawping mob at a street corner. Riding Snowdrop gave me, even with an urvivel's lack of height compared to a zorca's, a vantage point. The crowd surrounded a sorcerer. He was going through his repertoire of tricks and surprises. He was a sorcerer and not a magician, as a single glance confirmed. His gown was liberally splattered with mystic symbols, and what he was doing was beyond mere magic tricks. I rode on. I had no idea of the man's discipline or what society of the many societies of sorcerers there are on Kregen he belonged to. Although it may sound unlikely to say a sorcerer was down on his luck, occasionally they, like any mortal, go through bad patches. Deb-Lu-Quienyin had been very down when we'd gone adventuring together. As a Wizard of Loh, among the most respected of all Kregan thaumaturges, he had bounced back and was now resident in Vallia. But the item that caused me most concern in this trifling encounter with a sorcerer on a street corner was its reminder that Queen Fahia now openly trafficked with wizards of all kinds. When we went up against her, we must be wary of occult powers arrayed against us.

In Noran's courtyard, the duty slaves closing the gates after me under the intolerant scrutiny of the gatekeepers, I walked across to the fountain. The Och crone gave me a cup of water and my ob vanished in its usual miraculous fashion. Noran had hired himself a new cadade to replace the old chief of his guards, but the new man, a Chulik, was not to be seen. I left Snowdrop in the charge of hostlers and went through with an underchamberlain to escort me. Cool shadows dropped down from the columns and arches. The streaming light of the suns lay across the stone flags. I followed the underchamberlain across one anteroom and we passed through double folding doors into a reception room.

The men gathered into a group talking easily among themselves swung around as I entered. I was aware of much finery, much gold and silver lace, a multitude of feathers, glittering jewelry.

A voice lifted, a strong lion-voice.

"Jak the Sturr! A spy! This man is a spy! Seize him!"

The group of men obeyed instantly. As one they unsheathed their swords and rushed upon me.

There was no time to think, no time to cry out that I was not a spy, for they would not have believed me. There was time only to rip out my thraxter and parry the first fierce blows.

The fashion in which the order had been obeyed made me realize that these men were disciplined, and now they

"The lion-man reached for a polearm."

tried to seize me as ordered and not kill me. So I did not make any attempt to slay them but beat away their weapons and sought a means of escape. The swords rang. The lion-man stepped to one side, reaching for a polearm leaning against the wall. I recognized the halberd as I recognized the lion-man, for this numim was Naghan the Doorn, whom I had last seen deep underground when we struggled through that subterranean vault of horror called the Moder. I shouted.

"Naghan the Doorn! I am no spy! I am here by invitation of Vad Noran. Call your men off before blood is spilled."

The swords flickered and flashed before my eyes. I leaped and swatted the blades away and circled back toward the door.

Footsteps sounded at my back.

There was no need to think. Instantly I leaped to the side and whirled, blade up. Two or three of the fine fancy young men rushed after me, and I was forced to thump a couple with the hilt. As they collapsed I saw that Vad Noran had entered the room, and with him, Ariane nal Amklana. I found no surprise she should be here, for the numim with the halberd, Naghan the Doorn, was her chief retainer. Ariane had not, when all was said and done, come out too well from the adventure down the Moder. Her yellow hair, secured by a jeweled band, fell to her shoulders, and her high-colored face turned toward me. She moved with all the old imperiousness. Her white gown did not fall sheer to her ankles but was cinctured by a broad golden belt. From the belt swung a thaxter in a jeweled scabbard. Even as I ducked a wild blow and so thunked the last one of that three and spun about to face any fresh attack, I reflected that the lady Ariane felt that to bear her part as a conspirator she must wear a sword. That was like her. Her gray-green eyes stared into mine for a heartbeat as I leaped away from the expected attack.

"My lady!" I shouted, in almost a yodel. "Call off your hound dogs before they are hurt."

Noran was fussing and throwing up his hands and exclaiming.

"Stop, stop!" he shouted. "What is all this trouble in my house?"

"Ask Naghan and his lady, notor," I yelled, skipping away and flailing a convey of swords from my shins. Now that it was going to be all right, I could allow the stupid feelings of the ludicrousness of the situation full flower.

"Jak the Sturr!"

"Aye, my lady—Lahal. Now call your men off or I will strive in real earnest."

She had seen something of our fighting down in the Moder where we sought treasures and magics among monsters. She gave the order in her high hectoring tones, and the men fell back. I shook my arms and thrust the thraxter back into the scabbard.

"Lahal, Jak the Sturr. And you are one of us now?"

"Aye, my lady. As Vad Noran is my witness."

"It is true, my lady," babbled Noran. A single glance told me his sorry story and the state he was in. He was besotted with the lady Ariane, who as a kovneva, so I had been told, outranked him. If he could marry her and lay his hands on the estates and the money, he might aspire to rise a step and become a kov himself. "Jak is a valued associate of the prince."

"I never thought to see you alive again. You or the prince." She wrinkled up her pretty nose. "You must tell me how you escaped. We had a most dreadful time."

I forbore to mention the manner of her leaving us. I said, "The prince has been unavoidably detained. He will be here as soon as he possibly can."

At this Ariane pouted. It was clear she detested having her wishes flouted in the slightest particular.

Avec Parlin had been right. There was a powerful noble in the shadows masterminding the conspiracy and using Vad Noran, but it was not a man, it was a woman.

Much of the mystery surrounding this Ariane nal Amklana had been cleared up by this meeting. She had ventured down into the terrors of the Moder in order to secure some thaumaturgical advantage, and it was easy to guess why. If she was determined to overthrow Queen Fahia and take her place, she would need occult assistance to combat the queen's new sorcerers. And Noran would be her willing tool. As the men I had knocked down stood up, shaking their heads and looking miserable, Noran and Ariane moved on, just like a regal couple at a levee. Their words to each other confirmed my diagnosis of the situation. Ariane had Noran firmly wrapped around her little finger, wrapped and knotted tight.

Naghan the Doorn, stroking his whiskers, came over. The numim looked me up and down.

"You were nearly—" he began.

I said, "You are zealous for the welfare of your mistress. Just remember, I'm on your side."

Then he said something that, although it should not have surprised me, did so.

"When we left you and those others, down there in that underground hellhole, I was not—was not pleased. I am glad to see you escaped." He fidgeted with the halberd. "And the others? How did they fare? Did you all escape?"

"Yes, thank Huvon the Lightning. But it was a bonny time."

"I can imagine."

We talked for a space, and the men from Amklana went back to talking among themselves, and presently Prince Tyfar was announced. I wondered if all this open naming of names was the right way for conspirators to carry on. Certainly, other folk I'd tangled with had used cover names, and carried on deception as a mere simple precaution for survival. The answer—and at the same time as I delighted in it I felt the chill—must be that Ariane was supremely confident that whatever spell it was she had obtained would smooth her path over all difficulties.

During that meeting we began to flesh out the plans. We began to put forces in order, and decide where the bribery should be used or where the knife in the night was the answer. Men would march from Amklana and other of the provinces of Hyrklana inimical to the queen. Tyfar would assign his Hamalese soldiers. Soon specific functions were being allocated. It began to look as though these people not only meant business, but knew how to run it.

I caught the task of guard to the principals. That, on the face of it, seemed appropriate. Everyone assumed I would sell my life to protect Ariane and Noran, and joy in the doing of it to the greater glory of Hyrklana and the soon-to-be Queen Ariane. I did not disabuse them of that idea. If there was to be any laying down of lives on that account, it would be theirs and not mine. If Tyfar or Jaezila ran into trouble, that was entirely different.

The meetings continued on an irregular basis for the next few sennights, and I did not attend all of them. On the occasions I did attend I was aware of the forward movement of events. It seemed a sound idea to keep myself under cover as much as possible, and I did not venture too much abroad from The Silver Fluttrell and Noran's villa, and when I did I kept a sharp lookout on the backtrail. I was not followed, was not being spied on. I trusted this happy state applied to all the conspirators.

Ariane's men were close to the city; much gold had been spent. Noran, although a vad and not the highest of the nobility, a kov, was one of the richest men in Huringa. This, presumably, was the prime reason Ariane had selected him to be her dupe. She oohed and aahed well enough when they were together, but it did not take a sharp eye to see the true situation. He dreamed of becoming the King of Hyrklana. Fat chance!

Almost at the end of planning, for Ariane had matured her schemes for a goodly time, we met to discuss what was to be done with some of the important personages of Huringa who had refused to declare for the usurper to the queen. All they had done was to indicate their loyalty to Fahia, for Ariane had not revealed herself. The list was carefully considered. They came to the name of Orlan Mahmud nal Yrmcelt.

"He must be killed," said Ariane. She spoke spitefully, her words biting. "He is not devoted to Fahia, I know, but he refuses to aid me. And I have spoken to him. He detests the Hamalese, and would not aid me in my schemes when I am queen."

Tyfar looked upset. "Is it necessary to kill him? He could be banished—"

"No! Our alliance must be founded on rock, prince. When I am queen and you carry back word to Thyllis in Ruathytu that I will join with her in the glorious conquests, I do not want men at my back who will not support me, men who will work against me and the greater glory of Hyrklana and Hamal."

"I see that," said Tyfar. "But I do not like it. I think—"

I put a hand to my mouth. This woman Ariane would ally herself with Thyllis! She would place Hyrklana into bondage to Hamal! Yes, Tyfar would seize on this, as a good Hamalese. He was a prince of Hamal and eggs get smashed making omelettes, and no doubt he fancied Hyrklana's willing help would tilt the balance in favor of Hamal and thus end the war swiftly. As well it might. Hyrklana might be smaller than Hamal, but the island realm had been untouched by the war raging on the mainland and up north. The people were tough and hardy, certain with weapons, grown ferocious through the constant raiding by the Shanks, the fish heads, from over the curve of the world. My evil dream of bringing Hyrklana into the war was being realized—realized from the other side!

When we rose to leave, my thoughts were still in a turmoil. Noran spoke to Ariane, who nodded. She turned with her wide smile to Tyfar, to whom she was now exquisitely polite, seeing she had lost the influence she might once have had over him through her conduct in the Moder.

"Prince! The time grows nearer. Noran suggests you should live here until we strike. It seems a good plan to me."

Tyfar nodded agreement, so, perforce, I was to stay, too. Jaezila said she would see about collecting our things from The Silver Fluttrell, and Noran's majordomo saw about allocating quarters to us. The villa was palatial enough to have housed a regiment or two.

We settled in for the few days remaining. Tyfar was now possessed of an eagerness to strike very becoming in a proud young prince. I racked my brains to think of a way to scupper the plot. The obvious way seemed the best. When Fahia's guards burst in on my betrayal, I would see to it that Tyfar and Jaezila were safely away. I attempted to leave the villa, acting naturally, but was stopped. The new cadade, a Chulik, explained.

"No one leaves now. It is the vad's order. Security."

To have fought my way out might have served, once. I would only betray me, instead of the plotters. This night saw the last meeting. Kov Naghan na Hanak had at last decided to throw in his lot with the conspirators. We need wait no longer, for he brought a strong acquisition of strength. And I decided that I could probably deal more easily with Queen Ariane than with Queen Fahia. I'd let the plot succeed, and then see about stopping this ominous alliance of Hamal and Hyrklana.

By this time I knew my way around the less-private parts of Noran's villa. The meeting was to be held in a sumptuous reception room in the heart of the Strigicaw Complex. The room was a mass of crystal. Jaezila had brought all our gear from the tavern, so I could put on a scarlet breechclout, which still made Tyfar frown, and strap up a useful assortment of weaponry. Going down the stone stairs and out under the light of the Maiden with the Many Smiles, fat and pink through scattered clouds, I walked across to the Strigicaw Complex. I did not feel at all like a conspirator ready to topple a kingdom and install a new queen. Jaezila and Tyfar came toward me as I walked in the light of the moon.

"Jak!" Jaezila's voice held an edge. "The lady Ariane bids you guard them well tonight. You are to take post at the far end of the colonnade."

I was surprised.

"Very well. That is some distance from the meeting place."

"If we do not hurry, we will be late," said Tyfar.

"There is time," said Jaezila. "I want to show you something you ought to see, a trinket they have here in a glass case. Come on, Ty! You will delight in it, for it is from Balintol, and then we can go into the meeting. Tomorrow—we strike!"

When one mentions a trinket from Balintol, which is a mysterious place, by Vox, one is always interested. Tyfar looked at the moon, telling the time, and then we went along the colonnade.

"This had better be good, young lady," said Tyfar. "To keep a revolution waiting!"

Noran's villa, like any well-furnished palace on Kregen, was stuffed with curios, objets d'art, fascinating treasures from all over the world gathered together through the centuries. We had time to inspect this item Jaezila had marked before the meeting began. The Maiden with the Many Smiles cast down a fuzzy pink light. Shadows burned pink, and the night air smelled sweet. The moonblooms were out. We walked along toward the building that formed an extension to the Strigicaw Complex, and a frightful hubbub broke out at our backs.

Tyfar whirled. We looked back along the colonnade.

"That's not Kov Naghan," said Tyfar.

Dark figures ran under the arches, and the sounds of wood smashing told us the door was being broken in. The jangle of steel broke brilliantly into the night.

He whipped out his sword and started to run back, and I caught him by his belt and hauled him in.

"Wait, Tyfar, wait."

"But—"

Those dark figures ran fleetly toward us. They looked demonic, agile, and the glitter of their weapons struck an edged note of horror.

"We have been discovered by the queen!"

"Then we must fight them!" said Jaezila. Her rapier gleamed liquid silver. She took two paces.

Tyfar put a hand on her arm and looked at me. I let his belt go. "You stop Jaezila, Tyfar, as I stop you. If we have been betrayed, there is nothing more to be saved by getting killed."

"But my honor—"

"I respect your honor, prince. But my honor says that you will take Jaezila and move back through the colonnade. I will hold them until you reach a good spot."

I stopped talking then for an arrow spat from nowhere and pierced Jaezila through her left arm. She did not cry out, but she gasped. She staggered. Tyfar caught her and glared wildly at me.

"There, you see!" I cried, annoyed. "Now take Jaezila and go! Do not argue."

I reached out with the thraxter and flicked a second arrow away. Dodging behind a column, I shouted most fiercely toward Tyfar and Jaezila. "She's in pain and you dillydally, prince? Where is your famous honor? Save Jaezila—*that* is your duty!"

"But—you—Jak—"

"By Krun! I've never met a man who'd argue when a girl needs to be saved."

I almost thought I'd overdone it. But he scooped Jaezila and ran like a scuttling locrofer, bent above her in his arms, and as he ran he flung back: "I will run and I will save Jaezila, Jak, you may depend on that. But for the sake of our comradeship I will not forget why I ran or who made me run away from a fight."

So I, Dray Prescot, laughed. In the next seconds my sword crossed with the first of the guards who sought to pass me and rush after my comrades and take them. The steel slithered and scraped. I took the first one cleanly and skipped away and so nicked the second. The third and fourth came on together and tried to sandwich me, whereat I let them come in and then, with the old one-two-hop, avoided them and clouted their heads together. They were Rhaclaws with domed heads as wide as their shoulders. They slumped to the stone floor of the colonnade. One remained, and he came on bravely, so that I dazzled him, and hit him with the hilt.

At the far end under the roof of the colonnade the shadows clustered. I trusted Tyfar would have the wit to keep on running. This was no time to hang around or make a stand. More guards were running up, and the noise from the meeting room smashed into the night air.

Ariane's plot had been discovered and was in the process of being shattered.

There was absolutely no doubt in my mind what the lady Ariane would be doing now. She would follow the same course of conduct as that she had adopted down in the Moder where among the crazed mob she sought only to save herself and refused to aid others. Tyfar had seen that. Only his own code of honor maintained his civility toward Ariane. So now she'd be running and if Naghan the Doorn got himself killed protecting her, well, that was what he was paid for, and Ariane would soon hire a new retainer with a halberd. So I held no brief for her.

As for the other plotters, they must take their chances.

So, with slumbering guards strewing the stone flags of the colonnade, I took myself off. Tyfar and Jaezila were well away by now. Heading for a narrow alley between sumptuous buildings leading to the outside wall, I heard that typical ringing sliding susurration of bronze links above my head. I leaped. The net dropped on me. They are very cunning with metal nets in Hyrklana. The mesh enfolded me as an octopus engulfs its prey. I thrashed about, entangled, and they trotted up and bashed me on the head, just to be on the safe side.

Chapter Nine

Red for the Ruby Drang

The brilliance of the twin Suns of Scorpio, Zim and Genodras, beat down into the stone-walled yard. The sand strewing the floor was not the silver sand of the Arena, but coarse stuff suitable for a training area where coys were given a few rudiments of the craft before being sent out to face death. About two hundred miserable wights sat or stood about in the heat. I suppose I ought to consider myself lucky I was there at all, arena fodder, rather than lying in some pit with my head tucked neatly under my arm.

A certain amount of guile had been necessary to achieve this end. Using the painful art taught me by Deb-

Lu-Quienyin, I had put on a doleful, moronic face and passed myself off as merely a hired guard who knew nothing—as Havil the Green was my witness!—of what went on among the great lords. Victims for the arenas of the many Jikhorkduns of Hyrklana were always needed. As a mere hired guard, who knew nothing, it was not even worth putting me to the question, and with the other guards captured I'd been packed off to the Jikhorkdun.

"Stand up! Stand up! Get in line, you no-good rasts!"

The bulky man with the whip walked along slashing about, and we cowed souls formed up into a long line. At the far end of the enclosure stood four men. They wore armor and carried weapons. Other arena guards were positioned at strategic points. We were all naked and weaponless, browbeaten in line.

As I took stock of what was taking place and the line shuffled toward the four men, I saw that as a coy reached the end of the line he walked to one of the four armored men in rotation, and then went through a doorway at the rear. The four men and the four doorways were marked. Over each door a splash of color stood out vividly in the suns. The four men each wore a colored favor. The line inched along toward the four men and the four doors.

A simple calculation told me that when I reached the head of the line I would, in my turn, have to walk toward the man with the flaunting green feathers in his helmet.

Now, had those feathers been yellow, or blue, even, I do not think I would have cared a jot. I'd simply have walked along and gone through the yellow or blue door. But green! Well, I had long since overcome my irrational, as it turned out, detestation of green. But, for some reason that I did not care to fathom out, I pushed in front of the fellow before me and checked him and so marched smartly toward the man wearing the red feathers. Again, I might in avoiding the green have walked to join the yellows or blues, and I do not think I would have cared. Fate, if it was fate, sent me once again to fight with the Ruby Drang.

"What are they going to do, dom?" said a young Rapa, his beaked face unhappy, his feathers limp.

"You have never sat in the stands?"

"No—I work on my father's farm, and—"

I said, "Do not lose heart, fight as hard as you can, and die well." I turned away. I would not make acquaintances, let alone friends, among men marked for death.

The manhandlers with whips and spears—and all wearing red favors—sorted out us fifty recruits who had been apportioned to the Ruby Drang. They went about their work with methodical thoroughness; this they had done many times before.

"You—over here! You—over there!" The whips snapped.

No one ran berserk, trying to escape. We were all too cowed. As for me, I had to bide my chances and stay alive.

"Spearmen, stand there. Swordsmen, stand there. Archers, here." They sorted us out and, after a moment's wondering if it might be useful to stand with the archers, I went over to the small group of men who claimed to be able to handle a sword. The managers of the Jikhorkdun had the nasty habit of sending archers up against unpleasant flying animals. Everything was carried out with punctiliousness and yet with an air of boredom, as though mere repetition dulled the alertness of the manhandlers. I knew that was false. One attempt to escape, a single try, and the retribution would be swift, I knew.

We were given red breechclouts and a cloth band to tie around our foreheads to keep our hair tidy and to hold a single red feather. The men stuck the feathers in awkwardly, talking in frightened whispers. Like a fool, I own, when I put the red feather into the cloth headband I felt—not a thrill, dear Zair, no!—but a kind of spine-stiffener, a flood of memories, a final reminder of where I was.

The blow on my head which had caused those famous old Bells of Beng Kishi to chime in my skull could be used as an excuse for stupid behavior. Not one of us was damaged goods, for the arena managers were strict; but some of us were in a sorry state, right enough. The face I now had was my own, if rather hangdog. The cheldur strutted out and stood on his pedestal and rested his fists on the wooden rail. His face was a mere mass of scars, although he still had both eyes. His red jerkin and his saffron kilt and his silver greaves made of him a figure of splendor. But it was his sword that marked him off from us, for we stood sullenly before him unarmed.

He shouted in his bullfrog bellow.

"Coys! You now fight for the Ruby Drang. If you live you may become kaidurs. If you die—die well! There is gold and wine and women and ease for those who live."

He swelled there above us on his pedestal. "I am Hundal the Oivon! You do as I say and you do nothing else. Or by the glass eye and brass sword of Beng Thrax you *will* do nothing else—ever!"

We believed him.

A sense of much greater speed in all the aspects of the Arena was clearly apparent from the days before the great war on the continent. We coys were assigned quarters and given some sketchy training with tricks and stratagems. But it seemed to me the blood fever gripped these people, clasping them helplessly in its grip. Spectacle was demanded, and more spectacle. The hunger for sensation, for blood and death, was insatiable.

Hundal the Oivon sweated over us. Like anyone closely involved with his color faction, he wanted the reds to win. At the moment the blues, devotees of the sapphire graint, were in the ascendant. We, we were informed, if we lived would help to redress that balance and once again place the red of the ruby drang at the summit of the victory poles. These cheldurs who train up the apprentices for the Arena are singular to Kregen, it seems, for although they have wide privileges, they do not have the same opportunities as the old Roman lanistae. Hundal sweated over us—and he made us sweat, by Kaidun!

Well aware that the first fight I got into was likely to be the last, and that this first encounter out on the silver sand carried more danger by reason of the surroundings, I felt relief mixed with annoyance that a group of us was chosen to test out some apprentice yellows. It was to be a sword and shield encounter, a minor bout during a slack time, mainly to determine what quality the new material might be. Well, the spectacle of the amphitheater with the tiered seating lofting up into the sky, the rows of eager, blood-obsessed faces, the yelling and the infernal din, the stink of blood and animals, the smell of sweat and oiled leather . . . Yes, the Jikhorkdun can get under a man's skin, well enough, once he is a kaidur and understands what he fights for. I would have none of it. I intended to keep a whole skin and get out of here as fast as possible.

The coys went in awe of the kaidurs and hyr-kaidurs, who strode about like gods. To face one of those superlative fighting men would be the end, and yet, in many and many a breast beat a heart that would thrill to the kaiderin of it all, before it was stilled forever . . .

To perform a High Kaidur, that was the dream . . .

Preparations were still very thorough. Hundal chose an interesting mix of men; half were those who in training appeared more likely to cut off their own ears than their opponents', and the other half consisted of men who showed promise. We waited behind the iron-barred gate and the racket from the Arena, this close, dinned in our ears maddeningly. Fristle women poured the coarse red wine, called Beng Thrax's spit, into leather cups for us to refresh ourselves in the dust and heat. And I still did not know that drink was spiced with drugs that inflamed a man and turned him into an insensate fighting fury. So we waited until it was our turn to step out into that oval of death, a melting pot of passion, a crucible of conflict, and stake our lives for the enjoyment of the populace of Huringa.

The storm of emotions that hit me as I stepped out onto the silver sand! Instinctively I turned to look up at the royal box, glittering and high; the place gaped empty. Fahia would not waste her time on a program filler like this. As a devotee of everything pertaining to the Jikhorkdun, a woman who could recite the names of hyrkaidurs for seasons past together with the kaidurs they had performed, she reserved her patronage for the best displays.

"By Havil, Chaadur! Don't stand gawping! Here come the yellows!" Norhan yelled at me.

Chaadur was the name I had given. I looked across the Arena and the yellow coys, shrieking and yelling and waving their swords, charged toward us. Hundal had warned us. "They'll come out like evil spirits from Cottmer's Caverns. Don't let that worry you. Just get stuck in."

So we did.

The fight proved Hundal's eye. The yellows' training had been just as thorough as our own in the time, I daresay. I recognized a few men who had waited in line with me to be chosen in the yard. Of the reds, we lost all those who had failed to measure up, and the yellows lost all except one, who ran shrieking about the Arena, under the wall, with the crowd yelling at him to stand and fight. A couple of our blood-crazed reds ran after him. It was left to a couple of the Arena guards to step out from a pillared area offset from the queen's box and feather him as he ran. He sank down, and that was the last of the yellows. The red totem would move up by a fraction of a notch. It would take a much more important kaidur than this to make any significant changes. Yet, as we walked back, feeling the aches and the aftereffects, Hundal greeted us warmly, and pointing out that we had lifted the ruby drang, not depressed the red, and that was as it should be.

Norhan, a shock-headed fellow with a twist to his lips and a remarkably evil eye, said, "You were moonstruck in there, at first, Chaadur. It is just as well I am quick-witted."

"Indubitably, Norhan. And my thanks."

He cocked that fishy eye of his at me and licked his lips, and we trailed off to the barracks.

During the next few days we trained hard and fought twice more, and Hundal and Oivon called me aside as we washed ourselves of the blood and filth after a grueling set-to with a pack of blegs of the blues. We'd drawn. And, with the old fever for the ruby drang hot upon me, I raged that we had not won.

"We are gaining strength, Chaadur," said Hundal. He glowered at me, a bluff, ruddy-faced professional cheldur. "I see you are of the reds."

"Aye."

"And also, Chaadur, I think you have fought before. You were a paktun, a mercenary, perhaps?"

That seemed the easiest thing to agree to. I nodded as I sluiced water. The basins ran red.

"You will make kaidur very soon. It is in my mind to try you single tomorrow."

Again I sluiced water, and nodded. The quicker I could rid myself of being a coy and apprentice, start to climb the ladder of victories, win my way to a position as kaidur, the quicker I would get a freer run of this place. We were prisoners. There was no easy way past the guards, as I well knew. I did not intend to rot here until I was killed. This was my route out.

"Tomorrow, then. You fight a churgur of the greens. As ever, by Kaidun, he will be good. I rely on you, Chaadur."

So it was fixed. I did not doubt there were wagers even on so small a match. The pairs paraded in their armor and feathers across the silver sand, the trumpets pealed, the suns cast down their mingled streaming lights, and we fought. Afterwards, as I washed myself again, Hundal said, "You may count that as your first victory, Chaadur."

We stood by the door and the noise of splashing water and yelling almost obscured the footfalls. I turned, warily.

Hundal said, "Lahal, Cleitar. Did you see Chaadur just now? Have you come to sniff him out for yourself?"

Cleitar Adria still appeared a little strange to me, with the dead scar tissue glistening down the left half of his face and the lifeless socket that had once been an eye. He looked just as tough and ruthless as he had when we'd been taken up together as slaves and fought in the arena. I had won free, with help, and Cleitar had gone on to become a hyr-kaidur and then a senior cheldur. I noticed Hundal's respectful attitude, despite his pointed remarks about another trainer looking over his men. I had to speak up sharply, and yet not arouse suspicions.

"Lahal, cheldur," I said. "I am new here, very new. It is all strange. But if you—"

And then Hundal's outraged bellow silenced me.

"Coy! You do not speak until spoken to! And especially to a kai-cheldur! Impudent fambly! Onker!"

But Cleitar had taken the message. He understood, for I had told him in a drinking den here in the Jikhorkdun, that I worked in secret for Queen Fahia. As a story, I had taken some good mileage out of that, by Kaidun! Now he nodded, very much the superior officer, and said that he had seen me fight and was faintly interested. "All the new young coys are flatfish these days. It is pleasant to find a man who can use a sword."

"He can, Cleitar, he can," burbled Hundal.

They talked on and I stood back respectfully. Cleitar might give me considerable assistance to escape, and I was not going to miss that opportunity. They knew how to manage men in the Jikhorkdun, especially recalcitrant men.

The proof of that came very quickly when I got Cleitar alone for a few words. His scarred face sobered me, dashed my hopes. "Escape, Chaadur? No, dom, that is not possible. Not for you, until you become a hyr-kaidur again, as you will."

"In that case will you see that Hundal arranges fights? You know what I mean. I have to get out of here—"

At that, Cleitar's slashed lips curved into a mocking smile.

"Don't they all, by the brass sword and glass eye of Beng Thrax!"

My reactions might have puzzled me had I dwelled on them. I did not feel the biting sense of frustration I ought to have experienced. I was desperate to get away; and yet

I felt that in a remote, disinterested fashion. It was not just that I was caught up again in fighting for the ruby drang. That was far below the worth of my feelings. But undoubtedly, although conscious of my duty to get away, I felt nothing was being lost.

"You were a hyr-kaidur once, Chaadur, when you fought under the name of Drak the Sword." I had known, then, that Cleitar Adria resented the bestowal of that name on me. "And you say you escaped by the queen's connivance? Then, why—?"

This, I had foreseen.

"Doing the queen's bidding is a hard road, Cleitar. I must get out of here and see her, for I do not think she can know I fight for the ruby drang again." That was true, by Vox! If fat Queen Fahia knew that Dray Prescot fought in her arena, she'd nigh choke herself laughing. Then—then she'd probably be highly unpleasant. She must by this time know who I was. It was not all gloom. Cleitar took in news of the outer world, and I learned that, yes, there had been a conspiracy against the queen, the latest in a long series, and the plotters had been taken up, except the ringleaders. They had escaped. It was known that Vad Noran was the chief criminal, and he was being sought over all Hyrklana.

"And the others?"

"There is a rumor, denied from the palace, which says that the visiting prince of Hamal was involved. It is a story not believed." Cleitar moved his shoulders. "I do not believe it."

"It is not very likely."

"No. Anyway, this prince has returned home."

My first and only genuine feeling was one of relief. Tyfar had gotten clean away, and that helped to make my own capture and incarceration and combats worthwhile . . .

He promised to do what he could to secure me promising contests. When I pointed out that, if Beng Thrax turned his glass eye favorably upon me and used his brass sword for instead of against me, Cleitar could pick up easy winnings, he merely smiled and tapped his nose and laughed, the scar glistening.

"That is what friends are for."

While not necessarily agreeing with that, I had to admit that friends are vital to both an emperor and a man trying to stay alive in and get out of the Jikhorkdun. Now I will pass rapidly over the ensuing period, for it was a simple round of combats in which I was concerned to keep a whole skin, and to pick up every scrap of information I could. By this time I was nowhere near the flamboyant fighter with the sword I once had been, although always preferring neatness and economy. Since my encounter beside the caravan with Mefto the Kazzur I had taken great thought to sword fighting. I was better than ever, but, as always the thought remained with me that I could easily meet a man far superior to me out on the silver sand. If I did, if I met another such as Prince Mefto, then all my plots and stratagems would go for naught.

So I did not take this period lightly.

Norhan said, on one day of madness filled with the shriek of sword and the ragged swellings of death, "Chaadur! You are the simplest swordsman I have ever seen. You seem to do nothing, and yet you do everything."

I turned away. I remembered another man who had said that to me, laughing, bright, eager—Barty Vessler, who was dead. I turned back. "Better to be quick and safe, than showy and dead."

"True. I prefer a pot of combustibles, myself."

The guards were herding in a bunch of miserable felons, men and women shackled together and doomed. They were to be turned out with a short sword between two of them to face wild beasts. It would be horrible and unpleasant. And yet many had chosen this death to life in the Arena . . .

"That must be why they call you Norhan the Flame."

"Smart with a pot of the right stuff, and a light, that's me." His high opinion of himself, I saw, extended to his skill with combustibles. All the same, it was difficult not to respond to his brashness, for there was nothing repellent in it, nothing to make a dour old fighting man like myself dub him an empty braggart.

A woman fell among the chained ranks and was hoisted up and prodded on. This hideous aspect of the arena gave me always the chill of revulsion and of death. It was not necessary for me, one of the new and upcoming kaidurs, to interfere. As I stepped forward I was surprised that Norhan the Flame stepped up, too. We remonstrated with the guard, a burly Brokelsh, and although anything we could achieve in these circumstances was of ludicrous insignificance, as we turned away, Norhan said, "I don't think he'll prod a poor chained woman so quickly, next time." The Brokelsh sat up on the dusty ground, his mouth bleeding. Norhan sucked his knuckles.

And then I stopped dead in my tracks.

A man beside the woman, chained to her, attempting to help her, said, "It will not be long now, Mina, and, by Spikatur Hunting Sword, it cannot come too fast for me."

I looked back at the coffle. The chains clanked. The man looked exhausted, and his arms were broken and strapped up across his chest, so that he could do little for the woman Mina. A single step I took, and another, and then the furious form of the guard Jiktar roared down, purple of face, protuberant of eye, and the coffle whisked away between ironbound doors that thudded dolorously together.

"What is it, Chaadur?"

I swallowed. "A nothing, Norhan. Let us—"

"Aye, by Sarkalak! Let us go for a wet."

That had not been in my mind; now that Norhan mentioned the subject it seemed the appropriate thing to do.

Chapter Ten

Of Spikatur and Princess Lilah

The first really hard information I obtained about the secret society calling itself Spikatur Hunting Sword came from a strong-faced swordsman who had parried a trifle too late, and taken a nasty thrust through his side. He had recovered and gone on to beat his man, a Rapa of the blues, but in the barracks he lay in pain on his pallet waiting for the needleman. I stayed at his side. He called for water and I fetched it. Helping to prop up his head so that he might drink more easily, I heard his sunken whisper of thanks. "By Sasco! I think I am done for."

"Nonsense, Pergon. The needleman will have you right in a trice." I bent closer. The stubble on his chin glistened. "Tell me about Spikatur. I do not think you are going to die, but—"

"I feel my death on me." His eyes rolled. We were alone in the barracks. He sweated with a chill that would be deathly if the doctor did not come soon. Norhan had gone for him and I had faith enough in the Flame to leave that in his hands. I knew that men who were involved with Spikatur used the oath "By Sasco!" In Pergon's weakened condition, near, as he thought, to death, he talked freely, telling me what he knew. What it boiled down to was not a lot. People had banded together into a hunting society, devoted to Spikatur, the mighty hunter, and they met in secret places in many parts of Hyrklana.

"And in the Dawn Lands, and in Pandahem. I cannot speak for the wild lands to the west of the central mountains of Havilfar, for that is remote and unknown. But Spikatur grows in strength—" He paused, and I gave him more water and wiped his forehead. I thought that he was going to die.

"All these lands," I said, "Pandahem, the Dawn Lands, Hyrklana where we are now—"

"Aye." He choked and blood dribbled down his chin, so that I thought the end had come and he would die before the needleman arrived to ease his pain. "Aye, Chaadur! We surround! We build. Soon we will strike!"

"Who leads you?"

"No leader." After that he became incoherent so that what he said was impossible to understand. He mentioned Faol and Ifilion, other countries of Havilfar. The doctor arrived toward the end. He was a crotchety old fellow, with a stoop, and he thumped his bag down and glared at Pergon as though the dying man had done him an injury. "This kaidur is dying. Nothing can save him. Why was my time wasted?"

I stood up. I looked at the doctor. I said, "Open your bag and take out your needles. Use them. Ease his pain."

He chomped his jaws in offended fury. He did not understand the situation. "I am a doctor! You are just a kaidur! Stand aside and let me pass, there is nothing I can do for this man."

"There is. I am a kaidur, and have nothing to lose. You are a needleman and have a deal to lose. I do not think you would relish inspecting your own backbone. Ease Pergon's pain, now."

"You are mad—"

"*Do it!*"

He did it. He inserted his acupuncture needles so that Pergon could die in peace. He kept muttering to himself. Norhan ran in with the basket of fruit he had stopped to fetch, and I shook my head. What had just occurred gave me no pleasure. It was symptomatic of the bestiality with which we were surrounded.

So Pergon died and was taken outside and buried along with the rest.

He was dead; but what he had said about Spikatur Hunting Sword lived on.

Norham rubbed his jaw, which was lean and blue. "As San Blarnoi says," he observed, quoting a saint whose aphorisms are trotted out to confuse and offend, " 'It is a flinty heart that is not softened by a fist in the jaws.' That needleman will ply his skill more freely in future, I think."

"Like the Brokelsh you took to task for hitting the woman? I wonder. Mayhap it will make them more savage."

"If they are they must be made to rue it!"

"You cannot run people's lives by fear, Norhan—"

He stared at me. "Fambly! How do you think the world turns?"

In no mood for argument, I let the subject drop as we went into the kaidur's drinking den and, avoiding dopa, which is the drink of fools, sat down with tankards of ale. Norhan knew nothing of Spikatur Hunting Sword. But two days later another man mentioned Spikatur—before he was chopped, so I guessed that a group of Spikatur's adherents had been taken up for the Arena. This made me realize that Fahia might know. Perhaps all the great ones of the world knew, and took steps to crush the Spikatur conspiracy. I might be the Emperor of Vallia, but I would not regard myself as one of the great ones of the world, for that way lay megalomania. All the same . . . If all I had to do to find out was ask one of my people in the Imperial Palace in Vondium . . . !

Somehow, I did not think it was like that at all.

By judicious arrangements, Cleitar assured that I met top-class opposition, and so rapidly made my way up the ladder. This was dangerous. Not just because I might get myself killed—that is an occupational hazard of those who step out onto the silver sand. But aficionados might cast their minds back and remember Drak the Sword. I had been a hyr-kaidur, yes, but my time here had not been too long, and perhaps the most spectacular fight at the end would be the fight that would be remembered. All the same, I fought along all the time expecting some well-meaning idiot in the stands to bellow: "Drak the Sword!

Kaidur!" Then Queen Fahia would sit up on her silks and furs and peer down, and her fat jowls would quiver like those of her damned spotted strowgers as they chomped on portions of people's anatomies.

Talk about tightropes and razors' edges!

During these days the ruby drang lifted up the red totem on the victory pole so that we no longer rested in the lowest position. The blues still lorded it over the others, but the greens were giving them a hard tussle. Hundal the Oivon, our cheldur responsible for our barracks, had money laid out on us reds overtaking the yellows—which we had done and he had collected—and he reinvested his winnings on our taking the greens. He found many folk willing to take his wagers. The odds against the reds were quoted at variously high figures, for the strength in the ongoing tussle for the moment lay with the blues and greens. This continuing fascination was a part of the Jikhorkdun's aura, the partisanship that led to incredible feats of bravery in the Arena when the stands went wild. I had pledged myself I would have none of it, none of the blood and death and degradation; that meant I would have none of the high striving and the passion to excel and the sacrifice. I would have none of it. I was the Emperor of Vallia and I had a job to do, a daunting task to bring Hyrklana in against Hamal and then to subdue Hamal so that we might all stand shoulder to shoulder against the reiving fishheads from the other side of the world.

So be it.

But the passions of the Jikhorkdun got into my blood, and I rattled my blade along the iron bars, and shrieked out with the others when the reds triumphed, and roared and screamed when the reds went down to bloody defeat. So the days passed and I got to know Norhan a little more, against my inclinations, and Frandu the Franch. Frandu was a Fristle with a very high opinion of himself—hence his nickname—equipped with a sharp tongue. But he was a doughty fighter on the silver sand.

Because we were kaidurs of the middle rankings, we no longer had to face some of the more primitive horrors in the arena. We had fought our way through those perils. Now we were reserved for the professional combats, skills against skills, in which the most educated and knowledgeable of the Jikhorkdun aficionados delighted. We returned one day from an interesting confrontation with a group of Khibils of the yellows. We had bested them, even though the foxy-faced, reddish-whiskered Khibils are fine fighters. Queen Fahia had not been present, and at the end of the fights the crowd had been uncharacteristically generous, and the victorious reds had been allowed to give the beaten yellows their lives. That rarely happened when the queen graced the games with her presence.

"It was a bonny little ding-dong, by the Golden Splendor of Numi-Hyrjiv himself!" quoth Frandu, spitting and taking an immense gulp of water. We sprawled on the benches waiting to return to our barracks. "And I recognized one of the Khibils and would have been loath to slay him, onker though he is."

"Not as smart as us, Frandu?" said Norhan.

"Not as smart as me, Norhan. I took him with the same cut I gave the Chulik who tried to spit him on the stairs when they tried to slay Princess Lilah."

I looked across. Names—well, there are many men and women on Kregen, and many of them bear the same names, as they do on Earth. I listened, saying nothing.

Norhan guffawed. "What do you know of princesses, Frandu?"

Now, the miserable folk herded into the arena seldom spoke of the reasons that brought them there. Sometimes, if they allowed themselves the foolishness of making friends, they would exchange confidences. Not often. But Frandu felt his honor impugned. He wiped water drops from his whiskers. His cat's face screwed up, all abristle, and his eyes looked dangerous, slitted, catlike.

"I guarded the Princess Lilah for many seasons, onker."

Norhan, offhandedly, taunting, said, "If you mean the Princess Lilah who was twin sister to Queen Fahia, then you surely jest. She has been dead and gone for many seasons."

"You are the onker!" Frandu was wrought up. "She was kept in a tower with her husband for season after season. I can talk of these things now, for we are all dead men. At the time I was sworn to a vow of secrecy, which I kept."

Norhan didn't believe the Fristle, and said so. Frandu's whiskers bristled. "She came back to Hyrklana seasons ago, and the queen immediately imprisoned her. Well, she would, wouldn't she?"

"Lilah is dead, onker."

"Yes, now. The Chuliks saw to that. And I am in the Arena."

I leaned forward "Who married the Princess Lilah?"

"Who? Why, that silly fellow Arrian nal Amklana."

I sat back. It seemed to me that the clouds parted above the Jikhorkdun and the mingled rays of the red and green suns struck through, illuminating everything they touched. Here was the key. Here was the key to turn the lock—if nature's natural course had followed. I had rescued Princess Lilah from the Manhounds and she had flown home and no one had heard of her from that day to this. And now . . . !

I said, "And the child?"

"Her?" Frandu shook his head. "I am a Fristle and she is an apim, but I own I have seldom seen a fairer girl in all the world."

"She lives?"

"Aye. The Chuliks slew Lilah and Arrian, and I nearly came by my death. But little Princess Lildra lives safely."

A somber feeling of sadness for the senseless death and, from what Frandu said, the even more senseless life, of Princess Lilah kept me silent as the crowd roar burst out as the pairs on the silver sand battled down to a finish and the blues' victory notched up their totem yet again. Lilah had been marked, it seemed to me, for a woeful destiny, and yet—and yet—could I have done anything else than I had done? No—and the Star Lords had kept me working hard for them at the time. I would have liked to have spoken to her again. But—she had a daughter, Princess Lildra.

So, as we walked back to the barracks carrying our armor and weapons, the red towels draped over our shoulders—for we were not yet far advanced enough to warrant slaves to carry our armor—I said, "And Ariane nal Amklana hired Chuliks to murder Lilah, and Ariane's own twin brother as well?"

"She did, the bitch." Frandu nodded vehemently. "And they nearly did for me, too."

I pondered the inhumanity of woman toward man. By these dreadful means Ariane hoped to prove a spurious legitimacy to the throne. She would use the old means of force and coercion to gain lawful ends, what Kregans call the steel bokkertu. Her twin brother was married to the sister of the queen—was not that reason and proof enough, Ariane would claim, to take the throne, seeing that Queen Fahia was dead? Well, it hadn't worked out like that. I made up my mind to find Princess Lildra.

One other point needed to be resolved, although I doubted if Frandu would have that knowledge.

"Do you know what the queen did about the bitch of Amklana?"

"We rescued Princess Lildra and took her to a safe place. I worked for the queen for many seasons and obeyed her in all things. But then I—" He glanced at Norhan, who was not overly interested, and hitched up his armor. "If you laugh, Norhan the Flame, I will singe your rear with one of your own pots! A charming Fristle fifi and I were very happy and she got me drunk and I was late reporting. There was a great hullabaloo. There had been an attempt to rescue the young princess. I was instantly suspected of plotting—well, I hadn't been, but I was—"

"A credulous fambly!" chortled Norhan. "Falling for the oldest trick in the world! A little Fristle fifi—she could have taken your uniform and weapons and armor while you snored, aye, and your keys! She gave them to her lover and they broke into the tower—you are a fambly!"

"It was not like that—and I warned you—"

"Save it," I said.

They looked at me. Frandu took a breath and Norhan shook his head. Before they had time to lacerate me with their barbed wit, I went on: "This story is interesting. But unless you can tell me who it was who tried to rescue Princess Lildra from the queen's imprisonment in the tower, I am going for a wet—now!"

"We will go for a wet, too," rumbled Norhan.

"All I know," said Frandu, "for they beat me severely, is that I overheard one of the queen's guards say that it must have been a great lord, for the money and the skill and the knowledge. But who it was, no one could say." He looked across the dusty alley toward our drinking den. "And all this talk has made me thirsty, by Harg!"

We went into the drinking den to slake our thirsts before we went to wash up. Frandu might not know who the great noble was. It was not Vad Noran, for a certainty. But I had an idea I knew who had tried to bring Princess Lildra out of imprisonment so that she might be made Queen of Huringa. By Kaidun, yes!

Chapter Eleven

Concerning a Silver Sinver and a Water Jar

"Watch out!" called Hundal the Oivon, running into our barrack room. "Here comes Tipp the Thrax. Get lost!"

At once a scramble began to get out of the confines of the barrack room and into the labyrinth of alleys and arcades fringing the arena. Fifty men, all stout fighting kaidurs, struggling to run away from a little, limping, lopsided Gon! But, this shriveled-up, shaven-headed Gon was Kyr Tipp the Thrax. He was a Queen's Cheldur. We all knew what he wanted and we all prayed he did not have our names written down on his note pad. He had a gimlet eye, and a nose and chin in too close proximity, and Queen Fahia looked on him with great favor.

We scattered into the alleys between practice rings and yards, running under the high walls of barrack blocks and armories, even getting away toward the menagerie areas. If our names were not written down then we had a chance. If Tipp the Thrax could not see us, he could not lift that crooked staff of his and beckon us over. We'd have to go. Tipp fixed up the bouts for the Queen's Kaidurs, and as the youngest child in Huringa knew, the Queen's Kaidurs always won. Or nearly always. While it was true that the queen would more often allow a champion beaten by her kaidurs the opportunity of his life, out there in the Arena, than she would in fights between the four color corners, no one could be absolutely sure she would not condemn the vanquished. Of course, if a kaidur got himself chopped in the heat of combat, well—wasn't that always the possibility of this life? So, we rough tough kaidurs fled.

Frandu the Franch hauled up under a striped awning over an opening in the wall where soft drinks might be bought by those with money. Sometimes the cheldurs would give us small sums out of their winnings. Slaves moved about, busy as slaves always pretend to be busy, the suns shone, the shadows lay dark and slanting, and Frandu said, "By Harg! I'm not running anymore. If Tipp picks me I'll—"

"You'll come up against a Queen's Kaidur," said Norhan, "and he'll thrash you. They always do."

The queen recruited her own champions from the ranks of the greatest hyr-kaidurs. They were good, there was no doubt of that.

"One of these days, if I live, I will be a Queen's Kaidur."

"I wish you well of it, and may the glass eye of Beng Thrax smile upon you."

So they started another wrangle. The four color quarters within the enormous space of the Jikhorkdun were like small towns in themselves. If Tipp didn't have our names written down, selected by observance of performance, we were safe. This, of course, was another danger faced by any man aspiring to become a hyr-kaidur. But the managers selected promising material and would exclude them from those kaidurs sent up against the queen's champions. To do otherwise would have been folly. When I'd been a hyr-kaidur, as Drak the Sword, I had gone through the danger zone fast, and in part that was due to the personal fracas and reconciliation I'd had with Fahia. I didn't want to go through that performance again, by Zair!

Watchful guards prowled every exit from the secure inner sections, and to escape, as I knew, you'd have to have outside help. If you were a topman you had the run of the place. But I was not a topman, yet.

All the same, this incident together with what Frandu had told me of Princess Lilah's daughter, Princess Lildra, made me look again at the chances of escape. I left Norhan the Flame and Frandu the Franch arguing away by the soft-drinks counter and walked off. I had resolutely refused to make friends, and this attitude was common enough. So I walked along with a new spring to my step, reasoning that now that I had a lead to a promising fresh series of plots and stratagems, the quicker I got out of here and shed the false glamour and allure of the Jikhorkdun the quicker I could be about my proper business. And, to be perfectly honest, with this resolve to escape burning in me, I experienced a touch of disappointment that I would not be here to see the red of the ruby drang finally ascend to the top of the victory pole . . .

We had overcome the yellow of the diamond zhantil, and had almost reached the green of the emerald neemu. Then it was the blue of the sapphire graint—and triumph!

The decision to make a break for it, right here and now, was sudden and unexpected. It swept over me like a rashoon of the inner sea, the Eye of the World. By Zim-Zair! What was I doing, allowing myself to be sucked in by the excitement of the Jikhorkdun? Instantly, with no further hesitation, I knew I would escape—now!

It would have to be daring and quick and without doubts. It would have to be simple. I like simple plans. Swift and direct, childish, even, and I'd walk out of here.

In the shadows of a low-doomed archway leading onto the outer sections of the area where the public came to see and admire their favorites after the games, and to stroll in the reflected glow of the Arena's thrills, I watched the guard. He was apim. He carried a stabbing spear as well as his sword, and his uniform might just fit. He was not alone. His comrade, a Rapa whose vulturine face appeared relaxed, laughed and picked up two pots swinging from long handles. He walked off with a casual remark about Beng Dikkane the patron saint of ale drinkers.

I looked back. Two slaves carrying a bronze cauldron on poles took no notice of me. A man stepped from the shadows of a doorway twenty paces back. He turned away at once, without looking toward me. At sight of him I bristled up, for he looked a fierce, barbaric, savage kind of man, in the way he walked and held himself, in the limber length of him and the breadth of his shoulders. But he took no notice of me and walked off. He was a man I'd not care to cross or to meet in enmity up a dark alley on a moonless night, by Krun!

I said to the guard, "I have found a silver sinver which is probably great wealth to the poor soul who lost it." I advanced, my empty hand clenched as though on a silver coin.

"That's funny," said the guard. "I dropped a sinver only this morning and you must have found—"

He did not say any more by reason of the fact that the clenched fist he so dearly wished to inspect put him peacefully to sleep. His harness came off in the shadows like the skin off a rabbit. I donned the leather straps and gear, buckled up the sword, settled the helmet on my head and seized the fallen spear.

Then I set off boldly, marching as though on parade, out

through the public sectors. There would be more gates to pass through, but a guard obviously on business could, with a word or two of gruff comradely greeting, pass where a kaidur would be instantly stopped. There was no sign of the man's Rapa comrade. There would be time to get lost among the people out there and find myself a civilian's outfit. If this sounds easy, do not believe it. Escapees made the same old mistakes and were caught in the same old way. That apim guard had been lax—he had been lax and a fool. But then, a silver sinver. . . !

Had I mentioned a golden deldy, he would have been suspicious on the instant, and a copper ob would not have moved him. No, I fancied I had pitched it just right.

By the time I was dressed in a neat blue tunic with a silver hem, the distant sounds of shouting wafted across the intervening walls. The owner of the tunic slumbered under a bench against a wall. I slapped his thraxter down into the scabbard, for the sword was a private one, of fine workmanship, far superior to the issue sword of the guard. Then I put a simple, innocent face on, which stung confoundedly, and walked casually off toward the flight of steps leading to the nearest exit. The noise faded. The Rapa must have found his comrade, and now there was hell to pay. I felt sorry for the guard, but he had been lax in his duty, through greed, no doubt of it. That was no justification, of course, but I recalled the way Prince Tyfar regarded these affairs.

Walking up to the villa, which was as sumptuous as Tyfar had indicated it was, I felt the freedom. There was more to this feeling of liberation than merely walking outside the walls of the Jikhorkdun. The freedom was a liberation of spirit.

The day was on the wane. But there was no point in delaying. Escape wasn't quite as easy as I have indicated, and the Queen's Guards would scour the city. The civilian would describe his clothes. Any others I filched would likewise be traced. I had to press on as quickly as I could, trusting in the truth of my deductions.

The villa looked impregnable, but there would be a way in.

My face was now bedeviling me with a myriad beestings. I let the facial control relax, and that old beakhead that is Dray Prescot's glared out again. I'd put on another new face when the time was right. Getting over the wall was not too difficult, and only a few smashed frames and ruined fruit on the other side witnessed my descent. This was merely the outer wall. The man I wanted to see, if he was here, would be at ease in his own apartments. To reach those I could adopt the guise of a slave, or a guard, or try to bluff my way in as a horter on business.

Well, slaves get everywhere and are unremarked, especially if they are carrying something and look busy. There is the notorious case of the soldier who walked about camp all day carrying a piece of paper and looking important, and thereby escaped all manner of duties. The first slave I ran across was carrying a water jar. Now—laugh all you like—I realized I was extraordinarily reluctant to hit him. He had done me no harm, not even the negative harm the guard had done by merely being there. I looked the slave up and down and he trembled.

"Slave!"

"Yes, master?" He was apim, with a gray slave breechclout and he quavered, gray with fear. This was not promising.

"Is your master at home?"

"Yes, master. At home. I know, for Lettie told me—"

"Very well." My first ridiculous notion had been to ask him to give me his breechclout and jar of water in exchange for my fine blue tunic. I sighed. I said, "Slave, I bear you no ill will. But it is necessary that I hit you—"

"Do not beat me, master! I know I did wrong, but I have been punished enough—I was forced—"

So, in something of a state of self-contempt, I put him to sleep. I stowed the blue tunic and the sword under a bush and put on his breechclout. I picked up the jar of water and hoisted it. Then, with a hangdog look on my face, I trailed off toward the house.

One way or the other, I was not going to be long about this.

Considerable activity was taking place at the front, with carriages and saddle animals arriving and guests entering. This was bad news. I pushed on and went in through the slave entrance at the back, the jar of water concealing my face, and walked along bare corridors toward the front of the house. The door that led out of the slave quarters into the master's portions of the villa was marked by a hanging lamp and a thin-faced Rapa guard. I just hoisted the pot higher and walked on with that sad slave's shuffle. I went through without a word.

The villa *was* sumptuous. Tyfar had been right. The layout followed that of many of the better-class houses, and I decided that if I found an imposing series of doors along the next floor where an outside balcony ran the length of the house, I'd be on the right tracks. Slaves pitter-pattered past. There were a few guards stationed at various doors. A parcel of women, all beautifully dressed and dripping furs and jewelry, passed me and I shrank back. They were laughing and talking, refined, the great ladies to the life, and they just did not see me. I was grateful for that.

Their menfolk would be off somewhere talking business while they enjoyed themselves with gossip and scandal—and also with arranging affairs to suit themselves when they talked to their husbands again, I did not doubt. Two Khibil guards stopped me at a door studded with gold, and with golden zhantilheads for handles.

"Water, masters, water," I whined.

They let me through. They would be punished if they stopped the water being brought, as the slave would be if he spilled any on the priceless carpets of Walfarg weave. I walked on.

Voices sounded from the next room, which was large and domed, and with many lamps shedding a mellow light. I passed the open door and saw the men in there, brilliantly attired, full fleshed of face, assured, dominant. They were organizing the affairs of their world, without a doubt. I passed on and went through the small door at the side which would lead into the ablution area. My plan was simpleminded; it had worked so far, but now I was likely to come to a dead end.

The room was large and furnished with a variety of exotic wares—statues and ceramic pots of curious design, fountains and sinks of running water, ferns and flowers growing in tubs, and one whole area at the side was given over to the hot-air recreation lounge. The place was empty as I entered and, by Vox! I felt more than a little stupid with my pitiful pot of water. All the same, here I was, and no doubt in entirely the wrong place for the water jar. The door from the main room opened, admitting the buzz of conversation. The door closed. I busied myself with a mop snatched up from a corner, sloshing my precious water down and sluicing the mop back and forth. I did not look up. The two men talked in loud tones, ignoring me—not even seeing me, I had little doubt. Their conversation was of the foolish, fleshy, man-of-the-world kind so obnoxious in the real world. They finished up and looked about for towels. From a wicker booth offset to the side emerged a Fristle woman. She wore a decent robe of yellow, and there were thick-soled wooden sandals on her feet. She carried on a silver tray a pile of fluffy yellow towels.

She'd been there all the time, watching, waiting to perform her duty, and she, in her turn, had taken no notice of me.

The men left. The Fristle woman collected her towels and went back into her wicker booth. I let out a breath. The warm scent of perfumes on the air, the steam from the adjoining sections, the continual rush and susurration of running water, all added up to a weird rhythm. I blinked. I took a breath and the door opened again and a man stepped in. Because, I suppose, I was not bent over, mopping, or doing something slaves are expected to do, he looked at me.

He looked. My face was my own. He stared, and came closer.

He rocked back on his heels and looked me up and down.

Very calmly, I waited, looking back at Orlan Mahmud nal Yrmcelt.

He put a finger to his lips. His eyes were brilliant upon me. He wet his lips. "I do not—I cannot believe—Dray Prescot! It is Dray Prescot, that was Drak the Sword!"

Chapter Twelve

The Star Lords Astonish Me

"I did not think you would remember me—"

"Not remember!" He threw his head back, brilliant, laughing, suffused. There was a tremble in him that came from some hidden knowledge that gave him quick and sudden joy. "Not remember the man who, when we first met, told me I was an onker? Told me to run? A man who with a word might have had the queen throw me to her pet neemus?" He took his hand away from his mouth and looked back at the door. The heavy wood cut off all sound. "Not remember the man who threw the leem's tail? The man who fought the boloth and was taken up in a voller? My friend, you undervalue the stir you caused in Huringa those seasons ago."

"And yet you see me now wearing the gray slave breechclout—"

"I do not believe that. I have followed your story. Of course!" He replied to my surprised unspoken query. "I know you. And I believe it is Opaz himself, manifest through the Invisible Twins, who has brought at this hour into Huringa the Emperor of Vallia!"

"So you know—"

"I know a great deal. Not all. Not why you are here. We do not know each other, we met for heartbeats, and have not seen each other for seasons. But I have spies, I learn, I know what happens in the world, and how you thrash those Opaz-forsaken cramphs of Hamal." His voice thickened on the last words, and he almost spat out his hatred and contempt for the Hamalese.

I sighed. I had formed a favorable impression of Orlan Mahmud. He had been reckless and uncaring—yet he had been involved in a conspiracy against the queen. Now that he had succeeded to his father as the queen's chief pallan he still reminded me of the young man who had kicked me free of that damned great slate slab. He wore a costly evening gown, much laced with gold, of a deep plum color. His brown hair still clustered in curls and the fleck of green in his eyes still gave him that quicksilver look. A clever man, Orlan Mahmud.

"Why are you here to see me, majister?"

The way he said that, the way he brought out the "majister" in so unaffected a way, gave me pause. His quick words had lulled me. I could be in deadly danger. The Fristle attendant could now be bringing up guards. I stared at Orlan Mahmud.

"How was it you failed in your attempt to rescue Princess Lildra?"

He gasped and took a step back. It was not theatrical. He was genuinely shocked.

"Quiet, I beg you!" He looked about, and the color fled. "How—how could you know? If it is known—the Jikhorkdun—"

"Aye. She would have sport with you."

"Yes. I have come to detest the Arena of late."

"By your mien I guess you hold a meeting tonight with

those who share the queen's favors—as do you—and not with those who share your true desires."

He nodded and said, "A formal reception. Tiresome. I am married and with two sets of twins. I have responsibilities. What do you know of Princess Lildra, whom Opaz preserve?"

"I fight—at the moment—against Hamal. I know of plots to bring Hyrklana into the Hamalese camp. For the sake of Vallia I do not care for that. I think if Queen Lildra sat on the throne instead of Queen Fahia, the world would smile more cheerfully."

"Then you know Fahia inclines toward Hamal, after all this time? She believes there is much gain for her. The ordinary folk do not like the Hamalese, as you know. I have much support."

I looked him straight in the eye. He drew in his chin, facing me, looking back. He was, after all, a queen's chief minister.

"Do you desire to make yourself King of Hyrklana, Orlan?"

"No, majister." His answer came back like a bowshot. I believed him. He had always exercised power from the background.

Before I could question him further, he said, "It is not safe for you to stay here like this. I will find clothes and weapons." Trust a good Kregan to bracket those together! "Then we can talk. After this damned reception. In my chambers."

"Very well. First—where does Fahia hide Princess Lildra?"

"The Jasmine Tower in the Castle of Afferatu."

There clung to him that quivering air of excitement. I suppose one could suggest, without too much megalomania, that he was impressed by having an emperor dressed up in slave's gear in his ablutions; there was something else, and that something else puzzled me. It seemed he was expecting me to say what he waited for me to say. I stretched my back and looked toward the door.

"Yes, it is a good idea for me to leave. I came here to see you. Is there anything else you have to say?" I studied him and, by Vox, he started to smile like a grinning lurfing. This meeting had been prosaic enough, Opaz knew. I said, and I own my voice was a trifle tinged with impatience, "You do not seem very surprised to see me."

"I am, I am. And, yet, majister—no." He laughed

openly. "I am astonished to find you dressed up in slaves' gear when you could have come with an embassy to the front door. As the Emperor of Vallia you would be welcome—"

"I, Drak the Sword, welcome in Queen Fahia's eyes?"

"No. Of course not. But—why, majister, did you come if it was not to add to your son's pleas?"

I gaped.

"My son?"

"Of course. Prince Jaidur. He has been working on the lords and ladies of Huringa to bring them into alliance with Vallia, acting on your instructions."

Had I been wearing a hat I would have snatched it off, hurled it to the floor and jumped on it.

By the disgusting diseased liver and lights of Makki-Grodno!

"Jaidur—*here*?"

"You are telling me you did not know?"

Sometimes emperors have the opportunity to exercise a right which in others would be rudeness. I did not answer directly. I said, "Let me get into a safe bolthole, with some clothes and weapons, and then I'll have a word with that young imp Jaidur."

"At once, majister."

The doors moved and then started to open and at once the blast of noise from the meeting burst in. Orlan looked stricken. He glared about like a hunted beast seeking asylum from the pack.

"You must hide, majister! Quickly—"

I just picked up the mop and bent over.

"Take no notice of me, and neither will they. Is the Fristle woman trustworthy? Not now. Later."

Four young men in high spirits caroused into the ablutions and began skylarking about, throwing water. Orlan stepped forward and the strongest desire in me to laugh had to be suppressed. The change in demeanor in those four foolish young men was remarkable. Well, as I had to keep reminding myself: Orlan Mahmud was Queen Fahia's principal minister. With a quantity of hangdoggery and sheep-facery, and quickly sloshed water, the four lads departed.

"All the same, Orlan," I said, when the door closed, "I will avail myself of your kind offer right away. Where do I go?"

"I will fetch you myself."

We went out through the smaller door into the corridors and anterooms, and as a slave I shuffled along half a dozen paces in rear. Orlan was clever. No doubt he had dealt with spies in a similar manner. Eventually, up a dark blackwood stair, I found myself in a small room, smelling faintly of dust and ripe apples, with a bed and table and not much else. Orlan closed the door, which was locked by a monstrous great bronze and iron contraption.

"You will be safe here. Only I have the key. I must get back to that tiresome reception."

"Assuredly. Tell me, before you go, what was Arrian nal Amklana like, as a man?"

"He was a friend. He was frothy, yes, but his heart was sound. He was with me in the cavern when you held up the slate slab so that we might all escape."

The feeling of satisfaction within me, almost like that of digestive juices moving, came from two sources. I was pleased that Princess Lilah had loved a man. Of course, when the Star Lords sent their damned great blue Scorpion to snatch me up and deposit me somewhere else to do their bidding I more often than not remained in ignorance of just who it was I had rescued. I'd not known in this case; now I thought I did.

Orlan hesitated at the door and turned diffidently. "Arrian won Princess Lilah. He was a true man, and there was nothing I could say to that, for I loved her myself. He chose to go into captivity with her—as I would have done." And he went out and locked the bronze and iron contraption after him.

In the nal Amklana family, it seemed clear, the twin sister was the hard and ruthless one, the twin brother the easygoing and softhearted one. Perhaps his daughter would prove a broken reed; perhaps she would be embittered and vicious in her hatred of everyone. All I knew was that I had to rescue her and see about helping the rebellion along . . .

A most gorgeously formed Sybli wearing a slit shushchiff of laypom-yellow material, her baby face bouncy with smiles, brought me food and drink. Through the half-open door I caught a glimpse of a giant Khibil, a massive glimmer of steel, dangling Orlan's key ring. So he did trust someone other than himself in his villa . . . In only a few burs, Orlan returned. He looked weary, and his face was whiter and more strained than it ought to be. He moved a hand despondently.

"The queen is set on her course, majister. We must depose her and install the Princess Lildra as queen!"

"Agreed. I'll get along to the Castle of Afferatu."

He sat down on the bed. "Yes. I will send word. We have people down there, but they are despondent after the last failure."

I thought to say, "Can you tell me anything of Spikatur Hunting Sword, Orlan?"

"By Harg! I was approached recently and I think other lords also. Then I heard nothing. And then arrests were made and men and women were sent to the Jikhorkdun. It was done by Kov Hogan who is a spymaster it would be better not to cross. He says he is a queen's man, but I know he has been bought by Hamalese gold. He hates me."

We talked for a space and I told him that Spikatur Hunting Sword was a conspiracy directed against Hamal. "They claim to have no leaders, which probably means local chapters each doing what it can and reporting back—but to whom? They assassinate Hamalese. They burn voller factories. They attempt to be a thorn in the flesh of Hamal and her friends."

It occurred to me that if the local chapter of Spikatur had not been broken up then Tyfar would have been in serious danger.

"What can you tell me of the plot formulated by Vad Noran?"

"He was betrayed. By whom, I do not know." Orlan spread his hands. "There are always plots and always, always, always, those who will betray for money."

"Or ideals."

"Those as well. It comes down to the same thing in the end. Men and women broken or turned out into the Arena."

"Yet you persist?"

"I must. There is no other way."

From this nighttime meeting in a small room smelling of dust and apples we both learned much. He was eager to ally with Vallia and Djanduin and whoever else would stand against Hamal. I spoke to him of the Shanks, or Shants, Schtarkins, the fishheads from the other side of the world, and he shared my dreams of a great confederation to stand against these leem-loving reivers.

"I have sent word to Prince Jaidur, and he will come, I

have no doubt, as soon as possible to see his father. He is a busy young man."

"Aye," I said. "Busy."

The Sybli in her slinky shush-chiff, that alluring evening gown worn by Kregan girls on holiday or festive occasions, brought us wine and we drank a little companionably. Orlan left late, and I debated if it was wise for me to wait for Jaidur. He was still resentful that I was his father, although he had proved himself a fine young man and a splendid son to his mother. I'd give him until the morning, I told myself, and then I'd be off, and the little dusty-apple-smelling room tinged with a lambent blueness.

My first reaction was one of complete stupidity. Not stupefaction, for whatever tricks the Star Lords and their Scorpion got up to would not, I thought, surprise me. I shook my head. I slumped down on the bed. "Not now," I said aloud. "Not bloody now!"

And the gigantic form of the Scorpion leered down on me, gloating. Far larger than the modest confines of the room, that enormous shape glowed with blue fire, and I felt the winds sweeping me up and the coldness chilling my flesh and I went whirling away end over end, yelling my foolish head off that I wouldn't go, by the putrid diseased left eyeball of Makki-Grodno.

But—I went.

In the next few heartbeats I expected to be hurled down all naked and unarmed somewhere on Kregen's savage surface to rescue some poor devils at the whim of the Star Lords. The Everoinye, the Star Lords, cared not a whit for what I might be doing. If I rebelled against them I could be hurled back to Earth and left to rot. Once, I had rotted on Earth for twenty-one years.

Never again—not ever again, could I allow that . . .

By the exercise of willpower I had accomplished that defiance. My own puny mortal will had been set against the superhuman demands of the Everoinye. And I had influenced events. Mind you, they'd gotten their revenge in flinging me to Earth and leaving me there to molder away until, in the fullness of time and with the help of other forces, I had returned to Kregen.

So now, tentatively, I tried to resist.

Suppose I were thrown down into Segesthes, miles away to the east, or Turismond, miles away to the west? Suppose they dumped me down in the Eye of the World? I fought them. I had to go to the Castle of Afferatu to res-

"The gigantic form of the scorpion leered down at me."

cue a princess. The will of the Star Lords, I thought, being superhuman, must overwhelm my own desires. They were usually aloof, and although there was dissension among them with the young Star Lord, Ahrinye, demanding a greater share of power, they just did not bother about humanity. So I thought in my ignorance. And so, thinking that, I struggled against them.

A voice whispered in, like a dagger.

"You swore, Dray Prescot, there was a compact between us."

By three things I knew this was not the voice of Ahrinye. First: The blueness tinged with a deep crimson, and there was no sign of the acid green associated with Ahrinye. Second: The voice was not his, although superhuman and remote, not drilling in my head like a white-hot auger. And, third: I had no compact with him, and had at best a ramshackle kind of agreement with the Everoinye themselves.

So I said, "I hear you, Star Lords. Have I not done your bidding well and faithfully? And I know you have no thought or care for humankind, so that anything I might say will not move you."

Into the rushing wind swirling about me seeped that macabre silence and stillness found in the eye of a storm. The blueness of the Scorpion faded as the pulsating crimson brightened. I looked in vain for the first glimmerings of friendly yellow. The voice husked now, as though speaking in my ear, and yet I knew I sat on a bed in a dusty apple-smelling room in Orlan Mahmud's villa. All around me the crimson stretched, and gradually it coalesced beneath me and broadened and lifted above into a hollow vault.

"You have obeyed, Dray Prescot, although we know your resentment of us."

I marveled. These beings, although once human, were no longer a part of the human race. How could they be? I did not know. I was confused.

"What do you want of me now? I have work to do—"

"We released you for your work in Vallia. Now you will work for us in Hyrklana, as you did once before, just the other day. And your work here is goodly in our eyes."

I just didn't believe this.

"Goodly—my work? You mock me, Star Lords!"

"Mockery is for fools. No doubt that is why you mock others so much."

I clenched my fists. I was no longer sitting on the bed, I was standing on a hard crimson floor and the vault above blazed with white stars through the crimson curve. I stared, sick.

"What—"

"Listen! You will be sent to where you wish to go. In this thing our wishes coincide. Also, a bundle will go with you, for it grows heavy in the transsubstantiated state. It seems to us, Dray Prescot, that you are not as other men. You are reckless, foolish, headstrong and cunning. Also, you have striven to resist us. As a Kregoinye, one who serves us on Kregen, you have done well despite yourself. Continue to do well."

I held myself in check. If I angered the Everoinye I could be back on Earth instantly, stranded on the world of my birth.

Yet I could not hold back: "I do not admit to being a Kregoinye—"

"Yet you are."

The hardness of the crimson floor seemed to me to be no illusion. A soft wind blew. I thought I could see distant shapes, insubstantial, gossamer, floating at the extremity of vision. I appeared to be standing on the floor of an impossible vast hall, vaulted with star-pierced crimson. Somewhere there was music. I breathed deeply. Was that a face, a face of enormous size, peering down at me? Were those eyes, as large as suns, shooting forth crimson light within the crimson immensity? I shut my own eyes, dazzled.

I felt the coldness of a damp wind on my naked skin and the earthly sough of tree branches stirred by wind. I opened my eyes and I was standing at the edge of a wood, dark in the light of two of Kregen's lesser moons hurtling past low above. I looked about. The breeze blew damp and chill. The grass was wet. The trees sighed, black masses flogging in the coming gale, and I sucked in a breath of air vastly different from the last lungful I had breathed in that supernal chamber.

My foot kicked a solid bundle, and I looked down. Wrapped in an old gray blanket, the bundle looked—odd. I bent and undid the rope knots and threw the blanket back. I stared.

That gray blanket reeked with a repellent odor of fish.

Inside, a short scarlet cape showed the typical thin and elegant gold embroidery of Valka. I lifted it aside to reveal a rapier and main gauche of fine Vallian manufacture.

There was a first-class thraxter that had been taken at the Battle of Jholaix. I touched the old scarlet breechclout and fingered the broad lesten-hide belt with the dulled silver buckle. The breast and back gleamed with the luster of oiled armor, their chasings and embossings superb examples of the armorer-decorator's art. The helmet was really a plain steel cap with a rim of trimmed ling fur and a flaunting tuft of scarlet feathers I remembered I'd not cared for but had worn to show my position to my men in battle.

No surprise at all that the very first item I picked up, holding in my fists, and staring deeply, was that special sword Naghan the Gnat and I had designed and forged and built in the armory of Esser Rarioch, in Valka. That sword was as good a copy as we could contrive of the superlative Krozair longsword.

Well!

Yes, I knew this bundle of clothing and weapons. I'd last seen these swords, this armor, when I'd defied the Star Lords and been thrown back to Earth for twenty-one years. They had tried to bribe me then by hurling me down into action for them with my gear still intact. Usually—always—I was naked and unarmed. Slowly, I picked up the gear, looking at it, feeling it, expecting it to evaporate into moonshine as the pseudo-weapons from the Moder had done. But the metal felt hard and ridged under my fingers, the scarlet breechclout snugged neatly and the plain lesten-hide belt cinched tightly with the silver buckle.

I tore out half the flaunting scarlet feather from the steel cap and I hoped, as I donned the armor, that it would be taken as a favor of the ruby drang. For I was still in Hyrklana, and those lights beyond the curve of the wood must be the Castle of Afferatu.

With the rain-laden wind blustering about my ears, head down, I started off to rescue a princess from a guarded tower.

Chapter Thirteen

At the Castle of Afferatu

I should really have said to rescue a princess from a dragon-guarded tower. For her jailers had four captive risslacas, dinosaurs of ferocious aspect, chained up at the inner and outer gates. The walls towered. The arrow slits were narrow and deep. The moat was brimming and the drawbridge was up.

"No hope," said Dogon the Lansetter as we stood under a tree that dripped water on our heads and shoulders and down our necks.

The local rebels were very disheartened, dispirited, seeing nothing but failure ahead after their last failure. They'd been easy enough to find and identify from the information Orlan Mahmud had given me. We skulked in the woods and spied on the castle and we might as well have been on the first of Kregen's seven moons, the Maiden with the Many Smiles. There were perhaps twenty-five of us—I say perhaps, for I wouldn't care to try half of them in action. Men and women, boys and girls, both diff and apim, they looked up apathetically as Dogon the Lansetter and I trailed into the camp. Everything was sodden. There were no tents. And the waterproofs were wet inside and out. As for a fire—ha!

"There has to be a way to get in, to rescue the princess, and get out with all of us alive." I spoke commandingly.

A gap-toothed rascal looked across and unwedged his jaws from a cold ponsho chop. His gappy teeth showed as he spoke.

"We don't know you. You quote names at us—I say you are a damned spy come to trap us all without trouble."

"Aye!" shouted an apim with carroty hair and a spotty face.

The four Fristle fifis huddled under a blanket looked out wide-eyed. Pretty, they surely were. But now, they were wet . . .

"Which one of you organized Frandu the Franch?"

At this there were squeals and giggling; then there were certain searching questions for me to answer. One of the fifis admitted to detaining Frandu, but: "Was no good. He didn't part with his keys."

"And we lost Naghan the Finger, and Ortyg the Lame and Hernon the Kramdu, all of them killed dead," said Dogon. He was a bulky fellow whose belt circumscribed bulges, but he was useful with an axe. He wore an iron cap. Most of the others had some kind of body armor, mostly leather, and an assortment of weapons. I refused to let my hope sink or to allow myself to become disheartened. After all, it wouldn't be the first time I'd ventured into dark and dragon-infested towers to rescue princesses, now would it? But I would prefer company on this occasion.

"By Harg! If only this rain would stop!" growled gap-tooth. He was not Gap-tooth Jimstye, for which I was grateful, but his mistrust of me, while perfectly natural, could have been awkward.

"We wait until tomorrow night," said Dogon.

I was fed up with waiting. I said so.

"Tomorrow we expect more men."

Gap-tooth cackled. "You could have more than a hundred men and you'd never bust in there. The castle's impregnated."

A girl with long fair hair started laughing. One or two others joined in. Gap-tooth glared about, not comprehending.

Then a blasted squall drove stinging rain onto us all and drenched us all over again. As I say, not a happy camp and not an auspicious start for a venture that should topple thrones.

The root words for impregnable and impregnated are not the same in Kregish either, but the minuscule jest remained, as if it were hovering in the rain-sodden air. I was still mentally dizzy from the encounter with the Everoinye. Superhuman beings of awesome power living God-alone knew where—yes, I feel I was entitled to be a little punch-drunk.

There was no time for self-pity.

Circumspection marked Orlan Mahmud's dealings with people of this stamp, and I'd introduced myself to them as coming from him in his cover name of Klanak the Tresh. Tresh means flag, and Klanak is the name of a mythical hero of Hyrklana, so that Orlan was in effect saying, rise up and follow the flag of your greater past.

No, I could not wait around for this kind of rebellion.

The rain pitter-pattered among the leaves and splashed among the huddled forms in their blankets. I looked hard at Dogon.

"What is the name of the guard commander tonight?"

"Now, by the belly and brains of Beng Brandaj, how am I supposed to know that?"

"Rebels have to know things like that."

Eventually, one of the Fristle fifis, not the one who had enticed Frandu, said it would probably be that lecherous Khibil devil with the big sword, Podar, who was a dwa-Hikdar now. Or, she added, her fur wet and bedraggled, or it might not be, and instead that passionate Fristle, Follando the Eye—and what an eye!—would have the Gate.

"If there are three guards in rotation, who has the third?"

"There is a Brokelsh called Ortyg the Bristle, and a Rapa called Rordnon the Andamak. They are ord-Deldars."

I did not chew my lip, for that would convey my own complete indecision. But I would not delay. They had no saddle animals, so I had to walk off in the rain to rescue the princess.

"Remberee!" they called. "We will try to rescue you from the dungeons only if—" I didn't bother to hang about to hear their stipulations.

Now the scarlet cloak and the armor I carried were not those of Hyrklana. A rapier and main gauche might be excused a dandyish officer who wished to be in fashion. The longsword was scabbarded down my back. There is a knack to drawing a blade from that position. But my equipment was clearly military and I was not inclined to toss it away and don a gray slave breechclout. For one thing, guarding a princess with your head forfeit if she escapes is vastly different from standing guard in a busy villa or palace; slaves would not be so free to move around in the Castle of Afferatu. I slogged on in the rain.

No handy soldier of the garrison popped up to be popped into the bag and his uniform donned. No one showed at all as I stood on the bank of the moat and helloed across toward the gatehouse.

The drawbridge lifted up, its bronze spikes very nasty. Lights shone from arrow slits. Everything looked gray and black and wet around those slits of light. The rain trickled down my neck. Among the vaguely discerned clumps of towers there was no telling which was the Jasmine Tower. As far as I could tell, I might have yelled my head off into Cottmer's Caverns for all the notice anyone took of me. There was no point in waiting further. The water of the moat rippled and danced in the slices of yellow light falling from the arrow slits. The rain pranced. It was all very wet indeed.

Only a few strokes took me across the moat. The water was not overly cold, for we were in Hyrklana. As for my weapons, during the time they had been in the care of the Star Lords they had been liberally coated with grease. Removing that protective covering from the hilts had been a thoroughly painstaking task. I hauled myself out under the rearing gray walls, running water between the stones, and unwound the rope I'd demanded and obtained from those miserable rebels. It was as slick as a buttered pole at a fair, so the knots would be vital. I looked up.

The rope would never reach the top of the wall. I crabbed along until I was below a slit in a tower. The first cast missed, the bronze hook clanging back with what sounded like an infernal din. No one heard. Or, hearing, took any notice. I cast again.

The hook lodged in the slit. Hand over hand, up I went.

Gaining the slit, I edged in sideways and braced myself against the smoother stone facings. Now for the tricky bit. The next upward cast would be blind. The hook swung below making a wide arc and then flew upward. I heard the bronze strike the stone, and down the thing plummeted. Seven times I cast upward and seven times the hook missed the arrow slit unseen over my head. Eight throws, and eight misses. I took a ragged breath. Nine . . .

On the ninth cast the hook caught and held. Not for nothing is nine the sacred and magical number on Kregen.

Dangling in the wind-driven rain over emptiness, up I went again and so wedged myself in the next arrow slit. Just before I gained that doubtful sanctuary I took a good though rapid look up and judged the remaining distance. Just, I estimated, just. This time the hook caught on the very first cast, for the top of the tower afforded a better purchase. The knots were hard-edged under my fists. The parapet bulged, with slits frowning down. I hooked a leg, crabbed out as though going up the Futtock Shrouds instead of through the lubber's hole, and so tumbled over onto the top platform.

A fellow muffled in a cloak stumbled out of the little canvas shelter the sentries had rigged up and tried to stick a spear into my throat. I swayed to the side, and as he rushed past helped him on his way. He went over the edge with a long wailing scream that was lost in the rush of the wind. I collected the rope and started for the head of the stone steps leading down.

Annoyance and regret over the foolish death of that fellow made me cross. Now I would have to find someone else to ask where away lay the Jasmine Tower.

The stairs curved down to aid defense and I paused at the landing to listen. The place might have been stuffed with corpses. At the foot the door was a tough oaken affair with iron bolts; they opened with not more than a regulation screech. The ward beyond lay rain-lashed, sodden and completely uninviting.

A few lights fell from interior windows, but most were shuttered. The rain sluiced down and the storm grew and the stars were expunged. What a foul night! Mind you, the very wetness of the night aided me. I recognize that. But the water trickled down my neck and my feet were sodden and my hair was plastered down to my scalp like a devotee of Curdium-Ferang's mud-oil caked hairstyle when they scalp the sacrifices.

"By Krun!" I said to myself. "The first door it is, and no mistake."

The first door led onto a stone corridor with a few cressets leading to a maze of storerooms. No one was there. Useless. Fuming, I barged out into the rain and plodded through pools of water among the uneven flags to the next door along. This was shut and bolted. I hit it with my fist, and then drew the thraxter and hammered on the thick wood.

"Open up! Open up!"

After a space the bolts shot back and the door eased in a crack. I put my shoulder to it and barged in. A man staggered back almost dropping his lantern. His hair fell over his eyes. His mouth opened.

"What is it? What's all the racket about?"

Beyond him in the dimness lay an anteroom of sorts with tables and chairs stacked against the walls, and tubs and barrels piled in the corners. A bed to one side showed where the man had staggered from. I lifted him up by the nearest portion of his anatomy to hand and said, "Where is the Jasmine Tower? You have two heartbeats to tell me before I push your face in."

He told me.

I put him gently on the bed and closed the door after me.

The second tower along, he'd said, the one with the lantern in a niche over the door. The lantern was out, drowned, as I hove up. I eyed the tower lofting above me, lost in darkness. Up there, in some room and well-guarded, waited Princess Lildra . . .

So far I had not been detected, but this was a busy castle where other things went on, I did not doubt, than the detention of a princess. Despite the rain and the foul night, guards would be changed, sentries prowl. Time was running short. The door was locked and bolted. I fumed. I bashed the sword hilt against the wood. After a time it pulled back and a light glowed dimly.

Before the man could say anything I bellowed. I was just a dark shape to him, lacerated with raindrops, squelching, foul of temper and brutal of tongue. I advised him of his antecedents and probable destination and roared on: "The lantern is out! You know the regulations! See to it before your backside is roasted, rast!"

He started to mumble and I bellowed him to silence. "You bungling fool! Out of my way." Then, pulling the name from the four given me by the Fristle fifi back at the rain-drenched camp: "Is Hikdar Podar awake, or does he sleep in a drunken stupor?"

"Hikdar Follando has the guard, notor, but, but—"

I was in. The light, weak though it was, dazzled. I squinted and took the fellow's throat between fingers and thumb. His face glared up. He was apim. The room was a mere box, pierced with arrow slits in three inner faces and with murdering holes above. I had little time to get out of this trap. The farther door stood open, with a wash of sorry-looking light across the stone walls.

Gently putting the man down, I stepped over him and went out of the door. The corridor led to the foot of the stairs in one direction. The other way the guardroom was open, without a door, and containing half a dozen men lounging on benches and half-asleep on tables. One shouted: "What was that infernal racket, Nath?"

I tried.

"The lantern is out—"

The man looked up from his folded arms. He was a Deldar, fleshy, an ale-lover, with an enormous mustach. His eyes went mean.

"Stand where you are, cramph." He lurched upright, dragging out his sword. "Seize him, you idiots!"

They were slow. If they subsequently blamed the tempestuous night and the pervading dampness, they might be right; more probably they subconsciously relaxed after the previous attempts to rescue Princess Lildra had failed. They were still standing up and drawing weapons as I went into them. My thaxter whistled about merrily. I thumped them smartly, on heads, behind ears, turning and dodging a few return blows and kicking out to finish the job. The six guards slumbered. I went back to the outer door and closed and bolted it. Then I started up the stairs.

Two guards came clattering down, all a jingle of weaponry, swords in fists, to discover the cause of the uproar below. They were tripped and fell headlong—always a nasty trick on stairs, that—and I went on and up.

The stone stairs smelled musty and fusty and damp as everywhere else, yet into that depressing scent scenery crept a strongly pungent tang of a smell I did not recognize. I sniffed as I padded up—something like old socks? No—that was from another time and another place. The smell reminded me of damp fleeces hung before a fire. The first landing was bare and with a torch sputtering in its bracket. Without needing a light on, I went up the next curving flight, alert for the next pack of guards to come rushing down. They were the queen's men, and they could be excused much on a night like this, but the fact remained, I'd not get out of this without a fight, by Krun!

Almost certainly Princess Lildra would be quartered at the topmost section of the Jasmine Tower. The next landing contained an enormous animal whose coat gave off that distinctive aroma, whose jaws opened and whose fangs gnashed—and whose yellow eyes regarded me malevolently from a face that was a mere mask of hatred. Instantly I hurled myself back, slipping on the damp stone, and the beast's charge carried him over the topmost step before the iron collar and iron chain hauled him up fast. He slavered after me, his tongue lolling and those glistening teeth clashing together.

His gums glistened black and his teeth stuck up like needles. His mouth spattered foam. Shaggy hair dangled like tangled seaweed. He growled and barked and snarled and leaped against the restraining chain. He was thoroughly at home on a vile night like this, being a hound dog from Thothangir in South Havilfar, and if he fastened those jaws in me he wouldn't let go without taking his hundredweight of flesh.

Then—and even I find this hard to credit—I heard myself saying, "Good dog, good dog."

He nearly took my outstretched hand off in one gulp.

Someone called down from above—a rough voice, most unfriendly.

"Quiet, Zarpedon, you hound of hell!"

The hound dog yowled and nearly tore his head off trying to get at me. I looked at him and drew in my breath.

"It's you or me, Zarpedon."

Even taking him with the flat presented an interesting problem, for he was quick. But then, I have been accounted quick also, and the sword blade thudded alongside his head. His eyes rolled. He fell over on his side and lay there, for all the world like a friendly collie taking a rest. I stepped over him, looking down, moving gingerly. Then I went on up. Zarpedon could not be blamed. He had raised an outcry, and the oaf above had taken no notice. Well, by Krun, that suited me.

At the head of the stairs I paused for a moment outside the door. The dog-abusing oaf had left it partially open, no doubt to hear if the dog made any more fuss, and to come out and shout again. I listened before I went in. That is a useful habit.

There were two voices, a woman's and a man's, and the dog-abuser was saying: ". . . hellhound. Worse than the risslacas at the main gate."

"Poor Zarpedon," said the woman's voice, a harsh, unpleasant croaking kind of voice. "You treat him shamefully."

"And you, you hag, treat him better than you do the prisoner."

"No worse than you, Charldo! No wors'n you!"

The sounds of a blow and a yelp were followed by dragging footsteps, and the woman's whining voice faded, mingled with the man's bad-tempered growlings. I pushed the door open and peered inside. Just an anteroom, with a few sleeping furs piled on a ramshackle bed and bits and pieces of furniture added to relieve the starkness. A light fell from a half-opened door in the far wall. Listening, moving soundlessly, I heard the man and woman grumbling again. But this time they had joined forces and were speaking in ugly tones to a third person.

The clank of iron and a heavy curse from the adjoining door made me realize that in there rested the guards. How many were there? However many, they would be considered by the queen to be up to the job of guarding her niece. I listened thoughtfully for a few moments, considering the thunderstorm outside, the dampness of the night and the hellhound dog below on the stairs.

"Now, then, missy.*" The woman fairly snarled the words. "No more nonsense out of you. Drink it up or Charldo will take the strap to you again."

The sounds as of a leather strap being thwacked down into an opened palm made me almost instantly burst in. But I peered carefully through a knothole. Charldo was beating his palm with a leather strap. He was a most venomous-looking Kataki, a race of whip-tailed diffs with lowering faces and jagged teeth with whom I have had my fill of trouble over the seasons. Interestingly enough, he had unstrapped the bladed steel from his tail, and the flexible appendage coiled like a whip above the bed. The woman was a bent-over Rapa woman, missing a quantity of feathers, and her drab clothes bulged here and there, hiding the person who lay on the bed. The Rapa woman held a pottery cup in her hands.

"Drink it, missy. Now!"

The Kataki's whip-tail flourished in time to the leather belt thwacking into his palm.

The girl on the bed spoke in a voice that trembled only a little, and the desperation in her and the low almost controlled words filled that dismal chamber with a courage anyone would respond to. Anyone except these two—and Queen Fahia and her guard.

"It is disgusting and I think it is taking away my reason. I will not drink it!"

Smack went the Kataki's tail down on the bed and that was quite enough of that.

"The princess will not drink your gunk today, kleeshes," I said, and jumped into the room—fast.

The Kataki fell down with a broken nose. I kicked him

* The Kregish word Prescot uses here is tikshvu, which I have translated as missy with that word's ominous connotations of reprimand and temporary superiority threatening a girl who, powerless, yet insists on rebelling. —A.B.A.

"I jumped into the room—fast."

as he lay there as I grabbed for the Rapa to silence her. I got a hand wrapped around her mouth and her big beak clashed and she tried to nip me so I hauled her in, still gripping her tightly.

"I do not, princess," I said, "much care for striking women. But sometimes—"

"Let me," said Princess Lildra.

Chapter Fourteen

Princess Lildra

She stepped over the Rapa woman and started to run for the door and I took her arm and said, "We can't just run out like that, princess. There are guards."

"Of course there are guards. There are always guards." She looked puzzled, hurt, not afraid but withdrawn. "I have planned long and long what to do when my prince rescues me. So I know. We—"

I didn't listen to any more. I was too wet and in too foul a temper. She carried herself well and was young although fully formed, and her long white nightdress would be no garment for a night like this. In her face the lineaments of her mother, Lilah, could be plainly discerned. Also, there was more than a hint of the startlingly fair beauty of Ariane nal Amklana, her aunt who had ordered her killed.

"Are you a great jikai or are you not? Who are you and why do you seek to rescue me if you are not my prince?"

"I see they allow you books to read in your imprisonment."

"You dillydally, fellow!"

"I am called Jak and have been called Jak the Sturr and Jak the Shot and Jak the Sudden. You may call me Jak the Onker, if you wish. Now, lady, put on some suitable clothes for a wild night."

She didn't care for my tone. I judged that before her parents had been murdered she'd led a life of some privilege, and these dolorous surroundings were relatively recent. As for her aunt, Queen Fahia, some credit—if credit is the right word—had to be given to that fat unhappy queen for refusing to slay her sister and sister's husband and child. And if we stood lallygagging around now we'd all wind up arguing on the way to the Ice Floes of Sicce.

"Get changed, lady. Move!"

She jumped and the flush stained her cheeks. But she went behind a holey curtain and rustles and clickings indicated she was putting on clothes better able to withstand the rain than her flimsy nightdress.

She still wore a dress, whereat I sighed. But perhaps she did not have anything else. I dragged a blanket from the bed and draped it across her head and shoulders. Her hair gleamed liquid gold in the lamplight.

"Keep your head down, keep behind me, and do not scream or run. Only run when I tell you to. And then, lady, *run*!"

She drew a breath and I took her shoulder, twisted her toward the door and started off.

The conventional view of a young girl in these circumstances did not require an intense imagination to visualize. Sympathy and a lively determination to escape safely with her might be all that was required of the average rescuer. But I fancied that her long absorption with the details of the rescue she was convinced would one day occur had acted as a kind of pre-sensitizing agent. Now that the long-awaited rescue was taking place the whole process acted on her as a drug. Her calmness, her decisiveness, the way she wanted this affair to run, all convinced me of her condition. As to my own expected feelings of sympathy and compassion—of course. I felt them as who—apart from those I have mentioned—would not? But Lildra's actions and ready acceptance of this rescue as a mere acted-out appendage to dream-planning afforded me the opportunity to move fast and not to fear she would collapse.

At the door she said, "The birds are stabled in the White Tower. They do not have them here. We must—"

"I do not think birds will relish flying tonight, lady. It is the rope for you."

Her eyes regarded me with a look I took to be incipient annoyance that her dream-plans were not going as expected.

There was little time before the guards below aroused themselves, but I said—and I own to a genuine curiosity:

"How do you plan to reach the White Tower from the Jasmine Tower?"

Her head went back. "Why, that is simple. You will fight your way through and I will follow you."

The hound dog on the landing below sent up a throat-growling sound, very hackle-raising. Poor Zarpedon was feeling sorry for himself. The guards in the adjoining room gave no sign of alertness, and Lildra and I padded softly up the last little flight of stone steps to the roof of the tower.

She saw the rope and she understood. The rain pelted down. Her dress melted against her body in moments. I fastened the bronze hook on the stone and lowered the rope down, not dropping it. There seemed no point in explaining to her that if we could not find an arrow slit, and if we could not wedge ourselves into it, the last part of the descent would be ropeless through thin air.

She said, "When you burst in and knocked Charldo over I took you for a jikai. But you refuse to follow the plan—I am not sure—"

"Just hold onto my harness. Grip tightly and do not let go."

I had to take her arms, wet and shining with rainwater, and place her hands on my leather gear. I cocked a leg over the parapet and let her weight come on me. The rope was like bristly butter under my fingers. Thank Zair the knots held! Carefully, with Lildra hanging from me, I started the descent.

My head was level with the crenelations when I felt a sudden and totally unexpected jolt and I slid down a hand's breadth. I looked up. The rope was slipping down the wall. In the rain the bronze hook looked a golden-brown smear against the stone. It opened. The bronze hook was bending open, the rope was slipping down the wall, and we dangled on the rope. In only a couple of heartbeats the bronze would straighten and we would plummet down.

One chance—just the one. My hands gripped the rope, found a knot, and hauled. The rope slid down and the bronze screamed on the stone. I got my left hand on the lip of the parapet and held. I dangled, twisting away, and the fire raked all through my arm as the muscles corkscrewed. We swung back. Lildra started to struggle.

"Keep still, girl!"

She quieted instantly, shocked into immobility.

Hanging from one hand, with a girl draped around my neck, I heaved up with my right hand. The rope fell. The rain hit me in my upturned face. Fingers scraping over stone, over rain-slick stone, I found a purchase, gripped, held. For a moment I just hung, dangling. Then I started to chin myself up.

At that moment the sky shattered itself into shards of jagged fire and vomited noise about our ears. Lildra jumped. The thunder and lightning sizzled and smashed again. Everything stood out in momentary flashes of light, the marching lines of rain glittering like the spears of a host. Then the night crushed us again in darkness.

Getting a knee over was difficult with the soft wet form of the girl in the way. But eventually, with cracking muscles and a final heave, we tumbled over the parapet.

Lildra sat up. She was a mere dark shadow, but the way she held herself told me she was furious.

"You should have done as I said, Jak the Onker! My mother told me about being rescued. I know. You seem to be very new or unskilled at being a jikai."

Laugh! Of course—but later on, later on.

"You seem to have the right of it, lady. Just make sure you do not get yourself chopped."

"I will take Charldo's sword."

So, down the stone steps we went and back to her room. Charldo still slumbered, so rapid had been the fiasco on the walls. Lildra picked up his sword, and swished it about. I jumped out of the way. She had mentioned her mother. This time, this time I'd see the whole thing out, sorry farce though it might be. This time I was doing what the Star Lords wanted.

"Get those wet things off. The blanket was useless—put on some of your friend Charldo's gear that will fit."

Again the flush stained along her cheekbones.

"It will be wet again when we fight our way out."

"True. But all the same—do it."

"I—"

"You will find it more convenient not to have a dress encumbering your legs."

"In that case—very well."

Very much the great lady in her poise, upheld by the drug of her rescue, this princess, and yet heartbreakingly unversed in the ways of the world outside her stone walls. By the way she held the sword I saw she had had some lessons but was unskilled in the unpleasant arts of actually using the weapon to kill anybody.

She went behind the screen to strip off the dress and I unbuckled Charldo's gear. It would wrap twice about Lildra, but she would find it more convenient. And the door burst open.

The guards from the adjoining room broke in, cursing and swearing, swishing their swords about, raving to get at me. They had heard our quick conversation, no doubt of that, and I had been lax in not anticipating that they might be required to make regular rounds.

The blades crossed in the lamplit chamber and the first of them was down with a severed neck—a judicious slicing blow that kissed his skin—even as my sword leaped away to parry the oncoming blows. The metal rang and clinked. They were in no doubt that they would overpower me and we crashed across the room in a furious bundle of smiting blades and striking limbs. Two were Katakis, and one of the tails chopped off from a neat little backhander. Its owner looked horrified and drew back, clasping the bloody stump in his hands. I wasted no more time on him but flashed my sword blade in the lamplight, dazzled the next long enough to sink the steel into his guts below the corselet.

The others still came on and I backed to make room and collided with the screen. Only by a reflex hop and skip was I able to clear the tangle. A sword swept down at Lildra's head. She was attempting to claw out of the screen and the racks of clothes, shouting not in terror but in fury. I parried the blow, twisted and sank a goodly length in Kataki flesh.

One of them, a bristle-pelted Brokelsh with the rank markings of an ord-Deldar, thrust past a stumbling Rapa to get at me. I parried his blow.

"Well, Ortyg the Bristle," I said, cheerfully, "either you back off and run or you spill your guts on the floor."

He showed his teeth and feinted cleverly and hacked back, but I wasn't where he expected me to be, and my sword was. So Ortyg the Bristle followed my prophecy in all things.

A sword flickered around my legs and I leaped away, swiveling, and Lildra slashed again, blindly. Her wet dress smothered her head. She had leaped up to get into the fray and the screen had gone over and now, here she was, raging and blindly slashing with the wetness gleaming silver and gold over her naked body. I said, "They are all gone."

She pulled the dress away from her head with a squelching sound. She flung it on the floor. She was mad clear through, panting, like a zhantilla aroused to magnificence.

"Why did you push into me, oaf! You knocked the screen all over me, old clothes and all!"

I pointed my blood-dripping sword. "Get yourself dressed. And be quick. They must have heard that racket by now."

She gave me a look that ought to have shriveled me and pulled on a tunic. She strapped up Charldo's leathers as I had said. Then, grasping the sword, she stormed toward the door.

She waited by the door, turning to glower across.

"You seem to forget I am a princess. I would not mention it ordinarily, particularly as you are supposed to be rescuing me and my mother was strict about that, but really—"

"Later," I said, going past and padding out onto the top landing. One thing gave me some hope; she had not fainted clean away at the sight of blood and dead bodies. Metal clanked below.

"They're on the way. Hurry, girl, we must reach the next landing before they do."

Her face expressed conflicting emotions, but there was no time. I seized her arm and hurried her along.

"Zarpedon," she said, on a breath. "He is fierce and will—"

"I sent him to sleep before, and will do worse if he tries to stop us now. Hurry!"

Down the stone steps we plunged and there was no need to steady Lildra. She ran fleetly. The shaggy hound dog glared with his demonic eyes and I jumped in, saying, "Good dog!" and clouted him again. He rolled over, stiff.

"You!" said Lildra.

"In here!" I pushed open the door to the adjoining room, which I expected to find deserted. There was no chance of making a stand. We had to get away. It is said, and with some truth, that a large number of lesser men may drag down one powerful man. True nor not, I did not fancy our chances of fighting through the pack below with Princess Lildra to be guaranteed safe. The room was not empty—rather, as we entered it was empty, but the opposite door leading out to the ramparts opened and a crowd of guards from the next tower along broke through. They had come to find out what the disturbance was all about. It was possible they had witnessed my attempts at climbing down the rope.

In an instant we were at hand strokes.

The closeness of the room, the chill dampness of the stone, the stamp of bronze-bound sandals on the floor and the clangor of combat brought instant bedlam. It was not easy to keep Lildra out of it. She insisted on jabbing her sword at the guards from under my arm, or around my side, and there was a fair amount of skipping and jumping. These men were hired warriors, I judged, mercenaries and not soldiers of the Hyrklanian army. Fahia preferred this, for she could control absolutely any rumor or news of the imprisonment of members of her family. So these paktuns were fighting men all. We had a right to-do, slashing away, and with the occasional short jab sending men screaming and, retching, staggering out of the fight.

Working around and with my left arm curved back and holding Lildra, I managed to maneuver so that we had the door through which the guards had run at our backs. That way lay the ramparts.

"The way is clear, lady," I said, and took a Rapa's beak off. "Run out onto the ramparts—"

"And leave you? Never!"

"Run out and see if anyone else is coming. I don't want cold steel at my back, girl!"

She saw the logic of this and darted back through the doorway. I own to a sense of freedom when she went, not having to spend most of my efforts keeping her out of trouble. I leaped headlong into the guards, smiting with an access of fury which I thought, coldly and calculatingly, would deter them more than mocking words. Two fell, not screaming but in the resigned way of the true professional at the moment of truth. The others drew back a space and a hulking great shaven-headed Gon bellowed: "Fetch bows! *Bratch*, you rasts."

If they were going to start shooting it was time for me to collect Lildra and depart.

I dodged back through the doorway and slammed the heavy oak.

Lildra crouched by the stone wall, dripping wet already and her new blanket sodden, staring along the rampart. More men were running up, presumably from the next tower along—although I had thought that clear. So there was nothing else for it.

The sky burst apart again with an almighty flash and bang; the Castle of Afferatu burned in limpid fire. The noise concussed and the light blinded, and in the ensuing darkness, blindly, I snatched up Princess Lildra, jumped onto the battlemented wall and leaped out into space.

We hurtled down through the air. Faintly and far off a voice shouted. The water hit us shrewdly, but we had twisted in our headlong fall and cleft the water not like two arrows but not like two tumbling carcasses, either. A few powerful strokes, and the surface broke around my ears and I started to swim across the moat with Lildra supported with her head out and in the air. She said nothing and I just hoped nothing was broken. Even then I was concerned for her reactions when the drug of her rescue wore off.

Climbing out on the other bank was a wet and muddy business. Halfway up we slipped and went sprawling into oozing slime. When we staggered up and started to run across the grass we were plastered head to foot with mud. We must have looked a doleful pair. Still Lildra said not a word; her breathing came fast and evenly, and she held herself as though restraining a fury that would undermine the pillars of the world.

So we ran off into the darkness. Thus was Princess Lildra of Hyrklana rescued.

The whole business was just atrociously *wet.*

Chapter Fifteen

Vampires of Sabal

In the days that followed, filled with suns' light and warmth, I began to believe I might feel dry once more. Lildra developed a snuffly little cold that annoyed her, and which made me feel sorry for her, the Savanti nal Aphrasöe having cured me of ailments of that troublesome kind. We joined up with the rebels and their numbers swelled so that soon we were a little army, ragged and ferociously ill-disciplined, but still the beginnings of the force that would topple Queen Fahia.

We cleared the area around the Castle of Afferatu and marched on, gathering strength. The news that Princess Lildra was come to liberate the country spread with the rapidity of sky-zorcas, and we found welcoming crowds of the poor folk everywhere we went, and the more cautious acceptance of the wealthy and lordly of the land. Orlan Mahmud nal Yrmcelt, the queen's chief minister, sent down a general to take command. The rebellion gathered momentum, for everyone awaited the arrival of Princess Lildra. She was the focal point. Without her, I now saw, the rebellion would never begin on any scale likely to succeed.

Orlan's general, a man whose parents had been brutally driven into the Arena because Fahia believed they plotted against her, was a quiet, thoughtful fellow with a bent nose. He called himself Nath the Retributor, although that was not, I judged, his real name. He tried to bring some kind of order to the ragged mob we had with us. I stayed discreetly in the background and kept an eye on Lildra. She, I knew, was the reason I was here, and her welfare was my first priority.

So we progressed northward through the island, our ultimate goal Huringa, the capital city itself. The locals would give up news of troop movements, and we avoided confrontations, garnering our strength. I was content to leave all this to Nath the Retributor. Soon enough our motley collection of rebels would be found by a force of Queen Fahia's soldiers, and then we would have to see just what the rebellion was made of.

During this time I talked a great deal with Lildra, and learned much of her story, for there was pitifully little to tell. She had been born in the kind of genteel captivity Fahia reserved for her sister, Princess Lilah. Lildra's education had been simple and direct, and there was much of which she was completely unaware. I found her one day in a little clearing slashing Charldo's sword about.

She looked at me commandingly.

"You are a great jikai, I think, a hyr-paktun, although you do not wear the zhantilhead at your throat. I have seen how you handle a thraxter and will have you teach me the art."

"If you desire it—"

"I command it!" She had taken to the adulation heaped

on her by the lords and ladies, hostile to Fahia, who now more and more thronged our rebel camp. I did not think this would spoil her. I could see a directness and a brightness of spirit in her very becoming a young lady who would be queen.

All the same, she joyed in letting me know she was a princess. "I command you to teach me the arts of swordplay, Jak!"

Gravely, I said, "I can't teach you. But it is only you and the spirit that can learn. Also, the arts of killing with the sword are not play."

She didn't like that. It clashed with her romantic notions. She hadn't liked it when I'd remarked, offhandedly, about our leap from the battlements of the Castle of Afferatu, that that was what castle moats were for, for heroes and heroines to jump into. And yet, and yet, with her fair beauty and her lissom figure, her high color and brave spirit, there was a bright aura of romance clinging about Princess Lildra, oh, yes, very much so . . .

"Well, Jak, the Onker, let us begin and you—"

A loud, raucous and mocking squawk cut rudely across Lildra's words. She took no notice and went on speaking. I knew she could not hear that croaking voice of doom. I looked up. Perched on a tree branch sat a resplendent bird, all gold and scarlet plumage, his head on one side, his beady eye fastened on me. Lildra could not hear or see him, for he was the Gdoinye, the messenger and spy of the Star Lords. I hadn't seen him for a time. He kept observation on me for the Everoinye, and we would insult each other as a matter of protocol—what the devil did he want now?

I ignored him and listened to Lildra, and presently the Gdoinye flew away. The Star Lords kept a watchful eye out on those who merited their attention. So Lildra and I fell to with our swords, and she was a quick learner and I felt confident she would develop—if she wished—into a fine sworder of the cunning and intelligent kind.

News came down fitfully of outside events. Hamal continued on her headstrong way of imperial conquest. The queen's son was grown into a tempestuous youth, determined to have his own way, and it was whispered that King Rogan had no part of his parentage. The Shanks had raided again, down in the southeast, and soldiers had been sent. This accounted for the paucity of opposition we had so far encountered. I did not say this to Lildra. The idea was bruited abroad that the lack of opposition came from men's reluctance to fight against Lildra for Fahia.

Orlan had not told Nath the Retributor who I truly was, and although a quiet, reserved man, he rubbed along well enough with me. For, and I own it with a half-smile, I occupied a special place of privilege, being the man who had rescued the princess. Nath the Retributor was in constant communication with Orlan. We even kept abreast of the fortunes of the four color corners in the Jikhorkdun. I listened avidly as the fortunes of the ruby drang rose and fell. We still had not caught the emerald neemu . . .

Then a shattering surprise burst about my head.

I just did not believe it. It couldn't be true. Why?

News came down secretly that the Princess Majestrix of Vallia intended to join our rebellion.

By this time I no longer automatically thought of Delia when the Princess Majestrix was mentioned. Delia was now the Empress of Vallia. Lela was the Princess Majestrix—and I hadn't seen her for so many years the pain gnawed mercilessly at me. I'd been flung cruelly back to Earth, and Lela had been sent adventuring for the Sisters of the Rose. That organization of women was secret to men, as it must be, and it was fruitless for any man to seek to uncover its mysteries. What the SoR did in secrecy was done for the good of Vallia and they did much good work for the poor and sick, men and women both. Useless to try to probe, and ultimately futile. As soon try to uncover the mysteries of the Krozairs of Zy. And, so my daughter Lela was coming to join the rebellion!

She had been some time in Hyrklana, so Nath the Retributor told me over the campfire one evening with the fat stars pulsing that shimmering Kregan nighttime glow over the camp. Sentries patrolled. We had eaten and drunk, and now we rested for the morrow's labors.

"She has been working in secret against those cramphs of Hamal. One day, Jak, we will have to stamp our heel upon the Hamalese—but it will be a stern task, for they are strong."

"The strong will fall to the shrewd blow."

"You quote San Blarnoi at me. Very well. It is true."

He knew nothing of Spikatur Hunting Sword.

"The Princess Majestrix brings sisterly greetings to our own Princess Lildra. Vallia fights gallantly against Hamal." Nath took a sip of wine, sparingly, as was his custom. "An alliance will be offered, I am sure. When Princess Lildra is queen then we will join with Vallia against Hamal."

"That," I said, "is a development devoutly to be wished." And, then somberly I added, "And will it be worth all the dead?"

"Of course, Jak! Of course."

Sometimes I wish I did not have this all-encompassing vision. It knocks the stuffing out of you when you least want that. We had to knock seven kinds of brick dust out of Hamal, and there was no getting over that this damned side of the Ice Floes of Sicce, no, by Vox!

Nath leaned forward and lowered his voice. "There is more, which is not general circulation. I am given to understand that the Princess Majestrix's father will also honor us."

I kept my wine jug steady. The red wine, a medium Mahemj, did not ripple. I lifted the jug and drank and wiped my lips with a mental, *By Mother Zinzu the Blessed! I needed that!* I looked hard at Nath the Retributor with the look that says you do not believe what you have just heard with your own ears.

"It is true. By Harg! Unlikely, but true. I had it from Orlan Mahmud's messenger personally and only tell you because you are very dear to the princess."

"Oh?" I said, intrigued by this idea. "I wouldn't have thought that."

The Retributor laughed and leaned back and drank, and there was no getting any more out of him that night.

I would like to know how it was that the Emperor of Vallia was going to join the camp he was already in, and how it was he did not know that interesting fact. Yes, by Krun!

When Orlan had received word that Lildra had been rescued by a hulking, scowling, rascally fellow he would have known that was me, and that our plan had worked. Knowing me, as he thought, he probably hadn't given a second thought to my method of departure from his villa. And that despite the key ring and the precautions.

A beautiful warm feeling began in me and continued to grow. The very fact that the Princess Majestrix of Vallia was coming to see Princess Lildra, that Vallia was willing to join hands with the Hyrklese in defending ourselves against Hamal, had a tonic effect on everyone and our ranks grew prodigiously. We were marching on Huringa, a growing tide of eager volunteers. And the name of Vallia meant something, even here, even this far away. So I felt the future glowed with promise.

The very next day as we marched into a town whose inhabitants turned out to cheer us, a contingent of the Hyrklanian army marched in from the other end. There were three regiments of foot and a cavalry regiment of totrixmen. Before an ugly scene developed, the soldiers began to cheer for Princess Lildra. Well! That proved we would win, so said everyone, and much wine flowed and gusts of laughter burst above the mingled camps.

And then, of course, we had news that because the Hyrklanian army was proving unsatisfactory, even disloyal, Queen Fahia was busily at work hiring mercenaries to fight us. A deal of hard talk went on among our people, and when the froth of declamations blew away, it did seem as though we would go on and fight and win. But the news deteriorated even further. More and more mercenaries were pouring into the country, paid for with broad Hyrklanian gold deldys, and we saw we had a fight on our hands.

When we reached the River Llindal we camped just above the water meadows near a corpse in which still stood the ruins of a temple to a half-forgotten god. Instead of sending for me when we wished to talk, as was the usual custom, Nath the Retributor sought me out as I dropped sticks onto the fire. By this time I had acquired a fine zorca to ride, and a tent and gear, and a cheerful helpmate in Wango the Mak, a shock-headed fellow who had run off from his master and whom I had taken it on myself to manumit. He was fetching the water. Nath walked up and then, glancing around and seeing we were unobserved, motioned for me to enter my tent. Intrigued, in I went. He followed. At once, the moment we were inside, he started to go into the full incline, that slavish Kregan bow of fulsome proportions, a hateful grovel.

"Stand up, man!" I said, somewhat testily, for of course I could guess what had happened.

"Majister!" said Nath the Retributor.

"Of Vallia, not of Hyrklana. Why do you know now, Nath?"

"I have word from Pallan Orlan Mahmud. The Princess Majestrix will ride in this evening—Orlan felt that you—"

"Considerate of him. And only you know about me?"

"Yes, majister."

"Well, leave it at Jak for the moment. We will see."

"Yes, majister."

By Zair! There we were, back again to the "Yes, majisters" all the time. Confound it!

The meeting during which our chiefs would meet the party who had ridden secretly from Huringa was to take place in the ruined temple. The twin suns slanted into the western sky. The half-forgotten god's name was, I believe, Rhampathey. Wango the Mak finished cooking the meal and I ate hugely and then went off to the River Llindal and, stripping off, plunged in. I did not swim but washed thoroughly. Then I had a Fristle fifi with her cunning scissors clip my hair and trim me up smartly. I took out the scarlet breechclout, neatly washed and pressed, and donned that old favorite, along with my armor and gear. I walked about the camp for a space, talking to no one, meeting no one's eye. When I saw Lildra walking toward me among the tents I turned sharply away and took myself off, pretending not to have seen her. I wandered about. I chewed my lip. I fiddled with my swords and harness. The suns sank . . . Presently the messenger came for me and, together with Nath the Retributor and others of our chiefs, off I went toward the Temple of Rhampathey.

At my express wish Nath's conduct toward me was no different from usual, and I was just one of the crowd as we went in among the ruins. The stone looked leached. Lichens splotched the pillars and fallen walls, forming ancient faces of mildew and decay. The Maiden with the Many Smiles and She of the Veils were already up, sailing above our heads and casting down their rose and golden radiance. Insects buzzed for a brief space, but the ruins absorbed sound and the place lay dead and silent.

A Chuktar next to me breathed hoarsely through his open mouth. He kept his fist wrapped around his sword hilt. I walked quietly. The place appeared ghostly, uncanny, and no one would have been surprised at ambush or the sudden apparition of skeleton men. All that happened was the approach of a body of people from the other direction, bearing lanterns, unnecessary in the light of the moons.

I stared eagerly toward those people illuminated by the lantern glow. Over there, walking toward me, was Lela!

I did not rush forward. I wanted to savor this moment, so I stayed a little way in rear, moving to the side, staring as the newcomers approached.

And then I saw among those strangers a familiar face.

She had doffed her blue tunic, and her black leathers shone liquidly in the radiance of the moons as though molded to her. Her legs—very long, very lovely legs—stamped along in her tall black boots. Her brown Vallian hair and brown Vallian eyes, the carriage of her, upright, defiant, all gave me a swift and poignant pang of affection and love for my Delia, for this Valona whom I had last met trying to slash me with her claw, while nothing like Delia, yet reminded me of her. She did not remind me of my middle daughter, Dayra, who was called Ros the Claw. But, even as the crowd closed around her, I remembered I had had that feeling I was reminded by her of someone I knew. There had been no time to puzzle out the riddle then, when we'd stormed through the deserted spaces of the Temple of Malab the Kazzin and found Tyfar tied up and then Jaezila, and not much since. All the same, the wearing of black leathers and tall black boots, the swishing about of a rapier, even brown Vallian eyes and hair, do not make two women look the same. Valona, who was not called Valona the Claw, did not resemble in any profound way Delia or Dayra or even Jilian.

We went on in the moon's light and I swallowed and licked my lips.

The idea occurred to me that no man would ever know the secrets of the Sisters of the Rose, nor even how many of them there were, or who wore the steel claw among them. Jilian Sweet Tooth was a good friend to Delia and me and she couldn't tell me so much as a spider's eyelash about the SoR. That Lela had preceded Dayra through Lancival, where these girls learned how with their claws to chop up nasties, seemed eminently logical.

The crowd bunched to pass between craggy buttresses of rotting stone, ancient and stained in the moonshadows, and I was pushed a little to the side. Bushes grew from cracks in the stones and paving flags. The smell of night flowers hung on the air. The two parties hurried forward. Lildra, with Nath in attendance, stepped out ahead.

From the bushes flanking us a movement caught my attention.

Dark forms leaped from their places of concealment. Sharp, acid-bitter faces, white as death, leered from hunched cloaks of shadow. Vampire fangs gleamed. Eyes glared hot and red. And steel blades shimmered death in the moonshadows.

"Sabals!" People screamed and the two bodies, confused, surged and swayed. "Vampires of Sabal!"

I was the nearest. This was a time for the headlong rush into danger, chancing destruction, no time for thought. If Lildra were harmed, I would feel sorrow and the Star Lords would exact vengeance. But if Lela were harmed. . .!!

My sword ripped free and I went into them like a battering ram. Dark forms shrieked about me, fangs struck, swords slashed. I managed to skewer the first and then it was a matter of ducking and dodging and slashing back. Lopping arms presents a small problem when your muscles are powered by a frenzy of fear for your daughter. Calculating the amount of force necessary to put a vampire thing out of action, and not spend overmuch force on that one, ready for the next, is difficult when your head is filled with a breathless panic. Heads rolled.

A lithe form surged into the fight alongside me. A sword struck with precision and economy. The vampire things, fangs glittering, red eyes like demons, screamed and sought to slay us and drink our blood. And we fought back. We fought them for a space and then other people joined in, and a wall of steel barred off the vampire horrors from the princess.

I looked at the girl who had fought at my side and felt the shock overpower me again.

"I thought you were dead, Jak," said Jaezila. She laughed, very splendid in that flowing light, her brown hair severely tied back, her russet leathers plain and workmanlike, her sword a bar of blood in her gloved fist. "Tyfar went back to Hamal and I—well—and what are you doing here?"

"Jaezila!" I said, like a fool. "I am with the rebellion."

"Queen Fahia is like one of her own pet neemus, frantic with fear and rage. So I thought I'd help out—but—" Her face clouded. "We are blade comrades, Jak, you and Ty and I. Yet—yet—"

"I am—glad—to see you, Jaezila. This is not the same silly kind of rebellion Vad Noran attempted. I heard that Tyfar had gone back to Hamal and rejoiced, knowing you and he were safe. But here you are, and very welcome, too."

There was an oddness about this meeting. Yes, I was overjoyed to see Jaezila again, for she was a girl dear to me, as you know. If Prince Tyfar could be along to share in the fun, such as it was, then that would be even more splendid. Then I realized my own stupidity, and chilled. Jaezila was looking at me cautiously. Of course! She thought I worked for Hamal, as did she, and how, then, she would be wondering, could I be a part of a rebellion aimed at seating a princess on the throne who had vowed to join with Vallia against Hamal? This would be tricky.

What was even more tricky was—what was she up to here? There was absolutely no possibility that I would allow harm to come to her if it was discovered she worked for Hamal. She must be attempting to aid the rebellion and unseat Fahia and then turn the coup to the advantage of Hamal. And—would that mean danger for Princess Lildra? I sweated under the night breeze. What a coil!

We walked back to join the two parties, who were now mingled together and all talking away, excited by the sudden attack of the Vampires of Sabal. These things are not your Dracula vampire at all, being creatures who like to guzzle human blood and who hide in out-of-the-way places and who will die by stroke of sword without holy water or a stake through the heart.

For all that, they are vampires, and horrible and mortal foes to humankind.

Valona came running up, waving her claw, which ran red with vampire blood. "Princess! You are safe!" She saw me and said, "Oh!"

"I am glad to see you are safe, princess," said Jaezila.

Staring at Valona, seeing her beauty, I smiled. I, Dray Prescot, smiled with a sudden overpowering gratitude. But, for all that, I said to Jaezila, "So you are a princess! Well, I might have guessed it, and I've been tangling with princesses for a long time now—"

"You—!" said Valona. "But you are the man who said—"

"And you are a princess, too," I said, half-laughing, wishing to tease her. "Jaezila and you are friends? That pleases me."

"We have been through many adventures together, Jak and I," said Jaezila. "He is a blade comrade. I rejoice to see him alive, for I thought he had given his life to save me and—and another. He will give praise to all the gods that Jak lives. She looked at Valona and, I admit it now for I felt it then, I felt a pang—just the smallest, most unworthy feeling—that if you wished to compare the two girls, then Jaezila far outshone Valona. And this was a base and vile thought.

Before any more could be said in this tangle, Nath the Retributor hurried across. With him strode a giant of a man—an apim—with a strong bulldoglike head and massive jaw, a warrior who wore armor and carried four swords. This impressive fighting man was introduced as Hardur Mortiljid, Trylon of Llanikar. I judged him true to his appearance. He bowed formally.

"I am here as escort to the Princess Majestrix of Vallia, bearing a warrant from Klanak the Tresh." Klanak the Tresh was Orlan's cover name, and I felt relief that he had the sense to continue to use it still. We weren't out of the wood yet. The Lahals were made, and then Hardur said to me, "I give you my thanks, horter, for the gallantry of your fight against the Sabals. They are news from the devil, by Harg!"

"The princess is unharmed," I said. I still felt this enormous glow of delight, so I could add, "All the princesses!"

Jaezila laughed. No one else appeared to consider the remark worthy of comment, the fact being that my brand of humor is often considered odd even by the phenomenally peculiar standards of Kregan humor. But Tyfar, Jaezila and I shared our own idiosyncratic laughs together, and the suns were warmer as a consequence. Erndor, the slim Vallian who had tried to spit Tyfar and had then thrown a brick at him, came over. Kaldu, Jaezila's retainer, hovered. Nath the Retributor coughed and cleared his throat. A ring formed with the mingled parties all staring at those in the center, the lantern light falling upon cheekbones and glittering in eyes. I stepped back. The moment approached.

The expectant silence fell oddly into that place of ruins. It trembled invisibly, yet was real, perfectly apparent to everyone. Nath stared at me in puzzlement. I looked back, waiting. And then—of course, onker that I was!—I saw the cause of his embarrassment.

He could not know how things stood between Lela and me. He didn't know that the Star Lords, by hurling me between the stars, had prevented my knowing my own daughter, as Lela's dedication to the SoR prevented her from knowing me. So we all stood about like loons when Nath and the others expected father and daughter to fly into each other's arms.

Valona was quite clearly keyed up. She glowed with excitement, staring about. What it would be—to have two daughters who flourished lethal steel claws!

Hardur Mortiljid slapped one of his swords up and down in the scabbard. He looked down at Nath.

"Well, by Harg, Nath! These Vallians are odd folk!"

Valona glanced up at Hardur.

Nath said, "I will—"

Erndor stepped forward.

"An explanation is owed you, Trylon Hardur, and you, Nath the Retributor, as to you all. If you will allow? We Vallians may be somewhat different from other folk, but in this, the vicissitudes of cruel fate have parted the Emperor of Vallia and the Princess Majestrix for many seasons. For very many seasons."

The crowd nodded as though perfectly understanding the blows of fate, and the oddness of folk who were not Hyrklese. I looked expectantly at Valona. She stood alertly, waiting . . . At her side Jaezila stared at Erndor, and then she looked away, searching among the crowd, and coming back again to gaze upon the Vallian. Valona remained bright-eyed and vivid, almost hopping with excitement.

Erndor went on, "So that I do not think one would recognize the other—"

At that revelation, and never mind the blows of fate, the crowd's shocked oohs and aahs were fitting comments on not only the conduct of Vallians, but the way a father had allowed so terrible a degradation of his relationship with his daughter. Even though they did not know of the Everoinye, I felt that censure deeply. I was just about to do something very foolish when Valona began to step forward. Jaezila took her arm and held her, and then my blade comrade said, "So there is no mystery here. Nath the Retributor, if you would kindly do the office of introducing the Emperor of Vallia, the Princess Majestrix will be in your debt." She smiled.

Valona sucked in a breath, and Hardur looked down his nose. The crowd fell silent. I did not move but looked at Valona. Nath was slow.

"Well, Nath the Retributor," said my blade comrade, Jaezila. "The Princess Majestrix is waiting. Is he not here? I would not be surprised. He never seems to be at hand when I need him. Whereabouts is my father skulking now?"

Chapter Sixteen

I Stake My Life on the Truth

The world of Kregen went up and down and over and over three times and I was clinging on her for dear life with bleeding fingers to stop being hurled off into a black void of insanity.

Jaezila!

Lela?

And then, the mind does work in strange ways in fraught moments like these, I thought, *So Tyfar will be my son-in-law—if all goes as nature intends. Deuced odd!*

I felt like a man turning a corner and being blown back by a sea wind gusting past force ten. I struggled to get a breath. Nath the Retributor, all smiles, was saying, "He is here, majestrix, standing here. Now you have explained, of course, of course. These things happen in imperial families."

He was, I am sure, quite unaware of any sarcasm.

"Here is Dray Prescot, Emperor of Vallia! Lahal, majister!"

Jaezila looked at me.

Dayra looked at me, I recalled with anguish from our first meeting, with loathing and contempt. How would my eldest daughter regard the father who kept on disappearing?

She was beautiful, yes, she was her mother's daughter, regal, commanding, impish—and now a frown dinted in between her eyebrows, and her lips drew down, and her eyes regarded me with a look I just could not fathom.

"Him?" she said. And, then: "Jak the Sturr—my father?" And, then: "He is a blade comrade, Jak, a friend, one who would give his life for me, as I for him, as we have proved. But—the Emperor of Vallia?"

"Jaezila—" I said.

A struggle was going on within her. She had not expected this thunderclap of a revelation. No more had I, by Zair!

But I was over the wonder now. This glorious girl was my daughter Lela. And the magic was—we were blade comrades!

What a splendid contrast to my dismal confrontations with Dayra, who was Ros the Claw!

And of course, Dayra was not evil, only misguided. Now I had an opportunity to talk to Jaezila—Lela—and discover more about Dayra, and find ways for reconciliation. Lela would know about her sister, there was no doubt about that. I confess to a most beautifully euphoric feeling bathing me in wonderful sensations.

Jaezila brought all this down to earth with a thump.

"Whatever my blade comrade has told you, and however much I love him, he is Jak, and not the Emperor of Vallia. I know. I own I am disappointed, for he would have been a good father to me."

"Jaezila," I said. "I mean, Lela—"

"It's not going to do you any good. By Vox! I'll see no harm comes to you. You know that. But the good of Vallia is in this, Jak, and even you cannot jeopardize that."

Just as Princess Lildra stepped forward to have her say, she was pushed aside by Hardur Mortiljid. The giant's face exhibited every indication of bursting. His eyebrows drew down, black with thunder. At his side Nath the Retributor was already drawing his sword. Other men crowded up.

"I stake my life on the Princess Majestrix!" bellowed Hardur. "She has spoken. This man is an impostor. Seize him up!"

Well—I was slow. But I felt as though I'd been hit over the head with a sandbag. They had bonds around my neck and wrists and ankles even as I tried to reason with Jaezila. She looked distraught. I could imagine her anguish.

"Jak!" she called over the hubbub.

The crowd pushed and shoved around us; I was dragged along, shoved up against a stone pillar and the ropes wound round and around pinioning me to the ancient stone. I felt a damned hard edge jabbing me in the back and it was nothing. I couldn't believe all this. Princess Lildra was shouting, but in the uproar her words went unheeded. These people had found a spy in their midst, and mob law was about to run its course.

"Kill him now! Spy!"

"No, make him tell his secrets!"

"Zigging Hamalese rast!"

Jaezila was tall, but Hardur overtopped her as he overtopped most people. Even Jaezila's savage retainer, Kaldu, looked a trifle shrunken as he stepped up to clear a space for his mistress. They were forming a ring around the pillar to which I was bound, and the noise and confusion brought fresh mobs running up from the camp. Lantern light splashed bloodily upon the stones, and the moons tinged the scene with rose and gold. A tiny night breeze blew and the scents of moon blooms filled the air. And I was like to bid good-bye to all this exotic world of Kregen.

Lildra looked flustered and, not so much frightened as overwhelmed. Hardur with his giant stature and giant voice dominated events, and his bellows drowned more rational thought. But I thought. I thought that Jaezila, my blade comrade, worked for Hamal. She might not be my daughter Lela. She disowned me; might not I therefore disown her? We would remain comrades, for the bonds between us were not to be broken lightly—and even this business which was very far from light would not sunder my feelings for her, or hers for me, I was confident. Perhaps, as a spy for Hamal, she had wormed her way in and under the guise of the Princess Majestrix of Vallia, worked a mischief against my country?

I looked toward the knot of chiefs, and they were arguing in their more elegant way, as the mobs were yelling and caterwauling, in their more vehement fashion. They wanted my skin, all of them. No doubt of that, by Vox!

Jaezila was shouting up at Hardur, fierce, like a tigress: "I love that man! If you harm him I will surely kill you!"

"But he is a spy for Hamal! He knows our secrets!"

Lildra screamed, "He is a hyr-paktun and he rescued me and he cannot be the emperor! But—but I do not want him killed, whatever he may have done!"

Nath shouted, "Klanak the Tresh vouches for him—"

"He can be deceived." Hardur boomed out. "I say kill him now, out of hand, as you put your foot upon a filthy rast that infests a dunghill."

I bellowed across, "You'd get a mucky foot, then, Hardur!"

And Jaezila laughed.

By Zair! If she was not my daughter, how I longed for her to be Lela!

Using his height and lungpower, Hardur battered away at his central point—killing me with all dispatch—in an attempt to convince Princess Lildra. He was a loyal man, if a trifle prone to blustering pigheadedness, and even in his passionate anger he saw he could not just top me in defiance of Lildra's wishes.

The wrangling went on, brute force against sentiment, common sense against sentimentality. If you catch a spy, you have to do what he expects will be done—sometimes. Nath was in a quandary, for he quite liked me and had had word from Orlan; yet my detractors were violent and persuasive. If the argument broke down the middle and it was party against party, we had the outnumbering of them, true. I did not think Hardur Mortiljid was a man to worry over that.

In the uproar and excitement I felt a soft touch on my arm, twisted up around the pillar. I said nothing. A voice whispered. "Make no sign. The Princess Majestrix bids me free you. I still wonder if I should have clawed you before you jumped down the trap."

My bonds fell away at the back and were held up so that while I was free the ropes would not betray me. Barely moving my mouth, I said, "My thanks, Valona. Would you believe I had thought you were my daughter?"

A soft amused snort, and: "You are a splendid paktun, no doubt. But an emperor? Ha! No one has seen me and they will not see me go. Give me four heartbeats to get clear or we will land the Princess Majestrix in trouble. Do you understand?"

"Yes."

Valona had crept from the shadows at the back, unseen. If I betrayed her by leaping free now, Jaezila would also be suspect. Perhaps they would turn on her. *Was* she Lela? And these were Hyrklese. Perhaps, they would think, this whole affair was a plot on the part of Hamal. It was very likely.

A fleeting succession of shapes passed before the rosily golden face of She of the Veils. For a small moment the moon silhouetted a group of flyers, winging down. Then they winged swiftly on. I looked toward the arguing crowds. Soon the tinder would light and they'd turn ugly. Time to depart. I would go with great regret. I own to a fondness for my own skin; I hungered to talk to Jaezila again, and to satisfy myself she was my daughter, as I was in no doubt I could convince her I was her father, given the time denied us so far. But if I yielded to that almost overpowering temptation, then my fondness for my skin would be set at naught; they'd chop me, for sure.

Valona had placed the severed ends of the bonds in my hands and I held them taut. When I cast them away and leaped from the pillar I would be seen at once. The hue and cry would begin. Maybe I would not depart. Running away was foreign to the nature of the Dray Prescot who had adventured over the face of Kregen, even if it was tending to feature more and more with the Dray Prescot who, in these latter days, shouldered the burdens of empire. By the stinking left nostril of Makki-Grodno! I damned well wouldn't run away! I knew what I'd do, and by Zim-Zair, I'd do it quick!

I threw the ropes away and belted like a hellhound for the arguing group around Jaezila. I could convince her—I would convince her. If she was not my daughter, if she was a Hamalese spy, then we were both done for. I cast aside all doubt. Jaezila was Lela, and both our lives hung on the truth of that.

Instantly I was seen. The hullabaloo started, with yells that the mad paktun was trying to assassinate Lildra, murder the Princess Majestrix, disembowel Hardur and decapitate Nath. I pelted on. Someone hurled a javelin and the stux flew past. On I raced, dodging and ducking, leaping idiots who tried to fling themselves at me. I ran with my hands empty and open, arms up, trying to indicate that, being unarmed, I could not hurt anyone.

Any Krozair of Zy, any Khamorro, would know the lie inherent in that, but it was all I could do.

"Jak!" yelled Jaezila.

"Jak!" screamed Lildra.

"You're running the wrong way!" Jaezila started at me, yelling, and I could see she was choked with laughter. By Krun! What a girl!

Hardur Mortiljid whipped out his sword. Like him, it was big. He rushed. His first swing was designed to part me along the middle and I swerved and hit him on the nose—I had to jump—and hurdled over his falling form. Then I was up to Lildra, who looked distraught, and Jaezila, who looked ready for a fight.

"If you are Lela," I shouted, "as I truly believe, then I have things to tell you that will show you I am—"

"Your back!"

I dodged and the javelin whistled past.

"Don't stand jibber-jabbering, you great fambly! Run for it!"

"I'm not in the habit of running—well, only recently—"

Nath stood back, eyeing me, and his chiefs were suddenly holding back the mobs, bellowing with authority at them. Hardur staggered up with his nose streaming blood black in the moonlight.

"Slay him, you rasts! Strike him down!"

"He is unarmed, Hardur!" roared Nath. "Let the Princess Majestrix hear him out!"

"My thanks, Nath—"

"He may fool her. He will not deceive me!" And Hardur launched himself headlong.

The breathing space I had gained would be gone if Hardur were allowed to overpower them again. I reached up and back and, bending forward, ripped the longsword free. The superb brand gleamed in the light of the moons. I spread my fists on the grip and faced Hardur. He did not check but came on in a gusty rushing charge, yelling a wild whoop, his sword swinging.

"Leave him to me!" bellowed the Mortiljid.

The first blows were delivered with skill and strength, but the Krozair brand deflected them with ease and I leaned to the side and twisted my hands over and so laid the flat against Hardur Mortiljid's head. He fell down.

For an instant a complete silence enveloped the mobs. Into that silence the massed beat of wings brought a rushing note of urgency. Saddle birds landed in flurries of wing-feathers, sending up the dust. Agile men leaped from the saddles. A voice shouted.

"Now what tomfoolery are you up to, father? What's he playing at *now*, Lela, for the sweet sake of Zair?"

And my lad Jaidur strode forward, very wroth, to confront me.

Chapter Seventeen

The Rebellion Falters

We rode hard for Huringa in a jingling, determined cavalcade, with a screen of aerial cavalry winging ahead. We were the Revolution. On our banners glowed the light of coming victory. With us rode Princess Lildra, who would be Queen Lildra. On we rode, confident, bursting with pride, and if we were vainglorious there seemed every reason for that fatuous state.

You cannot have everything in life. Useless to think that wishing will make it so. Everyday reality doesn't work like that. Wish fulfillment does happen, of course—after a deal of damned hard work and luck and the ability to ride with the punches or to come to terms with emotional situations you thought impossible. As for power fantasies, they are for the crippled, and as most of us are crippled in one way or another, ought to be put to a responsible therapeutic use.

Jaezila was Lela.

That was the wonder.

Jaidur, being my raffish, feckless young tearaway of a son, was here in Hyrklana stirring up as much trouble as he could for Hamal. Unable to buy fliers, he had had a hand in the burning of a few of the factories. And he knew somewhat of Spikatur Hunting Sword.

The news he brought from home reassured me. Delia and my comrades had returned to Vallia successfully after the storm that had separated me, and the empress's wishes had sufficed to prevent that hairy swarm of rogues from attempting to devastate Hyrklana and all points south. As for Lela, she had a tale to tell. As we rode toward Huringa through the streaming mingled lights of the Suns of Scorpio, I learned much of my daughter. The odd thing was—and not so odd, when I thought about it—I tended to think of her as Jaezila rather more than as Lela. She had tried to buy airboats in the Dawn Lands of Havilfar, and had not succeeded there. With Prince Tyfar of Hamal as cover, she had tried again here in Hyrklana. As to her true regard for that honorable prince, I asked her, and she told me, and I said, "Then when all this nonsense is over, we will have such a splendid wedding as Hamal and Vallia have never before witnessed."

"That presupposes he will have me."

"Tyfar is no fool."

"Is that an answer?"

"Yes, daughter, it is."

"And love?"

I laughed. Laughing was easy with Jaezila, as it was with Delia, her mother. "If I have never seen love in a man before, I have seen it in Tyfar when he looks at you."

She turned her head away as we rode along, with the rebellion riding along with us. So I went on, "And, talking of love, you have perhaps noticed what is afoot between your brother Jaidur and Princess Lildra?"

"I have."

"And?"

"It pleases me, as I hope it pleases you."

I nodded. Some people in their modern sophistication deny any such force as Mother Nature. They may be right. Here, whatever the force, be it Mother Nature or anything else, the lightnings had struck, the looks had been exchanged, the understandings given and taken. The speed had been breathtaking. Jaidur and Lildra had met and talked, and that was that. It seems I was in for two weddings, when all this nonsense was over.

As a man, I felt lively affection and sympathy. As a father, I felt concern and hope for the future and desire for happiness. And as a cynical old emperor, I looked at the political aspects, and found they could be worse, could be far worse, by Vox!

So we rode toward the capital city and gained a little strength day by day and heard the rumors and came upon the realities. Had those diabolical Shanks attacked in southern Hyrklana when we marched, it would have been our duty to march with the army of Hyrklana and all the mercenaries, and fling the damned Schtarkins back into the sea from whence they came. But they had retired, sailing away in their phenomenally fast ships, and the soldiers turned their attention to the rebellion.

We did not fare well.

On the day after a nasty skirmish when we had to run for it, Hardur Mortiljid breathed heavily, nursing a wounded arm. He said he had forgiven me for clouting him over the head, and I chose to believe him, and saw that I did not turn by back, just in case. Now he flung himself down by the campfire and seized up a stoup.

"We cannot break through," he grumped, and drank, and spat. "They are too strong for us."

Lildra looked unhappy. Whether she objected to his manners or his opinion was beside the point. "But," she said, and her voice faltered, "the rebellion? We must win!"

"What with? We have not enough real soldiers, and the mercenaries are well-paid and ferocious. How do we fight through?"

Lildra looked across at Jaezila. She was frowning.

"The problem is difficult. Fahia is as cunning as a leem."

"We need more men." Nath the Retributor walked across, looking worried. It seemed that all our high hopes had been crushed.

Much of this dismal feeling had been lost on me, wrapped up in the magic of finding my daughter. We spent hours just talking, finding our way to this new relationship, and all the time joyously aware of our friendship that had grown through the times we had spent together and the dangers we had faced. So we had to make an effort to adjust to the grim reality of the rebellion's lack of progress.

A few—not many but enough, damn 'em!—of the lords and ladies who had flocked to Princess Lildra's standards departed. Those who remained looked worried. The suggestion was bruited that we should contact Orlan Mahmud nal Yrmcelt, for messengers had failed to reach us for the past sennight or so, and find out the true situation and what to plan for the future. This was the euphemism for saying, "Whether or not we will continue the rebellion." In the end, I, Jaezila, Jaidur and a small party agreed to venture into Huringa to see Orlan. It would be perilous, and Lildra clung to Jaidur before she would let him go.

I said, "You don't have to come, Jaezila—"

She laughed and that was that. But all the same, I now realized that adventuring with my blade comrade Jaezila was to be even more fraught with anxiety for me. If that is a selfish way of putting it, so be it. I understood rather more of what was entailed than previously. I confess I didn't much care for the idea of my daughter swaggering

"We took the fluttrells and flew into Huringa."

off into danger swishing her rapier about, magnificent in her leathers and black boots.

But they would, they would, all of them . . .

And I would be the last person on Kregen to be able to deny them, for they were people as was I, and they did what they wanted to do.

We took the fluttrells and flew into Huringa. The saddle birds with the big ridiculous head vanes are sturdy and willing if not of the highest quality of saddle-flyers of Paz, and soon we circled over the next-but-one villa along from Orlan's. We spied out the land, and seeing no obvious signs of danger, flew in for a landing in a clump of woods in the gardens. Vad Noran's villa had been extensive, with his very own arena; Orlan's was even larger, and without an arena, although he had practice rings, glittering with swept and raked sand under the suns.

The first question of importance anyone asked about Huringa was whether or not the games were on. As we landed we could hear the roar from the Jikhorkdun. The games were, indeed, on.

It had rained earlier but now the skies were clear and the suns burned down as we walked cautiously up to the villa. We had a lord with us who was known to Orlan's servants, and we were assured we could gain an audience without trouble. The place bore the quiet, bored appearance all parts and all peoples of Huringa wore when they were not involved with the games. Our party walked on swiftly under shady trees and along graveled paths to a wicket gate where a dozing Moltingur guard had no time to argue before he was struck down. I said, "Do not slay him, for he may be loyal to Orlan."

Strom Hierayn, the lord who knew Orlan and would get us in, pushed on and we followed. A few slaves moved among the outbuildings and children were playing at kaidurs with wooden swords among the chickens as we passed. Before we attracted attention we were inside the main building. Strom Hierayn, a fattish man with too much paunch and too much jowl and not—quite—enough humility, pressed on down a corridor known to him. The place appeared near deserted. A slave told us that the lord rested in the Fountain Room, and thither Strom Hierayn led us. And, I began to get that uncomfortable old itch up my backbone.

I glanced at Jaezila. She looked at me, and that perfect face drew down into a scowl.

"You feel it too, Jak?"

She continued to call me Jak out of common caution. I nodded. "I do. It smells like Makki-Grodno's left armpit."

Jaidur said, "If that fat Hierayn has played us false . . . By Zogo the Hyrwhip! I'll have his inards for zorca harness."

One or two others of the party looked concerned, and Hierayn led through an ornate doorway—pale blue and seashell with fern fronds all adangling in marble—into a patio where fountains splashed and the rays of the suns lay muted through crystal. A few slaves moved about carrying towels and basins and a party of girls danced and laughed among the fountains. They saw us. With squeals and shrieks they darted away, and I surmised they had no business there. I saw Jaidur's fist wrap around his sword hilt.

Orlan Mahmud walked out from the shadows of the colonnade into the diffused light among the splashing fountains. He wore a plain blue tunic and he did not wear a sword or dagger. So that, alone, convinced me. He held up his left hand. He was not smiling. Hierayn moved forward quickly, his body wobbling, and called out a greeting. I guessed that fat Strom Hierayn was no part of the plot. But plot there was, by Krun!

"Into cover!" I shouted. "Run!"

Even as I shouted, Orlan threw himself sideways, and he shouted too. A high desperate call. "We are betrayed!"

The javelin that would have destroyed him for his refusal to betray us darted from the colonnade's shadows and barely missed. He was on a knee, stumbling, and then he was half up and staggering. The party with us was fleeing madly away, trying to find shelter. Jaezila, Jaidur and I remained—but only for a moment. Together, the three of us hurtled toward Orlan. Jaidur hoisted him up; Jaezila snapped up her bow and let fly into the colonnade shadows. She is a superb mistress of the bow, deadly with the fletched shaft. I went headlong, with her arrows cutting beside me, slap bang into whatever skulked in the shadows.

Queen Fahia's mercenaries were there, ready to snap us up. In that tricky half-light our blades flickered like quicksilver, erratic, and dreadfully quickly my brand fouled with blood. Jaidur roared into action at my side. Four of the paktuns were down with shafts skewering them, and a fifth, and the fight was too hot and close and Jaezila put her bow away and ripped into the fray with her sword. I truly believe we three would have done the business ourselves. The mercenaries were good, a mix of diff and apim, and we had the beating of them. But others of our party joined in, and Strom Hierayn laid about him with his sword, and after a space we stopped, for there were no foemen left.

Orlan came across. He looked distraught. "Thank Opaz, you are here! But—as you see—I have been betrayed."

"They were waiting for us!" said Jaidur. He spoke accusingly.

Orlan nodded and swallowed; he was sweating. "You were seen flying in. The games may be on, but the queen's paktuns do not sleep because of that."

"We suspected it was too easy," said Jaezila.

"It was that new damned spymaster from Hamal. He ferreted it out. I am finished in Huringa now." Orlan looked at his villa, the fountains, the colonnades, the glowing flowers. He shook his head. "It seems we are all finished."

"There will be more guards." I spoke in a nasty fashion, to brace them up. "And we are not finished yet. You will fly back to the camp, Orlan. With your family and whomever—"

"I have no saddle flyers. They have all been taken."

"Then we must all make room on ours."

"But—"

"Help Pallan Orlan," I said. "And be quick. We must be off and flying before anybody turns up to find out the cause of the disturbance here." And then I said, "*Bratch*!" in a most unlovely way, and some of them abruptly realized that they were being commanded by an emperor, so they bratched.

When we had it all sorted out, I had the opportunity for enough words with Orlan to have grasped the situation. He was very down. The queen's new mercenaries were her trump card, and we had nothing to pit against them. The army was divided. The people wanted the games in the Jikhorkdun, and excitement, and bread and wine, and whoever could give them those could be queen for all they cared. It was not quite like that, but Orlan's words conveyed those sentiments. The Hyrklese are a tough old lot, having survived on their isolated island for five thousand years or so against all who sought to subject them. The Shanks in their raiding had made of the Hyrklese a hard lot. I nodded when Orlan finished. Jaidur came up and said all was ready for departure.

"Good. Jaidur, you will have to look out for Jaezila—for Lela—"

He snorted derisive amusement. "She can look out for herself, as you well know."

"Good. I will not be flying back with you."

They stared. Then they started protesting. I quieted them.

"We need fighting men. We need a force inside the city to rise and strike when we attack from outside. By Vox! We did it with Vondium, we can do it with Huringa."

"But there is no great force in the city loyal to Lildra!" Orlan protested wearily, almost beaten. "There is no one in the city who will strike a blow for Lildra against Fahia."

"Oh yes there is," I said.

Jaidur perked up. "I will come with you—"

I glared at him. I own I glared in hot and frenzied fury.

"You will not! You will not come with me! You've been an imp of a son, hating me—"

He protested at this, shouting that he'd never hated me, only that his discovery of his parentage had been a shock.

"All right, Vax Neemusbane!" I bellowed at him. "But you've always been disrespectful and sullen and cheeky—and I don't care, for that is your right, now you are a grown man. But in this you will do as you are told, and lump it! You will not come with me!" I was shaking. By Zair! The idea of my lad Jaidur in the Jikhorkdun! "Hasn't your mother told you about the Arena and what goes on there? Don't you know what they did to her with their silver chains and that damned great boloth? Haven't you listened to Balass the Hawk, and Oby, and Naghan the Gnat? Well? They'd start you as a coy, greener than Havil, and you'd not last—"

"I'm as good a swordsman as you, any day!"

"Maybe. But they'd chuck you onto the silver sand with a little dagger to face a strigicaw, or a chavonth. Or maybe a hulking great Chulik in full armor would have a go at you with all his weapons and you with a short spear—"

"I can use a short spear—"

"And you'd have your insides all over the sand; they'd have the iron hook in your ankle and your mother would say what to that, hey? You perverse, ungrateful child!"

He was scarlet. He was bursting. He was a man, a great

warrior, a Krozair of Zy, and he worked in secret for Vallia through the Sisters of the Rose, and here he was being talked to as though he were a child. Well, by Zair, and wasn't that what I should have done when I was flung back to Earth instead?

All the same, I added, "You have the right to throw your life away in the Jikhorkdun. You have the right to do as you see fit. I can only advise you and try to guide you, and your honor is your own concern. My view of your honor in this pickle is for you to work for the rebellion and lead on what forces you can against the city as I get the kaidurs to rise inside. I think you would impugn your own honor if you did otherwise. But it is for you to decide. And listen to me, Jaidur, I respect you as my son too much to order you about."

Jaezila said, "Respect!" She did not laugh but her eyes were brilliant on me. And I think she understood even if my own stumbling unhappy words could only convey a tiny fraction of what I felt.

"Well, you've changed your tune," said Jaidur. "First it's 'You must not go,' like a weeping mother as her son goes off to war, and now it's 'You must do as you see fit,' like a Jikaidast mockingly advising an opponent on his next move. Well? You are supposed to be my father, and I your son, and this is Lela my sister, and what do we know of you—"

"Vax Neemusbane.* Jaezila."

"Yes, very well, I grant you—but to skulk outside while you have all the fun in the Jikhorkdun—"

That did it.

"*Fun*?" I lifted a fist. "In the Arena? *Fun*!"

"Well . . ."

"If I catch you so much as sniffing at the Arena, young Jaidur, I'll tan your backside so you won't ride a zorca for a month! What would your mother say? Think of her, for Zair's sake! Kregen is dangerous enough without asking for it."

Now Jaezila did laugh, and stepped forward, and in her own authoritative way said, "You are changing your tune once again, Jak. Jaidur sees which way lies his duty. We will bring all the forces we can against the city when we

* Vax Neemusbane (or Neemusjid): Name Vax taken by Jaidur in the Eye of the World. Cognomen from defeat of Athgar the Neemu. —A.B.A.

receive the signal that you are ready to rise. Sooner rather than later."

"Agreed."

"And father, may Opaz through the Invisible Twins guide your sword and strengthen your arm—" Jaezila looked woefully at me. "I don't like this at all, by Vox, not one little bit!"

"Well—" began Jaidur.

I settled it.

"Get flying. Keep up your spirits. When the signal comes, you must be ready, or we will all be chopped."

The woeful look on Jaezila's face, lightened only sporadically by her laughter, depressed me. She was a girl, although of strong mind and iron will, fashioned for sunshine and laughter. When Lela got down, the reasons were hard and cruel. Of course, I felt guilty about causing her unhappiness yet again.

Orlan confirmed that he had been arrested and confined in his own villa in order to trap messengers and visitors. He had not been put to the Question, although, no doubt, that would have followed when enough of the rebels had been captured. Fahia was alternating between confidence and doubt, and no man was safe in her presence. Her pet neemus, black as hell, fed to repletion.

The remberees were said softly and then the fluttrells lifted away. I stared up anxiously. If a Hyrklanian air patrol came sniffing around, or a skein of aerial cavalry investigated, my people up there would be in trouble. But on a day of the games, the games were the thing, and Huringa dozed outside the Arena. So, not without a premonitory shiver, I started off for the Jikhorkdun.

Foolish to run my head into fresh horror? Of course. But what else was there to do? It is easy enough now to think of a dozen different courses of action I might have taken, but of them all, none, I venture to think, would be as swift and efficacious as the course I was now embarked on. Through the level rays of jade and ruby I strode toward the lifting pile of the Jikhorkdun, with the high fortress of the Hakal rising alongside. The beast roars swelled and grew enormous as I approached.

How, I was already wondering, fared the ruby drang?

Chapter Eighteen

The Queen's Kaidur

"Not so well, Chaadur," said Cheldur Adria. "Not so well, by Kaidun!"

"Then it is opportune I have come back—"

"More fool you!"

"Mayhap, Cleitar, mayhap. But there is a task set to my hands."

We walked toward the local drinking den. Cleitar Adria, because of his position, could ease me back, saying in explanation that my absence had been caused by illness. There was, in these latter days of the Jikhorkdun, a certain laxness which worked to my advantage. The needleman was rubbish, as we all knew, and a word or two in the right direction settled that. There was no difficulty in getting myself into the Arena. The problems started when I began to lay out the plan of action.

"But you work for the queen, Chaadur!"

I knew this was going to be tricky. Cleitar believed I labored for Queen Fahia, and to this I owed immunity from a deal of unpleasantness. Now I had to persuade him I did not, that I wished him to join with me—more, to lead—a rebellion against the queen. Fahia was generally detested. The coils and twists and turns of intrigue are not particularly difficult to grasp for anyone involved in them; for a bluff cheldur like Cleitar Adria they presented a certain baffling front he failed to penetrate. But he would not admit to ignorance or lack of brainpower. He nodded wisely. He drank and nodded again, and drank more, and listened and I laid it all out.

"So you see, Cleitar, Princess Lildra will be a boon to us all. For a start, you will receive a handsome pension, and a title too, I don't doubt. There will be no need—unless you so desire—to act in the Jikhorkdun ever again."

I was on dangerous ground here, for the Jikhorkdun had been Cleitar's life. But his face and absent eye told their own story.

He drank again. He held onto the jug. "I am grown more weary of the Jikhorkdun than I could ever have believed. You see that in me, Chaadur?"

"Yes."

"Never make friends in the Arena. We were never true comrades when you were Drak the Sword. And we were wise. But—" He drank again. "But there was a Khibil lad, Kranlo, brought him up from a coy, very quick with a sword, a good eye—I made a friend of Kranlo, more fool me. He was chosen last sennight by Tipp the Thrax to fight the Queen's Kaidurs."

"I am sorry, Cleitar."

"Aye. Aye. They dragged him out."

His head hit the table and his arms flopped and the wine jug spewed purple Hamish over the floor. I hoisted him up and carted him off to his rooms and dumped him on his bed, and let his slaves care for him. Then I took myself off to the barracks.

Many new faces were apparent, and many faces that might have been new and might not have been, seeing a kaidur takes little notice of the regular passage of arena fodder. Frandu the Franch and Norhan the Flame were pleased to see me, and I more than pleased to see them. I had work for them.

Lights out varied, in these latter days, with the whims of the barracks cheldurs. A one-armed ex-kaidur bucking for cheldur and with a little authority—a nikcheldur—at last suggested we'd better turn the lights out and turn in. The talk of the day's fights went on for a space and then the barracks dropped away into darkness and silence. Not sleeping, I lay and planned what it would be possible to do, and as that was clearly not sufficient, what I would have to do to please the Star Lords and set Lildra on the throne of Hyrklana.

Once I had resurfaced within the structure of the Jikhorkdun there was no possibility of my avoiding notice, and so I had to fight in the days that followed. Hundal the Oivon as bluff and gruff as ever, our cheldur, got me some interesting combats, which I managed to survive. The name of Chaadur began to be mentioned. And, all the time, we sounded out the feelings of all those we deemed accessible. The mood of the Arena changed. Fahia was no longer the popular young queen; people were more and more seeing her in the light of the aging butcher. For all that, no rebellion could hope to succeed without inside and outside combination of forces. When Lildra's people attacked, we in the Jikhorkdun must rise. And our numbers grew—even though, by reason of our employment, our numbers were cruelly reduced from time to time when Fahia staged a bloodbath.

Any man who is lucky enough to escape from the Arena must be all kinds of idiot voluntarily to return. I kept telling myself that, yes, I was a right onker, a real idiot, but all the same, returning to the Jikhorkdun and rousing all the kaidurs whose personal grudges against those who had put them there would spur them to rebellion had to be clever. Surely? Clever or idiotic, this was the plan, and I was stuck with it. We had a tasty series of tussles with the other colors during a period of high junketings, and the ruby drang inched again up the victory poles. Again, I found myself becoming involved with the fate of the reds and the fortunes of the ruby drang. Then, of course, disaster struck. It could never be unexpected. It was just simply diabolically inconvenient.

I rounded the corner of the barracks, carrying my gear with blood everywhere from some poor devil who hadn't jumped quickly enough, anxious to get into the water and clean all the muck and blood and sweat off, and Kyr Tipp the Thrax limped up. The shriveled, shaven-headed Gon thumped his crooked staff down. It was banded in ivory and silver and glittered. He banged it down, his nutcracker nose and jaw snapping, and lifting it high, beckoned me over. It was a summons that was death to refuse.

I went over and stood looking down on him.

"Chaadur, is it? Yes, Chaadur. You have been mightily honored, mightily honored, by the glass eye and brass sword of Beng Thrax himself."

So, feeling my insides falling away, I said, "Get on with it, man, get on with it. When?"

If we could rise before this one-sided fight . . .

He snapped his nose and chin, his gimlet eye very nasty. "You would do well not to talk to me like that—"

"Do you want to tell me, or must I report that you are lax in your duty, Tipp? Well?"

He blinked. In a very menacing tone—very menacing—he said, "I will remember you, Chaadur. Tomorrow. You fight tomorrow."

I cursed. So soon! But that was the way of it. Tipp the Thrax limped off, with a final threatening curse, and I went on to wash up and to receive the commiserations of the kaidurs.

"It's the Ice Floes of Sicce for you, dom!" was the consensus of opinion. This was an estimation of the situation I found myself agreeing with and I detested that argument. Hundal the Oivon wanted to fuss, and Frandu and Norhan wanted to go out and get blind; but I said, "No, fanshos,* no. I am not important in the rebellion. But all the kaidurs, acting together, are."

Had the sounds of fights and arguments not been a common experience floating over the barracks of the kaidurs, someone might have come to investigate. They were all yelling away, belting fists into palms, swearing by all manner of gods and spirits. In the end we decided—I decided—that I must take my chances with the Queen's Kaidurs and the moment of the uprising would be brought forward. The quicker we struck, everyone felt, the more chance we stood. The longer we delayed, the more chances there were that we would be betrayed. As arranged, the message was sent out to our people on the outside.

On the morrow I would go up against an opponent—or opponents—selected from the Queen's Kaidurs. From such encounters few ever walked away, and they were never heard of again. Ever.

When Cleitar Adria found me he looked worried. He kept fiddling with his sword, shoving the thraxter up and down in the scabbard.

"This is a right mess, Chaadur. Couldn't you have ducked out of sight until tomorrow?"

"No chance. I just walked into the damned little Gon. Anyway, if we rise tomorrow as planned, and the message gets through, it will all turn out all right."

"You hope."

"There's no chance of my hiding—"

"No. You are now a marked man. You've seen the guards?"

"Aye. They dog my footsteps. Still, I could dispose of them—"

"That would ruin all. We've all laid our lives out on this plan of yours. This plan of ours." For I had insisted that Cleitar and the others join the planning discussions, and, in guiding them, made them feel a part of the conspiracy.

* Fanshos: "Comrades." "You guys." "Friends."

"I'll take my chances with the Queen's Kaidurs." Then, incongruously, I laughed. "I may be able to lift the ruby drang up the victory pole."

A kaidur destined to fight the queen's men did not spend that night in the barracks. The guards marched me off before lights out and quartered me in splendid isolation in a sumptuous room wherein much wine stood around in flagons and amphorae and the food was exotically lavish. I sent the dancing girls packing and, after a good meal and a modicum of wine, got my head down. I was in for a fight on the morrow, and I needed to concentrate on that. If, by any unfortunate chance, I met a champion as good as Prince Mefto the Kazzur, then my days on Kregen were numbered.

No good brooding. I slept.

The day dawned misty, which was a good omen, since I trusted that our rebel army was creeping up on Huringa. I ate a massive breakfast and began the preparation of my gear, for I would be fighting as a churgur, a sword and shield man, against an opponent similarly armed. Tipp the Thrax, very ugly, looked in to tell me I was fighting fourth and last. Three kaidurs from the other colors would be fighting first. Their names were known to me, and we were all halfway or so up the rankings, prime meat for the Queen's Kaidurs to chop. I snarled at Tipp and he scuttled off. As he went he spat out, "You'll sing a lot smaller when I've talked to you again."

I threw a boot at him and went on polishing my sword.

When he turned up next, about an hour before the fight was scheduled to begin, he smirked. He looked different, more pompous, more sure of himself, his shaven head a buttered glisten in the lamplight, for the room was shuttered, although the mist had cleared. With him were ten guards with nets and whips. Just in case . . .

What he told me gave me a clear understanding of why the Queen's Kaidurs always—or almost always—won out on the silver sand. He joyed in the telling.

"The men in black," he said, "with their tongs and their red-hot pincers and their bone-crushers, their gut-pullers and the rest of their clever inventions in the torture dungeons of the Hakal. If you do not lose, you will die such a death of agony as will make you regret most bitterly you did not lose. And you will make a fight of it before you lose. The queen demands spectacle. She wishes a good fight. You are a fighter, otherwise you would not have been chosen. So fight well. Fight hard. And make sure you lose convincingly." He snickered. "After all, the queen may be in a good mood and choose to spare you."

The men in black sniggered.

I eyed their whips and nets. It was the damned nets that would cause the trouble . . . Tipp saw my glance and read my intentions in my lowering face.

"Do not try to escape, Chaadur. The men in black are clever with their nets. And there are more outside. You would simply go straight down to the dungeons." He bit a fingernail. "I am told what is done there defies the imagination. Certainly, they do not bury whole bodies, only parts."

I turned my back on him, went on polishing the sword. If that sword went between his ribs now, then down under the Hakal I would go. The rebellion had to succeed, for the sake of Vallia. I'd fight the Queen's Kaidur. But I did not think I would choose to chance fat Queen Fahia's generosity of mood.

Tipp went on to describe in more detail some of the work that went on down in Fahia's torture dungeons, and some of it was stomach-churning, I can tell you. The men in black rattled their nets and flicked their whips. They were men happy in their work—if they were men, that is. I ignored the lot and saw to my gear and, by Vox, I believe if Tipp hadn't had the sense to stop talking and threatening and leave, I'd have lost control and gone headlong into the lot of them. But there was a better way than foolhardiness of that nature . . .

I could have postured and put on a different face, one which inflicted only a few painful beestings, and disappeared. But that would have aroused the guards and officials of the Jikhorkdun, and we of the rebellion wanted everything to go on as normal. So I sat and readied my weapons and waited to step out onto the silver sand to face an opponent who had a torture dungeon on his side.

Many a fine arena fighter had chosen to lose and die gracefully rather than face agony beyond belief. Yet I could not allow myself to be blinded by this nauseating trickery to the stark fact that the queen's champions were hyr-kaidurs of very high standing, men who had battled their way to the top. They would expect to win in any case. This intrigue of Tipp's was by way of insurance. And it occurred to me, also, that it was eminently possible that the champions had no knowledge of Tipp and the queen's underhanded dealings to insure the victory. The men chosen were, like myself, from the middle rankings, men the hyr-kaidurs would expect to defeat. Tipp's insurance extended to the one or two among them who had the makings of great champions and who might defeat the queen's man. Selah! What happened would happen, so I went on polishing up the sword and thinking of Delia, and of Jaezila and Jaidur, who ought to be nearing Huringa with our raggedy little army.

Jaezila had told me how she'd unexpectedly met men she knew when she'd tumbled down the trap in the Temple of Malab, and how she had had to be quick to make them see who she truly was, and therefore give them orders that no harm should befall us. That was why Tyfar had been bound and gagged and not slain, and Jaezila, also, out of the subterfuge. I knew Jaezila was a woman of immense resource and guile. And I knew Jaidur to be a right tearaway. With Nath the Retributor and Hardur Mortiljid they must break through quickly once the attack began.

So we were called and with the trumpets flinging brazen notes over us we marched up into the suns' shine of the Arena.

To catch the atmosphere of the Jikhorkdun! To grasp at the raw essentials of that horrific place! It repels in utter disgust, and, deeply and darkly, it draws on the ancient tides of blood, demanding sacrifice and dedication and adherence to ancient mysteries old before man stood upright. It was not a nice place. For some, it was the only place in all the wide world of Kregen that mattered.

As an earnest of my feelings, I will say that I felt disgruntled that in this, the last fight, I did not step out onto the silver sand from the red corner. My comrades over there rattled their swords along the iron bars, and yelled and screamed insults and encouragement, and I was debarred from them. We men selected to face the queen's champions were herded into a small space to one side of the overhanging mass of the royal box, and from the shadows we looked out upon blinding brilliance. Above us, unseen, sat Fahia and her courtiers, her pet neemus, her slave girls in their pearls and diaphanous gauzes. A square shadow offset to the side from the new balcony lay hard-edged in red and green, twinned shadows across the sand. That podium had not been there when I'd fought as Drak the

Sword. I thought I knew why it had been built and stuffed with ranks of archers.

The three other kaidurs sat on the bench and looked glum. A Fristle woman brought the leather bottles of raw red wine, Beng Thrax's Spit, and they drank. The heat stifled in our small slot of shadow. Out on the silver sand men fought and died. Herds of coys were driven out to be slaughtered in picturesque fashion. Animals squealed and slashed, struggled and, killing, died. The business of the day wore on. We were a prime fixture, and the stands and benches, the whole amphitheater, was crowded, a solid mass of sweating faces gleaming in the lights of the suns, waving arms and kerchiefs, the black cavities of open mouths screaming. A wall of sound lifted around the Arena. We sat and waited, and sweated.

The order in which we would step out to fight and lose was: Yellow, green, blue, red. This order had been arrived at by lot.

Of us all, the least glum was the adherent of the sapphire graint. He licked his lips. Wine drops clustered in his beard.

"The blues crown the victory pole," he said. "And don't you forget it."

The men of the diamond zhantil and the emerald neemu looked sullen. The yellow said, "By Nandig's belly! I wish I was home in Ystilbur, on my farm. I swear each vosk would be like a comrade, every chicken a friend."

"What does it matter what color wins?" said the green. "We are dead men."

The blue sniffed. "You knew that from the very first day you signed on."

"It makes it no easier to bear."

"Think of the men in black."

"By Harg! I think of nothing else. Suppose my sword slips, and I nick the queen's man, and he dies? What then?"

"Then, my friend, pieces of you will be scattered here and there. You have my condolences."

He merely said that; his mind was on his own problems.

I sat and said nothing.

By the way they talked, they exhibited the hardened toughness of the kaidur. They lived with death, and now they knew they were going to die. Fahia was not often generous. So there was no screaming and breast-beating, no wailing and panicky thrashings about. These men were kaidurs, and they did what kaidurs did, and when their deaths arrived, then their adherence was to the fight and their color, and their deaths were more codicils to the greater spectacle.

Familiarity with the Arena rarely breeds contempt. No man stepping out onto the silver sand often feels more than the impulses of the moment. The drive of the blood through bodies tensed for combat, the battering of noise from the mobs, the stink of spilled blood and the rank tang of a multitude of animal smells, the feeling of greatness and smallness and of impending doom—all these sensations and emotions flit through a man's concentration upon the single object ahead. He must go out and fight. He must win if he can; but, above all, he must fight.

The first marked for destruction stepped out onto the silver sand. He walked quietly to the designated place where he halted and turned to face the royal box. The high glitter from that place of regal power smote down. We waited in the shadows, unable to see the royal box but all able to see it in our minds' eyes. The yellow lifted his sword, and the first Queen's Kaidur stepped out. The golden trumpets rang. The crowds quieted, ready to be critical. This was no wallowing bloodbath, this was a contest of skills in which the favorite artifice of unequal combat lay not in the weapons but in the men themselves. Sword and shield against sword and shield, with a hyrkaidur ready to show the crowds his arts in combat against an opponent who was very good, but not quite so good as the queen's man. They liked that, these folk of Huringa.

Sometimes these fights turned into desperate affrays. Then the crowd's enjoyment was great. Our yellow comrade fought well, but he went down, and he did not go down from choice but because he was fairly bested. The green followed, and then it was blue's turn. He looked bloated, this man of the sapphire graint, his face sweating and scarlet with protuberant veins.

Tipp the Thrax was there, well guarded, walking into our place of confinement. It was clear he had been watching us.

"Remember! You lose well, or it is the men in black!"

Blue shivered all over. He took a fresh grip on his sword and shield and without a word strode out onto the sand.

"As for you," said Tipp, regarding me with his shriveled look of venom, "remember!"

I shook my sword at him, whereat he stepped back smartly, and his guards closed up. I did not bother to speak to him. Blue was fighting and he was worth the watching. He would, without doubt, have made hyr-kaidur in only a few more fair combats. He fought the queen's man with savage concentration, giving ground and then sidestepping and sweeping in with a clever flank attack. He drew blood. But in the end, he allowed his shield to sag and his thrust to falter, and the Queen's Kaidur chopped him, and blue went down, face first into the bloodied sand.

The trumpets roared, and out I stepped, and the heat of the Suns of Scorpio smote across my shoulders.

The royal box glittered with light.

I looked up, as the others had done. I neglected to give the formal salute, and I did not repeat that obscene sign I had once given Fahia. Instead, I settled myself and waited for my opponent to walk out and go through the formalities before we set to.

Although Kregans do not age much during their better than two hundred years of life, little signs can give you an idea of their age. This fellow looked young. He carried himself well. He must, of necessity, be very good, to be a Queen's Kaidur so young. His face was oval, with bright blue eyes and fair hair, but his nose was pinched and his lips were full and fleshy, glistening red and pouting with self-satisfaction and indulgence. The idea crossed my mind that he looked just like a spoiled brat, but that didn't make sense. His armor and weapons were of superb quality. He flourished his sword about and the thraxter splintered back light. He'd know a whole encyclopedia of tricks of the sworder's art . . .

As usual at the beginning of each combat, the uproar from the mobs quieted. We circled watchfully. He made a quick rush, feinted and stepped back. I did not move. I saw his face reveal his sudden annoyance that I had not reacted to his move. It was as though I had insulted him.

There was an odd feeling of wrongness about this. The three previous champions had been hyr-kaidurs, men I had seen fight before, hard-bitten and professional. If it made sense at all, this young fellow was an amateur, a dilettante, and you don't get many of those in the Arena, no, by the brass sword and glass eye of Beng Thrax!

Again he feinted and rushed, and again I did not move.

Some of the crowd started to barrack. The raucous

shouts came from the greens, the yellows and the blues, partisans who had seen their own men go down in bloody defeat. I circled again, still making no attack, trying to think in the heat and the noise and the stinks.

The smart young fellow came in confidently, and this time he meant it, so his thraxter had to be parried, and he had to be knocked away with the shield. These things were done, and he went staggering back. His face expressed the utmost surprise and savage resentment before he fell smack down on his rear end.

I stood back.

Standing up, he shook himself, set his shield, snouted his sword and came in with a ferocious rush. We tinker-hammered for a space, which is a pretty sight, but useless. Unless you can hack your opponent's shield rim through, this clanging away at shields merely blunts your sword. I gave him a final clout and put enough power into it to smash his shield back into his face. He yelped and skipped away. Over his shield rim his thin nose showed a dribble of blood.

He moved around more cautiously. He looked puzzled. When he came in again he hammered impetuously at my shield and thrust on. His sweating face was inches from my own. He snarled at me.

"Rast! You are supposed to let me win!"

I slid sideways, came back and landed a good welting blow with the flat against his backside. He spun about. His sword and shield went every which way. And the crowd began to laugh.

"Yetch!" he screamed. "Think of the men in black!"

Again I did not answer. The next flurry of action saw his shield failing to deflect a blow. His sword spun up in the air wrenched from his fingers, spinning, glittering end over end to thunk point-first into the sand. It quivered. He panted, staring from the sword to me and back again. I stepped back and bowed and with my own thraxter indicated his.

The crowd howled.

He wrenched the blade from the sand. "You onker! You are meant to let me win!"

"Maybe . . . It is not supposed to be easy for you, though, is it?"

He possessed a good and varied repertoire of tricks and stratagems and now he settled down to use them in real earnest. Many of the passages I recognized as being developed by hyr-kaidurs of the past, some were the old regulars; he had nothing new. He had been well-trained and his schooling had been thorough, but he lacked the fire, the spirit, the ultimate essence that makes a swordsman.

Breaking my usual habit when fighting, I fell into conversation with him. The incongruity of this did not escape me.

"You've had good teachers, lad. Fine swordmasters—"

"I have, rast!" And he leaped in, hacking and slashing and I foined him off and stood back as he went blundering past.

"All the same," I said, in a conversational voice as he floundered around to face me, "it is a puzzle that you have become a Queen's Kaidur. You don't have the wherewithal for the job."

He shrieked in an access of rage and rushed again, and I twirled his sword out of the way and then—it makes me feel odd to recall—I tripped him with an outstretched foot. It was a mean trick. He tumbled over again and this time he lost his grip on the shield as well as the sword. He lay for a space, winded.

Very gravely, I walked across and picked up his shield and sword. My own shield hung from a single grip on the arm, my own sword was stuck into the sand at my back. With a polite little bow I handed him his weapons. Instantly he was on his feet, the shield swished across and he took a lusty blow at me with his sword, slashing to take my head off. I skipped away.

The crowd booed!

They hadn't liked this display of boorishness. Not when I'd handed him his weapons, and myself without a sword.

This buffoonery went on for a time, and I started to undress him. This was done, I plead on my behalf, out of boredom and to give me something to do while I thought of my best course of action. His straps were slit through. His harness fell. He wore a tasty breechclout in green, so my heart hardened a trifle.

When he was practically mother naked, and still shrieking and sobbing and hurling himself on, telling me what the men in black would do to me, I began to play him a little in earnest. I confess he was run ragged. His face was a scarlet bloom. He gasped for breath. Any number of times he thought he was dead, and at the last minute my blade twitched away. I did give him a haircut though.

The crowd was now silent, with only the occasional long

susurration of indrawn breath, or an incongruous laugh at some buffoonery, to indicate aught went forward on the silver sands. He was out of breath now, panting, bursting, and his shield drooped and his sword wavered. Carefully, I chipped away the shield grips, and the shredded thing fell to the ground. Then his sword was upended and went flying through the air, a steel deadliness, spinning up and away to smack hilt-first into the sand.

He faced me, disheveled, sweating, gasping for air, unarmed and shieldless.

With a deliberate step I walked across. I showed him my sword. I was aware that the crossbowmen flanking the royal box were on the move. Out of the corner of my eye I could see them lifting their weapons. If they shafted me, that would not reflect well on the queen. I handed my own sword across to the lad, hilt first, with all the magniloquence of swordsmanship carried to absurd heights.

He did not know, I felt, that even with the sword he wouldn't easily kill a Krozair brother.

The silence in that place of noise was appalling.

I shouted.

"You're supposed to win, lad, if you're a Queen's Krozair. Well, let me help you a little."

The crowd exploded into violent laughter, enormously relishing all this absurdity. And then they fell silent. A single trumpet pealed a golden note. Cautiously keeping the lad in my sight, and taking my sword away, I stared up to the royal box.

The courtiers were bowing and scraping. The neemus were being drawn back on their silver chains and the gauzily clad slave girls huddled away in groups at each side. The fans kept on waving to bring fresher air into the royal box. The color and movement demanded attention from every eye.

Queen Fahia stood up.

She was simply a magnificent blur of color and jewels.

She lifted a hand and the suns struck splintering sparkles from her rings.

The silence was absolute.

"You have made mock of my son, Chaadur the Doomed! Give me one good reason why I should not tell my crossbowmen to loose and pierce you through with fifty bolts."

Her hair piled high with gems lent her a spurious dignity; her white face, painted and powdered, came into focus as I squinted up, seeing her blue eyes and the fair hair and the cosmetics laid on like butter on bread.

"So the lad is your son. He fought as well as he could. It is no discredit to meet a better swordsman in the Jikhorkdun. As to your question: because you and he have not lost yet and if you gave your bowmen the order to loose you would lose everything."

Her head went back and then slowly forward and she stared at me hard, hard.

"You are impertinent, Chaadur the Doomed!"

"You don't have to worry about that—you should be worrying about your lad, who has lost. What says the queen to that? Is he to live or is he to die? Choose!"

She put a hand to her lips. Even at that distance she could clearly be seen shaking uncontrollably. Then she thrust her hand out, pointing, her forefinger stiff and beringed, glittering on me.

"It is impossible! I know you. Drak the Sword! *Drak the Sword!*"

Chapter Nineteen

In the Dungeons of the High Fortress of the Hakal

There are dungeons and dungeons on Kregen and those beneath the high fortress of the Hakal in Huringa were in a class of their own. They were of a quite exceptional horror. The things done there turned men into drooling imbeciles. An item that confirmed my judgment that Fahia had sadly fallen away lofted to one side, an ornate area with seating and lounging facilities, with tables provided with the best of food and drink, it was quite simply a place of observation where Fahia could sit in her throne and enjoy what went on.

The iron rings stapled into the stone floor were no stronger for her pet neemus than they were for the poor devils out in the dungeon itself. The men in black busied themselves with their apparatus. I crouched in a small iron-barred box. This method of confining criminals and those reserved for judgment was the normal understandable system that insured the poor wight let out of the box would have his muscles so knotted up and be so writhing in pain with the flow of blood that he could be run into the next phase of his ordeal without protest. I knew. Unfortunately.

So it behooved me to attempt a few of the more esoteric Disciplines of the Krozairs. To force blood through constricted passageways was the devil of a job and one which high adepts mastered with difficulty. I did what little I could, using capillaries in the accepted fashions, but I knew my blood was still going to cause me considerable agony—euphemistically termed pins and needles—when I got out of the box. As for the muscles, these offered less of a problem, and by manipulations and tensing and relaxing, I hoped I'd have them limber enough. I did know, and with certainty, that I must leap about in a frenzy of action when they opened the box to lead me off to destruction, and I knew, also, that my body might decide not to obey the dictates of my will. I did not forget the slate slab. So I practiced the Disciplines and glared balefully at that elegant observation area where the lords and ladies in attendance on Fahia ogled with her the sufferings of the unfortunates below.

She had not yet arrived. The men in black moved about in a sullen and yet free way, cracking jokes, sharpening up their implements, oiling their tongs, stoking the braziers. In these pursuits they resembled humankind. When the queen arrived they would assume the stoic, calm, professional aloofness of the true torturer. Strange to attempt to evaluate the processes of another person's mind. What had brought these people to this? Perhaps here, as in some countries, the profession was handed down from father to son. Probably they took pride in their work. As they say on Earth and Kregen, it takes all sorts . . .

The layout of the torture equipment was of vital importance and the positions and relationship of the various items had to be judged exactly. Chains dangled from the rocky ceiling. At the moment they were free of the skeletons one assumed normally remained there until the chains were required again. A massive pot of oil bubbled and boiled. The metal glistened. The pot was of a size to have fed a cannibal city. Near it a rack with spikes and other strategically placed unpleasantnesses had been cleaned up reasonably well; only a few bloodstains remained. The rack was of a down-to-earth kind, a simple stretcher, but near it a device for turning the victim inside out frowned down far more ominously.

Slaves wearing black breechclouts in place of the more usual gray slave clouts stoked up the fire under the pot of boiling oil, and tended the braziers, occasionally poking the implements in further, or pulling them out to inspect their heat color. The whole place stank. I crouched knotted up in the iron-barred box and cursed fat Queen Fahia and longed for her to put in an appearance so we might begin.

When Fahia at last arrived she put on a regal show with all the trimmings. By that time I was aware that unless I could contrive a breathing space before they ran me up and strapped me into the first piece of their diabolical arsenal of devices, I was done for. Her pet neemus with their round heads and wicked fangs and glittering eyes were handled by experts with the silver chains. Her dancing girls were there—and I could only hope they would shut their eyes. The ranks of the courtiers were thinned, there being only a handful present. Her court wizard was there, a fellow of some discipline or other in which she believed devoutly, I felt sure, with his book of power and his wand and tall hat and his face that showed a too-great love of the wine jug. I glared evilly at the lot of them.

Fahia wore a mountain of clothing. It glittered in that dismal place. She walked over to me, and her walk was a waddle. She had been beautiful once. Never slender, her plumpness had been delightful. Now she was grotesque. Some glandular disaster must have struck, swelling her thighs and buttocks, coarsening her face, thickening her everywhere. The clothes disguised much; they could not conceal the pathetic truth.

"Drak the Sword," she said, and her voice came breathily, her lips red and bloated, "I should have recognized your style earlier."

If there was any one person in all Huringa who knew more about the Jikhorkdun than Queen Fahia then he was unknown. Looking at her and her grotesque barrel body and ravaged face, the pity in me was perfectly understandable. Her sister, Lilah, I judged, would never have come to this.

That thought made me say, "You did not treat Lilah well, Fahia."

She flinched. Her sway as queen was absolute.

"Yetch! You talk as crudely as ever. Now you will be sorry—"

"I think I am, a little, for you, fat woman."

That was cruel and unkind of me, but, by Zair. . . !

"Your death will not be easy, Drak the Sword. I remember you claimed to be Dray Prescot, and a multitude of other ridiculous names. We have heard of this Dray Prescot. He is the Emperor of Vallia. So you are forsworn. I do not think the Emperor of Vallia would be found fighting in my Jikhorkdun."

If they didn't let me out soon I'd never be able to move fast enough . . .

"Think what you will. I bore you no ill will. Now, you have forfeited what friendship I might have—"

"You were never a true friend to me! I thought you so once. But you escaped with that trollop of a slave girl—"

"Let them begin, mother!" The lad who had fought me spoke pettishly, not looking at me. "I want to see him scream and writhe and beg for mercy—for death he will not come by easily—"

"In a moment, Babb. In a moment."

This Babb, the queen's son, wore clothes of a cut that might have made me feel sorry for him. He could hardly be totally blamed for turning out as he had, given the circumstances of his upbringing, which were simple enough to surmise. Perhaps, had he possessed a tithe of the character of Prince Tyfar, he might have stood a chance.

The handful of nobles and the wizard came over to take a closer look at me. The wizard stank. The queen treated him with a marked respect. I had no idea of the sorcerer's powers, but I did not miss the look of loathing bestowed on him by Babb.

The conversation might be unreal in these surroundings, but Fahia was intrigued by the circumstances of my escape. I told her nothing, and insulted her a few more times. My limbs were dead as rotted timbers. The torturers hovered. She could take no more of my rudeness, and with a parting "You will suffer as only Lem knows how, Drak the Sword!" she waddled back to her throne.

The men in black clustered about my box and the locks were snapped open. The iron-barred side fell away.

Instantly, before any of them could reach down to grasp me, I was rolling. Like a bundled-up heap of laundry I rolled over and over across the stone floor. The internal torturers were at work. They inserted a red-hot needle into every joint and muscle, they trailed white-hot streams of agony through my veins. Still I had to keep on rolling. I hit the pot of boiling oil. It tipped. It overturned. Boiling oil foamed out in a broad flood. That was useful. In the abrupt yelling and shrieking, it was not yet enough. On I went, shaking and trembling, feeling as though I were being stretched out on the rack and being turned inside out on that fiendish device, on and toward the braziers. Slaves ran.

A black-clad tormentor jumped in the way, raking down to grab me. I hit him in the knees and he staggered and fell into a brazier. He screamed. Burning coals flew. The next brazier could be hooked over with a foot which felt nothing—there'd be a burn there the size of three deldys—and I had a wooden handle of a red-hot iron in my grip. I swung it about like a sword, and already I was beginning to overcome the cramps and the constrictions and the fresh surge of blood. I felt like a single scarlet bloom of agony, but I was getting back into action. The red-hot iron cleared a space.

The bedlam rang and boomed confusing echoes in the dungeon. Dungeons are called chundrogs on Kregen. Chun means jaws, and my jaws were tightly clenched so that their ache struck through as a welcome relief to the torments tying me up in knots. I caught a torturer an almighty thwack across the face with the red-hot iron and, branded, he shrieked and fell away. Others were running up, but I was getting back to being myself again. It was quick, thanks to the Krozair Disciplines. Without those I would have been a mere mewling bundle of agony writhing on the floor.

Fahia went nowhere these latter days without her guards. Now they clattered down from the observation area. They'd settle my hash too damn quick—if Fahia let them. The chances were she would order them to take me alive, for later attention. I slashed about and ran and dodged, clumsily, looking for the way out.

The boiling oil held up the guards. Fahia was shrieking at them: "Hurry, you rasts! Seize him up! Oh, my heart, my insides!" And then, in a veritable scream: "No! Babb! Do not go down to face him—he is a wild leem, a monster—Babb! Come back here!"

"I'll pull his insides out, mother—"

"He will chew you up and not spit out the pips! Babb! I am your mother and the queen! Do not go down!"

The red-hot iron went sizzling through a torturer's eyeball and I yanked it out and slashed away at another, and sent the pack of them running. I was becoming a little heated. There had to be a way out of this foul place. I saw Fahia, leaning on the shoulders of two of her courtiers. Her face was ghastly. Smoke lifted and the place smelled of oil and stink, and I jumped aside with something like my old agility as crossbowmen loosed.

The bolts whistled past. Everybody was shouting. The guards ran on. I whirled the iron which was cooling and blinked away sweat. Where was the confounded exit?

Up behind the observation area a door opened. It was opened from the other side. That, then, was my way out. I started to run for it, skipping past the edges of the spreading pool of oil. A man appeared in the doorway. He held a small earthenware pot. He threw the pot. It arched in the air, trailing smoke, and landed full among Fahia's guards. It burst. Fire vomited forth.

I looked up.

"Norhan the Flame!"

"Chaadur! Over here!"

Other men ran down into the dungeon from the doorway, kaidurs, men of the silver sand, men running with skilled weapons to destroy the queen's guards and those with her. She was screaming and screaming and nothing, it would seem, would stop her. Babb went down with a stux through his guts.

Frandu the Franch cut the wizard's head off. It was a quick and clever blow. The head bounced amid the feet of the slave damsels, and they shrieked and cowered away. It rolled among the black neemus and they devoured it, hissing and chomping. The great golden-bound book of power tumbled in a flutter of dried pages from the wizard's hands. So much for Fahia's hopes of sorcerous aid, stilled and stillborn by a Fristle's sword!

These courtiers in their silks and jewels had mocked and laughed as kaidurs bled and died. They paid gold to their mercenary guards to beat and humiliate the men of the silver sand. The kaidurs did not spare courtiers or guards. As for the neemus, golden-eyed, pricked of ear, they died, every one, struck through by stuxes hurled by experts. The damsels in their gauzes and pearls were not slain, being but poor deluded slaves, chattels just like the fighters of the Jikhorkdun. The dungeon fell to a sudden and eerie silence. I ran up to Frandu, who picked up the golden-bound book and shut it quickly. Smoke hung laced with the smell of charred flesh. The oil bubbled quietly.

Norhan came back with his sack of pots and his wicks and flame equipment and looked at Frandu and then at the dead wizard.

"He's headless!"

"Aye," said Frandu. "From the neck up."

"Well," I said, most unkindly, "it would be wise not to look into his eyes, which the neemus spat out, even though they had no head and the head no body."

Then the babble of reunions took place. The rebellion had begun and the kaidurs were running wild through the city. Ordinary citizens had retired to their houses and shops and barricaded them to await the outcome of the revolution.

"And our people outside?"

"They have begun their attack. We are assisting from within." Hundal the Oivon sweated the good news out. "We came to see what had happened to you. Our fanshos are fighting the mercenaries, and Cleitar Adria leads them on. The rasts are caught between two forces now."

"Then we will go up and help our comrades."

I looked about before we left. The dungeon presented a welcome sight with overturned and smashed torture equipment and dead tormentors in their black clothes lying twisted here and there. I gave thanks to Zair and Opaz and Djan that I had been spared.

Norhan the Flame said, "I thank Sarkalak we got here in time, Chaadur—although you had them worried; you had them worried."

As we went up through the chill stone corridors, Frandu laughed and stroked his whiskers and said, "Oh, we were much too smart for them."

Huringa roared to the skies with the noise of combat. We hurried to join the kaidurs who had attacked the mercenaries from the rear, and I was minded of my thoughts about dropping airborne troops here if we wished to take this city. Instead of warriors flying down astride saddle birds, or jumping from airboats, we had struck with a force already within the city, pent-up, trained, expert with arms and passionate with hatred for their oppressors.

Vollers sailed up against the brilliance of the sky, and we learned they carried the regiment of Hamalese. Those professional fighting men of Hamal knew when a battle was lost. Let the Hyrklese fight it out among themselves, the swods of the iron legion would have said, by Krun, let them kill themselves off so there are fewer to resist when we return. I wondered if their conduct would have been different if they'd known Vallia had taken a hand in this struggle.

Sandwiched between two forces and yet still fighting bravely, the mercenaries were worn down and hemmed in and, finally, forced to throw down their arms. There was a certain amount of revenge killing, but our chiefs, acting on the most stringent orders from the Princess Lildra, managed to restrain indiscriminate butchery. The paktuns might take service with Lildra, or leave Hyrklana.

The battle was over, our two forces met and the rejoicings began. The celebrations would thunder on for days.

Jaezila and Jaidur were safe, as were most of the chiefs. Nath the Retributor had taken a trifling wound, and Hardur Mortiljid had broken three swords in the fighting. Orlan beamed as his dreams began to be realized, and Princess Lildra was radiant. I asked after Gochert, the one-eyed man of mystery, and was told he had left the city after Vad Noran's failure, fearing he might be taken up as an accomplice. Of course, it had been Jaezila who had betrayed Noran. I could see that now, and the way she had attempted to save Tyfar and me, and would have, but for that damned stupid net. As for Ariane nal Amklana, it was rumored she had flown to Hamal to throw herself at the feet of the Empress Thyllis.

"Much good that will do her," said Jaezila.

"It is not over yet."

"No, it is not," said Jaidur. "But it is a beginning!"

I said, "Where is Queen Fahia?"

Huringa was searched, the high fortress of the Hakal, the villas of her adherents, everywhere. She was not found. Those of her pet neemus not slain in the dungeon, penned in luxury in one of her high palaces, looked sleek and well-fed. Well, it was a thought, and an interesting one. A brooch was found in the pen, a brooch slaves swore was Fahia's. But, for all that, no one in all Kregen ever saw Queen Fahia of Hyrklana again.

Chapter Twenty

A Wedding and a Promise

The high fortress of the Hakal in Huringa contained within its grim walls a palace of splendor and magnificence. I stood on a costly carpet of Walfarg weave and I said, "You may be desperately in love and willing to consign the world to oblivion to satisfy your passion, but you are not getting married without your mother present."

"But—"

"And there are no buts about it, Jaidur!"

"Queen Lildra—"

"She has not been crowned yet. But that is beside the point. Your mother didn't even know your sister Velia was married until after she was dead. D'you think I'll let you get married and not have your mother share in the joyous day?"

"Father—"

"Now, Jai, do listen," said Jaezila. "Look, I'll fly back home and tell mother."

"It might," I said, "be more becoming for Jaidur to fly himself and tell his mother he is going to be married."

Jaidur's nostrils pinched in. Jaezila looked at me and laughed. I stared back, no doubt wearing that grim old face of mine that, seemingly, had no power to arouse resentment in Jaezila.

"You said you wouldn't tell your children what to do or order them about, father. Well?"

I breathed hard. We'd won a resounding victory, the rebellion had been a triumph. Queen Fahia was gone no one knew where, and I doubted many cared. Prince Babb was dead. The wizards had fled the country. We were going to see that Lildra was properly crowned and seated on the throne and then we were going to turn our undivided attention on Hamal and mad Empress Thyllis. All this we would do. But here and now, my concern was for Delia. It was unthinkable to me that she should be deprived of the day of her son's wedding. And I'd said so.

About to state what seemed to be an obvious fact, that I was not ordering my lad about but merely pointing out to him what was seemly conduct, I was interrupted.

Lildra stepped forward. Jaidur watched her with the simmering violence of a volcano about to erupt.

"Majister," she said to me in her firm voice, "you are right and yet you are wrong. Jaidur owes love and respect to his mother, but it is we who are to live our lives together. We wish to begin aright, but we cannot allow the past to rule us."

That seemed fair enough, by Vox. But, all the same . . . Delia's half-brother, Vomanus, who had always seemed to us to be a feckless adventurer, had married in what amounted to secrecy. Valona, who was not Valona the Claw, was Vomanus's daughter. That explained the nagging feeling I'd had that she reminded me of someone I knew. But Delia had been—for her—put out that Vomanus had not told us of his wedding. If her own son Jaidur acted in what was to me a thoughtless fashion, then Delia would be hurt. And I couldn't allow that, if it was possible to prevent that damage.

I said so.

In the end the marriage was postponed for long enough for a fast flier to reach Vallia and return. I could well understand the urgency. The Queen of Hyrklana had to be seen to be firmly seated on the throne, and a powerful husband as king would give the added reassurance. There would be other factions besides ours still in the field. Vad Noran, for one. I wondered how he would view his new sovereign, and if he would take up arms against her. If he did—by Harg!—I'd chop him finer than best mincemeat. At least, that is what I said to Lildra, in reassurance.

Finishing the discussion, there in that sumptuous chamber in the palace of the high fortress of the Hakal, I said, "It is settled. I will fly to Vallia and tell the empress myself. I think she will put aside whatever is afoot to attend your wedding, Jaidur. But if she is absent about business for the Sisters of the Rose—"

"That will be all right." Jaezila spoke firmly. "I will come with you, Jak—father—oh, by Vox! Jak it is going to be."

That pleased me. We made quick preparations for the trip, choosing a voller of speed and comfort. "At least she will not break down, as the Hamalian vollers do," I said. We had still not settled that score with Hamal; now that we had Hyrklana as an ally we had circumvented that problem. The rankle remained.

Among the many urgent tasks to be done in Hyrklana, two very close to my heart would be extraordinarily difficult to deal with. I was a guest in this country. I had no power. All I could do was trust that Jaidur would carry out, not just my wishes, but actions I considered necessary and actions suited to the son of the Emperor of Vallia—even if those actions might not be regarded as expected of a King of Hyrklana. The young devil would find out a little of what being a king meant, then. I thrust aside the contemptible thought, that Jaidur's ascension to the throne, where he would co-reign with Lildra, might transform him into a tyrant. Zair forfend!

Quick and practical, Jaezila organized the flier and we took off for Vallia. I did not much like leaving Hyrklana at this moment, when rival factions might seek to oust Lildra before she was even crowned, but I was determined that Delia should be at her son's wedding. The voller was sleek and fast and superbly equipped, for she had come from Fahia's private flierdrome and was accounted a zorca of the skies. We flew for Vondium.

The reception was tumultuous. I will make no attempt to describe the crowded events of that brief visit. Suffice it to say that before I realized it I was up to my eyebrows in work—as usual. This time I had no intention of being waylaid by affairs of state. My return to Hyrklana was an affair of state. Let my pallans chew on that, by Vox! That a whole retinue of people should elect to accompany Delia, Jaezila and me seemed only natural.

Delia, after a first quick flash of an emotion I could identify and did not mention, was enraptured at the idea of Jaidur being married.

"He's always been a wild young tearaway. Marriage should steady him—although he has been splendid in doing what he has for the Sisters of the Rose."

"There are dark debts still outstanding . . ."

"I hate to think of them, but yes, my heart, there are . . ."

"It is in my mind that Vallia is entering a great period of prosperity. Our comrades do well everywhere."

"The whole island will be reunited soon. Events move on apace." Then she laughed and I felt the world give its topsy-turvy tug at my heart. "And another thing, Dray Prescot, Lela tells me you informed her you were married to some woman or other called Thylda. Well, husband, what have you to say to that?"

I groaned. "By Zair! You had to find out!"

Then, for a space, we shut out the grim world of Kregen and devoted ourselves to each other, and, later, Delia stretched like a drowsy cat before a fire, purring, and said, "Anyway, Thylda is not such a bad name, after all."

When we went down to the voller, Unmok the Nets limped up, out of the watching throngs. He cradled his middle left stump. He looked happy if a trifle dazed. He had been treated famously.

"So, Jak the Shot, your secret was a secret after all."

"Unmok! You Och rascal—and what are you doing now?"

It turned out he was, as he put it, "Still looking around."

I laughed. He looked surprised that I could laugh like that. I glanced at Delia. "Unmok will astonish us all one day, when he has decided what he will do in life."

Unmok made his peculiar Och grimace. "There is a nice little bangles and beads shop in the Kyro of Drak the Munificent I have seen. But also, I have been offered a part interest in a fancy mazilla silk works. As Ochenshum is my witness, I am not sure—"

"Well, just remember we are still partners."

"Partners! With the Emperor of Vallia?"

"Of course. I may be only a hairy apim, but I do not forget my debts." We talked for a space and then it was time to leave and we moved toward the voller. Unmok yelled the remberees.

Delia smiled. "I find Unmok absolutely charming!"

How gloriously superb she looked! Radiant, glowing, absolutely wonderful, the most fascinating, clever, willful, shrewd, the most absolute woman in two worlds. And she said to me as we walked toward the voller, "I've missed you, my heart. And now Jaidur is off and running. Drak manages things well. I own to no qualms for him. And Dayra—"

"Ros the Claw."

"Aye, Ros the Claw. Those villains she calls friends have been in hiding, lying low. But we have not heard the last of them. And now, you have told me nothing about this Princess Lildra."

"I told you of Princess Lilah, her mother, and the manhounds. Lildra is—rather nice. There is a lot she does not know, owing to her peculiar education and upbringing—"

"She gets on with Lela?"

Jaezila, our daughter Lela, walked ahead of us, swinging along in her russet leathers, her rapier cocked up, her brown hair brilliant in the lights of the suns. I nodded. "Yes. They get along famously."

"And do you think Lildra—?"

I laughed. We observed the fantamyrrh climbing into the airboat. And I laughed. "Silly woflo! She will love you as all men and women love you."

Delia turned to look at the half-ruined palace spread out beneath us and the proud city of Vondium below. She sighed.

"I do hope so, Dray. I really do hope so."

The Lord Farris spared airboats to take the wedding guests, on my assurances that they would be returned and with them a fleet of brand new vollers from the yards of Hyrklana. We took off and the flags fluttered and the trumpets pealed and the breezes blew in our faces. The windrush caught Delia's hair and swirled it back so that the outrageous auburn tints glowed. Her face regarded me with that look of love and passion to which I responded as I always have, as I always will, by Zair. We retired to the cabin for a space and the fleet flew on across the oceans to Hyrklana.

The relief I experienced when we landed at being told that nothing untoward had occurred during my absence revealed much of my own apprehension. Had Lildra been overthrown, had Jaidur been slain, I would not have been surprised and would have blamed myself . . .

The wedding was lavish.

It went on for ten days of riotous carousing and solemn ceremonies, of much pomp and magnificence and of quiet talk and planning. So many of our friends were there as to make the heart of a warrior kick with expected action.* So Delia's son and my son Jaidur wed his Princess Lildra, and immediately thereafter the pair were enthroned and crowned as King and Queen of Hyrklana. I tried not to regard this as nepotism gone mad, megalomania rife, but it was a near thing, I can tell you.

The dark shadow I feared lay across my mind during all these glittering ceremonies. Hyrklana rejoiced today; tomorrow her people must go up against Hamal. And then,

* Here Prescot gives in loving detail a list of all the wedding guests. It makes brave reading. —A.B.A.

when Hamal had been shown the true path, together, united with all Paz, we would face the menace of the Shanks, the true and fearsome enemies.

And after the Shanks, who knew what other monstrous foes we would face?

My son Drak said to me, "Well, I have seen that rascal Jaidur married off. Now I must fly back to Vallia. We have had disquieting news out of the southwest."

My ears pricked up, but all Drak would say was, "We defeated those rasts down there, but I begin to see another reason why you are so set against using mercenaries."

"You'd better tell me—"

"With your leave, I'll be off." A stiff-necked bunch, this family of mine. "It may come to nothing, and you have work here."

"I have. You'll be ready to march against Hamal?"

"The midlands are being cleared by Kov Turko. As soon as we can establish new frontiers and fresh bases, we will be clearer to march. If a job has to be done, it has best be done well."

"Vallia is in good hands with you and the council, Drak. I trust you. If you are having difficulty in the southwest—"

"It is nothing. Rumors only. Our spies are busy."

I sniffed.

He went on, "And Princess Lildra is lovely. Jaidur is a lucky fellow."

"She's a queen now, and Jaidur is a king. Deuced odd."

"Damned odd!"

And we both laughed.

Delia came in and Drak said the remberees. Jaezila would be staying with us. We had an invasion to plan and kingdoms to run. Delia and Jaidur spent a long time together. While that right tearaway I had first met as Vax, Vax Neemusjid, might regard me as a ruffian, he set great store by what Delia said. The world belonged to young people. And by Zim-Zair, I was young! The Savanti had insured that by their own superhuman powers. I felt young and hot and strong, and Hamal and danger lay ahead. I went galloping out for a gut-jolting ride astride a fine zorca and the blue radiance came stealthily dropping down over me.

The giant form of the Scorpion, limned in blue fire, hovered over me.

With the sound of a mighty rushing wind the crimson

radiance of the Star Lords enveloped all the world of Kregen. The thin voice keened.

"Dray Prescot! You are wanted urgently. There is a mission set to your hands—"

I interrupted. I took a whooping breath and started in calling the Everoinye all the blackguard names I could put my tongue to. I finished: "And I've a lot to do here that means much to me and Kregen, although not much to you, it seems. Have I not done as you wished, and is not Lildra now Queen of Hyrklana?"

"That is sooth. But you are your usual onkerish self. Listen! Our kregoinye has failed in Hamal. It is urgent that his task be concluded, for there is no time loop available. Why do you think we talk thus to you, when we could hurl you into Hamal without a second thought?"

"Why?"

"Debate that with yourself. The answer is obvious. You will go to Hamal and perform the task we set to your hands and then you may find advantages you had not bargained for."

I felt the amazement. The Star Lords? Talking like this?

The thin voice from the crimson radiance went on: "We have changed our plans, Dray Prescot, from the time when you were first brought to Kregen, all naked and raw. You seem to possess a spark of understanding we thought absent from you. Times are changing."

I gaped. These were the superhuman entities, who had once been men like me and were now aloof, remote, impossibly unknowable?

"Do you grant me a boon?"

I was talking about clothes and weapons, and they knew it.

"No."

"Well then, give me time to make the proper remberees to those I love here."

"That is granted you, Dray Prescot. With the first rays of the twin sons, you will be transmitted to Hamal."

The crimson radiance paled. There had been no interference from the acid green of Ahrinye nor from the warm yellow of Zena Iztar. The Scorpion leered down, and I fancied his bloated figure had a much more friendly appearance. I felt as though I were dreaming. The blue fire returned, the winds blew, and once again I was galloping astride the zorca headlong for Huringa.

Slowing that mad pace, I reflected on my future.

Jaidur, the King of Hyrklana, was now the man who must set in motion at least the most important stages of the coming campaign. He would have assistance. Also, I must entrust to him the promulgations of the two measures I knew he concurred with. Neither would be easy. Both would be diabolically difficult. But we must stamp out slavery in Hyrklana. And we must close the Jikhorkdun.

What two tasks could be more difficult?

Perhaps, just perhaps, what I faced in Hamal would tax the old nerve and sinews a trifle more. I did not know.

All I knew as I rode back to Huringa, the capital of Hyrklana, where King Jaidur and Queen Lildra reigned, was that I must once again say good-bye to Delia. Through the streaming mingled rays of the Suns of Scorpio I rode, the emerald and ruby lights falling about me, and the sweetness of the air intoxicating. This time, I vowed, the parting would not be long. This time I'd do what the Star Lords desired, and then I'd take Hamal to pieces and deal with mad Empress Thyllis as we had dealt with fat Queen Fahia.

And all this, all this, not because the Star Lords had commanded, but so that Delia and I might be together again.